Penguin Books
*The Nature of Passion*

KT-495-438

Ruth Prawer Jhabvala was born in Germany of Polish parents and came to England at the age of twelve. She was educated at Queen Mary College, London University, and began writing after graduation and marriage. Her published work includes four collections of short stories, *Like Birds, Like Fishes, How I Became a Holy Mother, A Stronger Climate* and *An Experience of India*; and the novels *To Whom She Will, Esmond in India, The Householder, Get Ready for Battle, A Backward Place, A New Dominion, Heat and Dust*, winner of the 1975 Booker Prize, and *In Search of Love and Beauty*.

She has also collaborated on several film scripts, among them *Shakespeare Wallah, Autobiography of a Princess, Quartet* and *The Europeans*. She has written several plays for television and the film script for the film of *Heat and Dust*, which had its world première at the beginning of 1983. Ruth Prawer Jhabvala won the Neil Gunn International Fellowship in 1978.

Her writing has won widespread acclaim: C.P. Snow said of her, 'Someone once said that the definition of the highest art is that one should feel that life is this and not otherwise. I do not know of a writer living who gives that feeling with more unqualified certainty than Mrs Jhabvala' and *The Sunday Times* called her 'a writer of genius ... of world class – a master storyteller'.

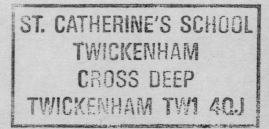

*Ruth Prawer Jhabvala*

*The Nature of Passion*

*Penguin Books*

PENGUIN BOOKS

Published by the Penguin Group
27 Wrights Lane, London W8 5TZ, England
Viking Penguin Inc., 40 West 23rd Street, New York, New York 10010, USA
Penguin Books Australia Ltd, Ringwood, Victoria, Australia
Penguin Books Canada Ltd, 2801 John Street, Markham, Ontario, Canada L3R 1B4
Penguin Books (NZ) Ltd, 182–190 Wairau Road, Auckland 10, New Zealand

Penguin Books Ltd, Registered Offices: Harmondsworth, Middlesex, England

First published by George Allen and Unwin 1956
Published in Penguin Books 1986
10 9 8 7 6 5 4 3

Made and printed in Great Britain by
Richard Clay Ltd, Bungay, Suffolk
Filmset in 9/11 Monophoto Times

TO M.A. AND P.A.

*Know thou Rajas to be of the nature of passion, giving rise to thirst (for pleasure) and attachment. It binds the embodied by attachment to action.*
Bhagavad Gita, XIV, 7. (Translated by Swami Paramananda)


Dr Radhakrishnan comments:

The three modes are present in all human beings, though in different degrees. No one is free from them and in each soul one or the other predominates. Men are said to be sattvika, rajasa or tamasa according to the mode which prevails . . . While the activities of a sattvika temperament are free, calm and selfless, the rajasa nature wishes to be always active and cannot sit still and its activities are tainted by selfish desires.

# Characters

Lala Narayan Dass Verma (Lalaji)

*His wife*

Phuphiji, *his sister*

Rani, *his eldest daughter*

Om Prakash, *his eldest son*

Chandra Prakash, *his second son*

Ved Prakash (Viddi), *his youngest son*

Usha, *his second daughter*

Nimmi, *his youngest daughter*

Shanta, *his daughter-in-law, wife of Om Prakash*

Kanta, *his daughter-in-law, wife of Chandra Prakash*

Dev Raj, *Shanta's father*

*Shanta's mother*

Lakshmi, *Shanta's cousin*

Rajen Mathur, *a friend of Nimmi's*

Pheroze Batliwala, *a friend of Nimmi's*

Tivari, *a journalist*

Zahir-ud-din, *a painter*

Bahwa, *a dramatist*

Kuku, *a fashionable young man*

Maee, *an old woman servant in Lalaji's house*

All the characters are entirely fictitious. If a name has been used that may suggest a reference to any real person, it has been used quite inadvertently.

# Part One

Lalaji himself was the only one in the house still to sleep outdoors. In the mornings it was almost chilly and he had to cover himself with a sheet, but he preferred to wake up to sky and hedge and crows rather than to the loneliness of his expensive bedroom. He did not like his bedroom. Nor did his wife with whom he shared it. It seemed wrong that just the two of them should sleep there, no children, no babies, no relatives come to stay, only pieces of strange and unnecessary furniture. Still, one had to keep up with one's money. A bedroom suite was a social necessity, so he had bought it. But he slept outdoors as long as he could; sometimes right up to early November. Now it was only early September, and he felt almost hot under his sheet. He pushed it aside and yawned and scratched his chest under the shirt.

The crows clapped clumsy black wings near his face and cawed angrily; but he did not mind them. All his life he had been wakened by ugly angry crows, and they reminded him of many people he had dealings with: such as the sharp thin Government officers who looked at him suspiciously over their regulation desks but had to be polite to him because he was a lala, a rich man, with influence in the highest quarters.

Groaning, for he was still stiff with sleep, he heaved himself from his bed and went to sit indoors in what they called the sitting-room. He sat in an armchair with his feet drawn up and picked little black grains from between his toes. The sitting-room had shiny English furniture, silk curtains and lampshades, novelty cigar boxes and coloured photographs in silver frames. It was very different from what he had grown up with and got used to.

Even the idea of having a separate sitting-room was alien to him. A room, for him and his like, had always been simply a room; it was all in all, one could eat there, sleep there, sit and talk and receive visitors. His ideas of interior decoration had been confined to patchily whitewashed walls and cracked cement floors; furniture meant string beds with the strings coming loose, earthenware water-containers and huge heavy trunks in which one kept one's clothes and blankets and silver pieces; beauty and decoration were provided by the highly-coloured, crudely-moulded clay toys brought

11

back from fairs and pilgrimages, and by the jasmine garlands hung reverently over the faded photographs of departed loved ones.

However, he had very soon managed to adjust himself to his new and foreign opulence. His costly, shiny possessions did not disconcert him. These things were, after all, his; he had paid for them. They were proof of his wealth, of his achievements. He felt at ease among them because he owned them; he mastered them. Tomorrow, if he wanted to, he could throw them out and buy new ones, more expensive ones, if more expensive ones could be got.

He looked very pensive as he sat there, picking his toes, but he was not really thinking of anything at all. He had learnt how to relax completely and switch off his thoughts. That was how he had managed to remain sound and healthy in the midst of all his business worries. But this morning something was vaguely troubling him, he did not know what. Not the usual things – the ten-lakh income tax arrears which the Government was demanding, the new Deputy Minister, the T— bribery and corruption case, his lawyer's latest report, and the twenty-five lakhs' worth of work which threatened to go to another contractor. None of these things, for these, or others like them, were constants and he had learnt to live with them, to switch them on or off at will. This thing that was so surprisingly troubling him was something smaller and more personal. If only he could think what it was . . .

A servant brought his soap and clean clothes, and he went out to wash. There were seven marble bathrooms in the house, but he preferred to wash by the garden-tap and clean his teeth with a twig from the margosa tree. Afterwards he prayed, very quickly and almost unconsciously. All the time this thing was nagging at him and when, back in the sitting-room, the servant handed him his cup of tea, he knew what it was. It was that his wife was not there. If she had been there, she would have handed him his tea, not a servant. He would not have spoken to her nor probably noticed her, but still – it would have been she who handed it to him, as she had done for the past thirty-seven years. She was part of his routine and he missed her.

Drinking his tea, he thought of the small annoyances that were in store for him. His food would not be cooked properly and he would be served by servants. Now he remembered that the cord in the pyjama trousers which the servant had handed to him had not been knotted in the way she knotted it. There would be many things like that to annoy him in the next few days. But there was no help for it; he made up his mind to it and was at once reconciled. If his wife had died, he would have made up his mind to it just like that, and been reconciled. He was used to making compromises and could fashion a life for himself under any conditions. But she had not died; she had only gone to the nursing-home to be with Shanta who was expecting another child. Perhaps the child had already come; though, if it had, they would have telephoned. Well, let it come; he would provide for it. As he provided for them all.

He read the newspaper. He read only the local reports on page three, skimming over them quickly to see if there was any mention of the T— bribery and corruption case. There was not; only a report of a man who had been arrested for offering a five-rupee bribe to a municipal officer. He shook his head: five rupees – what did the man expect? Though there had been a time when that was all he himself could offer. Five rupees – it was pitiful but it had got him on. From five rupees he had advanced to 50, to 500, to 5,000. One had to know how to do these things.

He turned to the advertisements, to the contract tenders: *'sealed tenders are invited for an Ayurvedic College . . .'* Not that there was any need for him to read them; he had information about all big work long before it came to be advertised. But he did it out of habit, because there had been a time when that was all he could do – read the advertisements and dream of the day when he himself would be rich enough, big enough, to tender.

Out of habit also he looked at the marriage offers: *'Wanted, for Punjabi boy, 21, wheat complexion, B. A., first-class family, a beautiful fair girl . . .'* He still had two to dispose of, Viddi and Nimmi, but there was no need for him to look at or insert advertisements. He needed only, in his own good time, to throw out a hint and all the richest men in Delhi would come eagerly forward with sons and daughters. But no hurry: the right time, the right opportunity, would come. His children could have and would have the best. First he had to establish Viddi, bring him into the business, make a man of him. He frowned a little, thinking of Viddi. The boy had been talking and behaving strangely ever since he had left College. But there was nothing really to get worried about, nothing that he, as a father, did not know how to put right. And Nimmi. He did not have to frown when he thought of Nimmi. His treasure, his pride, his finest achievement. Would there ever be anyone good enough for her? A prince, he thought, a prince I will get for her. Though he did not mean it literally: he would not have liked a prince in his family.

He threw the newspaper on the floor and yawned widely and loudly. It was only six o'clock and no one else was up yet. Only the children; he could hear them making a noise upstairs, then Om Prakash's voice, shouting at them. Why shout at them? It was good to wake up to the voices of children.

He went to the bottom of the stairs and called, 'Come down here, come down to your Dada!' Om Prakash's children came tumbling down the stairs, shouting, 'Dada, Dada!' – two of them, a boy and a girl. He laughed out loud with pleasure, then set them racing up and down the stairs. They raced, screaming.

'One rupee I will give to the winner!' he shouted. They screamed more and accused one another of cheating. He laughed uproariously. Om Prakash's voice came out of the bedroom, thick and sleepy and cursing horribly. His father laughed again but was inwardly shocked. To say such things to the children – he himself often had recourse to these expressions, but had never done so to his children. Om was too rough: it was a conclusion he often came to about his eldest son.

'I won!' the boy cried, and 'No, I!' the girl.

'Both have won,' Lalaji said. 'One rupee I will give to each.' The children screeched with delight, Om cursed again.

'Be quiet!' his father shouted at him. 'Give thanks to God that he has given you children!' and he gathered them into his arms, clumsily tender.

Nimmi cried, 'Please let me *sleep*!' and Lalaji chuckled and answered, 'Enough now, get up, let me see you.'

Om could be heard grumbling in his room, then he appeared at the door, his eyes still half shut, squinting down with ill-humour at his father and his children on the stairs. Lalaji laughed and told the children, 'Good, now you have got your father out of bed. All day he would sleep.'

Om Prakash in the doorway, heavy-jowled, folds of protruding stomach pushing out the crumpled kurta. His pyjama trousers had slipped down and his navel, deeply embedded in fat and hair, could be seen through the thin kurta.

'How can you sleep?' his father said. 'Go hurry to the hospital, see what has been given to you!'

Om impatiently shrugged, then turned back into his room, growled, 'Every morning this is done to me, is there no peace.'

Nimmi's door opened and she came out in a pink silk sleeping suit: 'Pitaji, why do you make so much noise? I was having a good dream.' Lalaji laughed and said, 'Come down, your life I will make better than any dream, my daughter.'

The telephone rang, a servant answered, then shouted, 'Babuji! Babuji! It is a girl!'

Lalaji ran down the stairs, snatched the telephone. 'A girl? It is all well? We are coming!' He dropped the receiver – from the other end a voice, dangling in the air, crackled, 'You are there?' – but he was already running up the stairs, shouting, 'Om, a daughter has been given to you! Nimmi! Viddi! Usha! A girl!'

14

Om, sitting on his bed, rubbing his hair, said, 'My God, not even a son.'

Nimmi in her pink silk sleeping suit chose to be blasé: 'Why are you so excited, Pitaji? Every day children are born.'

*'But are they my grandchildren?'* Lalaji roared.

Nimmi, leaning elegantly against a doorpost, twisted the end of one of her pigtails round her small slim fingers. 'Poor little thing,' she spoke into the air. 'What a life she will have.'

'What a life!' cried her father. 'The life of a queen she will have. What else? Like all the daughters born into my house!' He sat down on the stairs, smiling to himself. 'How beautiful she will be, like my Nimmi, like a queen. Such a wedding we will make for her, the best husband in the whole of Hindustan we will get for her, the richest, the fairest ... Om!' he shouted. 'Why do you not say something? Why are you not singing with joy? Viddi! Come out, hear what your eldest brother has achieved!'

Nimmi laughed and went back into her room. Usha was still fast asleep, snoring a little. Nimmi shook her by the shoulder and said, 'It is a girl. Pitaji is very excited.'

Usha grunted, then suddenly sat up: 'A girl?' Nimmi held her hand away from herself and studied the nails. 'A girl you say? Shanta has got a girl?' Nimmi nodded and showed herself more interested in her nails.

Lalaji was telling the children, 'A little sister you have got, a little sister like a pearl.'

'When will you give us our one rupee each, Dadaji? Now? This morning?' Om shouted for the servant.

Lalaji sat downstairs in the sitting-room with his legs supported on a chair. Usha was massaging them; she pressed them as hard as she could, kneeling on the floor, an expression of concentrated effort on her fat puffed face. 'Aah,' said her father with pleasure and pain every time she pressed. Nimmi, her plaits now piled up on her head, wearing a pale blue house-coat with a design of dark blue wistarias, read the cinema and restaurant advertisements in the newspaper while eating a banana.

'A girl,' Lalaji said dreamily. 'All the rich men in Delhi will run after her with their sons. The dowry I will give with her, no one will believe the figure.'

Nimmi said from behind her paper, 'Pitaji, you think you can buy everything with money.'

'With what else will you buy it?' her father answered simply. Om, eating a huge breakfast from a brass tray, took time off to laugh. His brother Viddi looked at him with loathing: 'Money, money, money,' he said. 'That is all anyone thinks of in this house.'

'You will learn, son,' his father said good-humouredly, and now Viddi looked at him with loathing.

'No,' Om said. 'He wants to be a sadhu and stand all day naked on one leg on the banks of the Jumna.'

'In winter also?' asked the father, and to Usha he said, 'Not so hard, daughter, I am only an old man.'

Viddi was scowling. This was his favourite expression nowadays: he felt very much misunderstood. If he had known that his scowl made him look even more like his eldest brother Om, he would have taken good care never to assume it. But even without it, there was an inescapable resemblance. Om had gone further down the path on which Viddi had only just started. Om's fat was loose and manifold, whereas Viddi's was still tight, still contained in firm young skin; but there was no doubt that in a few more years he too would spread and loosen up. Both sons took after the father who in himself was the prototype of what they would become. Massiveness was the only word for Lalaji. He had spread out so far that he was flat rather than round, the stomach hanging in huge folds, chins overlapping, eyes swamped in cheeks. Yet there was nothing inert about him: vitality quivered in the masses of flesh, the eyes though buried were bright and intelligent. He had always been a big man and knew how to carry, how to overcome, the additions the years had given him.

Nimmi tossed aside her newspaper and jumped lightly to her feet. 'I am going to College now,' she announced.

'And our new little daughter? You will not see our new little daughter?' her father protested, quite shocked.

'Today I have a class in English literature. We will learn about an English poet called Keats. None of you have heard about him, but he has written very beautiful poetry and that is why it is important for me to go.' She looked very proud as she said this, her head tossed back and her lower lip pushed out.

Om snorted. 'English literature! You can go and play your games, but what is the use when tomorrow we will find you a husband and your life will begin in earnest.'

'Not tomorrow,' Lalaji richly chuckled. 'Not quite tomorrow.' He looked fondly at his youngest daughter and noted with amusement how annoyed she was.

'The day after tomorrow then, what is the difference,' Om said. Nimmi turned her back on him and ostentatiously hummed a tune. 'This College,' said Om, talking more loudly, 'it is only a waste of time and of good money, and will perhaps even give her wrong ideas. Look at that one there,' he said, thrusting his chin towards Usha massaging her father's legs. 'How much money was spent on her education, and what has it all led to now? A betrothal today, a marriage tomorrow, children the day after. Only with her we were lucky: she is too stupid to get any harm out of education.'

Usha laughed. She had failed many times to pass her Inter, and reference to this always moved her to good-humoured laughter.

Nimmi, trembling with fury, picked up the newspaper again and pretended to read it. Lalaji and Om looked at her, the father with love, the brother cynically, but both conscious of her good looks and of her anger. The anger pleased Om and goaded him into continuing in the same vein: 'Do you know what I will do with that one?' he said, pointing at his little daughter playing marbles with her brother on the floor. 'When she is seven, I will find a good husband and betroth her. Then she can come back to the house and learn from her mother and her aunts to make chapatis and mango pickle. When she has learnt that well, and also how to manage servants and children, she can go to her husband's house and be a credit to us there.'

'Please do not think I am listening to you,' Nimmi said in a strained voice from behind her paper.

A servant came in with a pile of letters which he gave to Lalaji. Another servant came in with a pair of shoes for Om, who stretched out first one foot then the other, while he continued with his breakfast.

'Do not listen,' Viddi said to Nimmi. 'That is the only way to live in this house. Do not see and do not hear.'

Lalaji flicked aside one letter after the other. He stopped at one and opened it. 'My dear Nimmi,' he read aloud, rather laboriously. 'It is written in English.'

'My letter!' Nimmi cried and leapt to her feet.

Her father turned the envelope over and looked at the postmark. 'It is from Indonesia,' he announced. 'I did not know you had a friend in Indonesia.'

'Please give it to me, Pitaji. It is from my friend Neena. Her father,' she added casually, 'is Ambassador in Indonesia.'

'You have very great friends,' Lalaji said. 'Please read the letter to us. The handwriting is not very good.'

'Oh yes,' said Om, 'she has great friends. But wait till we find this husband for her, then no more Ambassadors.'

Nimmi sat curled up on the settee, engrossed in her letter. 'Read it aloud, we want to hear,' her father urged her. He took his legs from the chair and said, 'Enough,' to Usha, who was already very hot. The telephone rang. 'I cannot speak with anyone!' Lalaji shouted. 'I have a new granddaughter and am at the hospital.'

Om pushed his breakfast tray aside and got up to yawn and stretch. 'I would like to go straightaway to office,' he said. 'All my wife's relations will be at the hospital.'

'When my children were born,' Lalaji said, 'not one minute could I rest till I had seen them.'

'I will see her for the rest of my life,' Om replied gloomily.

The driver came to enquire which car was wanted. 'The big one,' Lalaji told him. 'We are all going to the hospital.'

'But I want to go to College, Pitaji,' Nimmi said, thrusting the letter into the pocket of her house-coat.

'First you must see our little one. What does your friend say is the price of cement in Indonesia?'

The nursing-home was a very expensive and very modern one. Each room had its own bathroom and veranda. The floor was grey and white mosaic, gleamingly scrubbed; there was a little bedside table of thin cold stainless steel and the bed had a foam-rubber mattress and a handle by which the top and bottom parts could be raised or lowered. Starched nurses shook thermometers and made notes on charts. Under the bed stood a disinfected bedpan. Lalaji's wife thought it was a most unsuitable place for any baby to be born in. Her own confinements – eight in all – had been at home, which still seemed to her the best and only possible place. Of course, times had been different then; they had not been so rich. But, she thought (as she often did), what was the use of so much wealth if all it did for you was to force you to abandon your own comfortable habits.

However, they had managed to make the nursing-home as much like home as possible. Their own charpais had been brought in for them to sleep on, their servant cooked for them on the veranda, their towels and the smell of their hair-oil were spread in the bathroom. And during the confinement they had been present in the labour-room. The doctor and the nurses had been almost an encumbrance – they could have managed much better by themselves – but still, they had given a good deal of advice to the doctor, so that, thank God! the labour had been quick and easy. Shanta was asleep now; she lay on the bed with her hair straggled over the pillow and her face sagging with exhaustion. Her mother sat beside her, waving a hand-fan in the sleeping face, though there was a perfectly good electric fan turning from the ceiling. Lalaji's wife – since the place of honour beside Shanta was taken – sat beside the baby's cot. It annoyed her that this was an ordinary cot which did not rock. At first she had thought that there must be something wrong with it and she had informed the nurse, but the nurse, who was an Anglo-Indian, had said rather sharply that it was a very good cot indeed, that rocking cots were out of fashion, that rocking itself was out of fashion because it did harm to the baby. Lalaji's wife had been annoyed at that, and she had wanted to answer, 'all my children have been rocked, and will you find finer children anywhere?' But she had not said it because she did not like the nurse, was even afraid of her because she had her hair cut short and spoke Hindustani with an English accent.

So she had to content herself with just sitting beside the baby and looking at it and making out whom it resembled. Thank God! it had a fair complexion, that was the most important thing. Sometimes she thought its features were like her husband's – the nose – sometimes she thought it looked like Om – the hair – sometimes like Usha – the hands; but mostly she thought it looked like Nimmi (all the girls born in the family were made out to resemble Nimmi, though none so far did). She stole a look at her husband's sister Phuphiji, lying on a charpai, sternly asleep: no, it did not in any way resemble Phuphiji. Her eyes strayed to Shanta's mother, and she noticed with surprise, and some satisfaction, that she too was asleep, the hand with the fan resting on Shanta's pillow. Lalaji's wife thought proudly that she herself had never gone to sleep by a daughter's bed. No, not if she had had three sleepless nights. She was feeling tired now, but nothing could induce *her* to go to sleep: who then would watch over Shanta and the new-born baby? Besides, she had too many things to worry her. She had to think all the time how they were at home, whether everything was as it should be, whether Lalaji's tea had had the correct quantity of milk and sugar, whether Usha had massaged her father's legs, whether Nimmi had had her glass of buttermilk and Viddi his parathas, whether the servants were not wasting coal or making havoc with the sugar and the ghee.

She sighed, thinking of all the things which would never be right unless she herself was there to look to them. She hated leaving home and never did so except under the stress of a daughter's confinement or a funeral or a marriage. But tonight, she thought, if all was well, she would go home; she had done her duty. And anyway, what was the use of her staying when Shanta's mother was set on hindering her from fulfilling all her duties? It had been so at Shanta's three previous confinements as well. Always Shanta's mother had thrust herself forward, done her best to exclude the mother-in-law. She looked angrily at the woman sleeping by the bedside: yes, she thought, you can sleep in peace because I am here to guard and provide for all. If only you had slept – this was her favourite reflection –

19

at the first confinement and let me manage alone, perhaps then my son Om Prakash would not have lost his first-born. She always held that the death of Shanta's first baby after one day was somehow the fault of Shanta's mother, though it had been an eight-month child, and they did say that an eight-month child never lived. Strange, the ways of God, that an eight-month child should die and a seven-month child should live. Nimmi, her own youngest, had been a seven-month child; such a small weak little being, four pounds she had weighed at birth, and yet she had grown up into the most beautiful child that ever was. Lalaji's wife sighed and hoped that Nimmi had taken her glass of buttermilk in the morning. If one was not there, children only neglected themselves.

Because she was lonely, with everyone asleep and no one to talk to, she called softly to Maee, the old woman servant, who was washing Shanta's clothes in the bathroom. Maee wiped her hands down her salwar and knelt at her mistress's feet to press her ankles. 'Look at that one there,' Lalaji's wife said with a cruel snigger, indicating Shanta's mother whose head nodded obliviously on her chins, 'see how well she is guarding her daughter.'

'O that one,' Maee said contemptuously. 'Why does she come here? We have no need of her here.' Her practised hands soothingly opened and shut over her mistress's ankles, the fingers feeling for tired bones and muscles.

'She thinks her right here is greater than ours,' Lalaji's wife said.

Maee gave a mocking laugh. 'And who is it,' she demanded, 'who feeds the daughter and sees to her comfort and the comfort of her children every day of the year? Is it she who does all this?'

'When she was in labour, Shanta cried out for me and it was I who had to hold her hand and help her to bear her pain. What a shame that was to her mother – all the nurses, and the doctor also, looked with big eyes to see that the mother-in-law was preferred to the mother. But it was to me she cried in her pain. "Mother-in-law," she cried.' This was a piece of convenient imagination; actually Shanta had cried to no one but her God.

'Naturally,' Maee said. 'In her hour of pain the girl knew where her heart was fastened.' She travelled from the ankles up to the calves, rubbing and squeezing.

'I do what I can for her,' Lalaji's wife said modestly. 'My son Om Prakash has brought her into my house. It is my duty. The left knee, Maee.'

'All the world knows what sort of a mother-in-law you are to your sons' wives. Here?'

Lalaji's wife nodded as Maee probed the left knee, and then her gaze travelled again to the baby. 'My Nimmi,' she murmured, 'exactly my Nimmi.' And she looked at the sleeping baby with great love. Maee also looked at it and echoed, 'Exactly,' and added, 'the same colour and see the hair and also the chin.'

'You do not think she looks a little like my Om Prakash too?'

Maee reflected for a while and then agreed: 'Yes, like the father, it is in the nose I think.'

'And there is something of my Usha also.'

'It is in the eyebrows. Such eyebrows are only to be found in our Usha daughter.'

'They should be here soon,' said Lalaji's wife. 'On the telephone he said, "at once we are coming". They will bring the sweetmeats and the fruit with them.'

'And *their* family – ?' Maee said, jerking her head in the direction of Shanta's sleeping mother.

Lalaji's wife uttered a sound of contempt. 'Soon enough they will come to disturb the poor child and hinder her from taking her proper rest. For that they will be here soon enough, though I do not know if we can look for many sweetmeats from them.'

Maee also looked contemptuous: 'They know only how to take. How to give they have not learnt.'

'It is how God has made them. And also there are so many poor relations in that family, Shanta's father has to provide for all his wife's family. All day they eat and sleep and not one of them does any work.'

Maee threw another derogatory look at Shanta's mother: 'Yes, it is plain enough what sort of family *she* comes from.' Shanta's mother slept peacefully.

'Go see if the boy is making tea ready,' said Lalaji's wife, withdrawing her feet from Maee's gentle fingers. Maee went out on the veranda, where the servant boy lay curled up on the floor, fast asleep. There was a bucket full of coals, but they were dead and black. 'Even the fire he has not lit,' Maee hissed into the room. Lalaji's wife shook her head and clicked her tongue and muttered curses. Soon they would be here and they would want tea – God knows what they had had at home: probably by this time the servants had drunk up all the tea and milk and sugar – and now nothing was ready. Everything was left to her, even the making of tea: the baby she had to guard, and Shanta, and even Shanta's mother. She set her mouth in a hard suffering line – well, it was good that she was still here and still strong and healthy enough to see to everyone's needs.

There was the sound of many feet trying to tread softly in the corridor outside and then the door opened and Lalaji's broad head was thrust in.

21

His wife laid her finger on her lips and beckoned him forward; Lalaji turned round with his finger on his lips and beckoned the others forward. They all tried to walk on tiptoe. Shanta's mother woke up with a start and at once began fanning Shanta's face again. She said, 'Be very quiet, you will disturb my daughter.' There was a gentle smile on Lalaji's face as he tiptoed to the baby's cot. He looked at the baby and then at his wife, who nodded, and then they both looked at the baby. 'She is like Rani,' Lalaji whispered. 'Rani!' his wife softly exclaimed. 'She is Nimmi, Nimmi exactly.' She bent down and picked the baby up and placed it in her husband's arms. He held it very tenderly and smiled down at it.

'The baby must not be picked up,' Shanta's mother said.

The others crowded round, all smiling, all tender. Nimmi forgot about being blasé; she clapped her hands and asked with subdued joy, 'May I hold it please?' Usha kissed its little finger and there were tears in her soft eyes as she did so. Om looked proud and possessive until his father transferred the baby to him and then he looked embarrassed. Lalaji slapped him on the back. Maee appeared in the door from the veranda, holding a teapot, and stood there looking at them. Everyone was smiling. Shanta's mother said, 'A baby is very delicate, great care must be taken.'

Servants came in with high baskets of fruit and boxes of sweetmeats which they at once began to unpack. Soon the room was brimming with bananas, pineapples, oranges, apples, nuts, pomegranates, and huge chunks of sweetmeats – green, white and pink, and covered with silver foil. Balls of coloured straw from out of the empty baskets and crumpled sheets of tissue-paper lay strewn over the floor. Phuphiji woke, sat up on her charpai and looked round severely, and then called to Maee for tea. Lalaji took out two one-hundred rupee notes and thrust one into each clenched fist of the sleeping baby: 'All your life may you have two fistfuls like that,' he wished. His wife looked triumphantly at Shanta's mother and was chagrined to find that she was not watching.

More footsteps could be heard in the corridor, the door opened and Shanta's relations came in. Behind them came servants with more sweetmeats and fruit. The room was very full now. Shanta's relations crowded round the baby's cot and Lalaji's wife said, 'It is not good for too many people to touch a baby.' Shanta's father also thrust two one-hundred rupee notes into the little baby fists. His wife looked at Lalaji's wife, saying, 'Yes, this child need have no worries, she has a good Nana to look to all her needs.' Shanta woke up. She lay for quite some time with her eyes open, but no one noticed; at last she said in a feeble voice, 'It is a girl? She has a fair complexion?'

They brought the baby to show it to her, and her two other children cried, 'Mamma!' and had to be pushed back. 'Fair as a Kashmiri girl,' they told Shanta and she went to sleep again.

More relations came in, looked at the baby and thrust money into its hands. Phuphiji collected all the money, but because she could not write she had to depute Viddi to keep an account of it; she dictated to him and watched sharply as he wrote. 'Five rupees,' she said scornfully, 'and this from Shanta's elder sister. Now you can see what sort of a family it is.'

Everybody ate sweets. The Anglo-Indian nurse came in, clapped her hands and cried, 'There are far too many people here; the mother must have rest.' They all agreed with her and each family looked meaningfully at the other, but no one left. The nurse also ate sweetmeats and then she softened and said, 'It is a beautiful baby.'

Lalaji was very happy – because he had a new granddaughter, because this was a family gathering and he loved family gatherings and because everyone else looked happy. He joked and laughed with the men, receiving and dealing out good-humoured insults, which was his favourite form of humour. The women meanwhile sat huddled round the bed, discussing pregnancies and miscarriages and other matters of interest. But whereas with the men the harmony was real and unsimulated, with the women it was very much a thing of the surface. The men had two lives, the women only one. If the men had business rivalries, they could forget them in private life; they could bitterly resent one another outside, but at home, and on an occasion like this, be the best of friends. For the women there was only that private family life, where a grievance was a grievance for ever and for all occasions. The women of Lalaji's family could never forget the occasion, at the betrothal ceremony between Om Prakash and Shanta twelve years ago, when a maternal aunt of Shanta's family had been given precedence over a paternal aunt of Om's family. The women of Shanta's family remembered with bitterness that when a baby had been born to Shanta's second cousin, Lalaji's eldest daughter Rani had failed to come and pay her respects. When Lalaji's wife's paternal uncle had died, one of Shanta's aunts had come in a coloured sari to the burning-ground; Lalaji's niece had given an inadequate present when Shanta's younger brother was married. No one ever forgot, and whenever they met these things, and a hundred others like them, itched under the surface of sweet harmoniousness. That surface never cracked (for the social decencies had to be meticulously observed – outright quarrels could only be indulged in with one's very nearest and dearest); but beneath it new insults were constantly being accumulated. Each remark could be construed into at least a slight, which had with the next remark to be effectively countered; and so it went on. Yet they met frequently, visiting in one another's houses. It would be true to say that they could not have lived without one another, if only because afterwards, after they parted, there was always so much to talk about, so many veiled insults to be brought to light. Life in the women's quarter was not always interesting, and some such stimulant was needed.

The men of the two families were aware of this strife but took no notice. What went on among the women did not concern them; theirs was a world apart. Anyway, nothing could ever disturb the good relations between Lalaji and Shanta's father, Dev Raj. Both were counted among the richest men in Delhi, and the wedding of Om and Shanta had been one of the costliest and most elaborate ever seen in the city. Lalaji spent many pleasurable moments in calculating how much money would come into his family on Dev Raj's death; and Dev Raj spent many equally pleasurable ones in calculating how much would come into his on Lalaji's death. But neither of them was disturbed by signs of unimpaired health and vigour in the other; their calculations were purely speculative, and both held that the world would be the poorer by the death of such a man as the other. On a happy occasion like this, they reserved the choicest and most jovial insults for one another; they poked each other's vast proud bellies and shouted, 'Like a tub of ghee he is only!' 'Like a pregnant woman in the last month he looks!' Their mutual esteem was very great. Each had worked his way up from negligible beginnings, so that each knew how to esteem the full measure of the other's achievements. Lalaji was a contractor, Dev Raj the owner of a fleet of buses and heavy lorries. Their business interests never clashed – on the contrary, they were often useful to one another, for both had extensive and valuable connec-tions.

Dev Raj's presence always had a doubly stimulating effect on Lalaji. First, because it did him good just to see the man – almost as rich, as expansive, as shrewd, as suave as himself. His equal, and there were few who could really esteem themselves that. Then, too, the sight of Dev Raj always brought to his mind some business problem which had been worrying him and with which the other might be able to help him. At the moment he was much troubled by the idea that the contract of the new building to be put up by the Happy Hindustan Trading Company, at a cost of twenty-five lakhs of rupees, might go to a rival contractor. But having discovered that one of the Directors of the Company was uncle to Dev Raj's cousin's sister-in-law, he felt much reassured. Dev Raj would speak to his relative; all would be well – ah, but it was good to be connected with such a man. And in return – for one should never take anything for nothing, nor give – there were those redundant Army lorries which one might be able to secure at a favourable price for a friend, since fortunately one had influence in Disposals.

These matters were lightly, very lightly, touched upon. 'I hear,' said Lalaji casually, when the first spurt of jovial insult was over, 'I hear,' he said, as they stood apart a little, the two rich men, the two heads of the family, 'that the Happy Hindustan Trading Company are investing in a building.' And when Dev Raj had registered this and knew what was wanted, Lalaji added, while helping himself to another sweetmeat, 'This morning I had a call from my friend in Disposals. Ah poor man, he is in a bad way. He wants to marry his daughter, but where is the money to come from?', pointing the way for Dev Raj, who very quickly apprehended it. No more was said; there was no need to say more, for each knew what the other wanted and knew that the other knew what he wanted. Such mutual benefits were to their liking: they blessed the new granddaughter all over again and each made a mental note to transmit 5,000 rupees into Om's bank account.

Lalaji's sister Phuphiji was meanwhile grimly busy counting the money that had been given to the baby. This done, she announced with satisfaction to the women round the bed that twenty-five rupees more had so far been given by Lalaji's family than by Dev Raj's. This was passed over in silence, Dev Raj's family pretending not to have heard, and Lalaji's putting on an air of being too polite to make any comment. However, it was treasured for future reference and private discussion among themselves. Shanta's mother was convinced that Phuphiji had deliberately falsified the account, and that in reality twenty-five rupees more had been given by Dev Raj's family. She looked forward to expounding this theory to her relations when they were alone. Meanwhile she said to Lalaji's wife: 'I have not seen your second son with his wife here this morning. I think they will soon be coming?'

Lalaji's wife was put out, though she had been expecting the question. She knew that the absence of Chandra Prakash and Kanta would not, could not, be allowed to pass without comment. And indeed it was very strange, not to say unprecedented, that the second son should fail to come and pay his respects when a child was born into the family. She had telephoned. She had said: 'Please come at once.' Kanta had replied, somewhat coldly: 'Of course.' And yet they had not come. She could not understand it. But then it was not often that she could understand her daughter-in-law Kanta. The girl had very strange ways ... Of course, she had always known that it would not be the same, that Kanta's ways would be different from their ways, but she had not suspected that they would be *so* different. Surely even in other communities, even in Kanta's community, daughters-in-law were expected to honour their mother-in-law, respect and submit to their husband's family? Kanta neither honoured nor respected nor submitted; she did not behave like a daughter-in-law at all.

But though at home, in her immediate family circle, Lalaji's wife often had occasion to deplore this fact, outside – and especially before Shanta's family – she never failed to defend Kanta. 'I think Chandra Prakash could not get away from office,' she said. 'These gazetted Government officers work very hard.' There was no gazetted Government officer in Shanta's family. 'Kanta could not get the car to come herself with the children,' she added.

Phuphiji disapproved very heartily of Kanta. She had been a violent and consistent opponent to Chandra's marriage with someone outside their immediate community, and further acquaintance with Kanta had done nothing but justify that opposition. But she said, 'Just now she telephoned. I spoke with her myself and she told me that one of the children had been taken sick. As soon as the doctor had been she will come, so she told me on the telephone.' She looked round severely, defying anyone to give her the lie.

Lalaji's eldest daughter Rani also did not like Kanta. Rani had always considered herself very modern and fashionable: she spent a lot of money on saris and jewels, her house was expensively furnished in what she presumed to be modern style, her children went to good schools and spoke English, and she was a member of a Club. But Kanta's children spoke English better; Kanta's clothes, though not so expensive, looked equally fashionable; Kanta knew how to do ballroom dancing and went to a superior Club. No wonder Rani could not altogether like her; and then, too – though of course she was modern in her outlook and did not set so much store by these things as her mother and Phuphiji – she could not help resenting the fact that Kanta failed to treat her with the respect due to an elder sister-in-law. However, she too said, 'Ah yes, when children are sick it is difficult to leave home, but Kanta will come as soon as she can.'

Shanta's mother smiled sympathetically and completely unbelieving, and said, 'The mother of young children never has an easy life.'

'Last year both Kanta's children had measles,' said Lalaji's wife rather desperately.

Rani said, 'My Kaka last year had pneumonia.'

Her younger sister Usha smiled happily at the recollection. It had been wonderful when little Kaka had pneumonia. She had been allowed to go and stay in the house of Rani's husband to help nurse Kaka, and all day she had sat by his cot and looked at him and pretended he was her own. Just as she was sitting now by the cot of the new-born baby, eating sweetmeats and imagining to herself that it was hers, her very own baby. Only if it had been hers, she would never have let it lie alone like this: she would have held it in her arms all the time and sung to it. She calculated how long it would be before she herself could have a baby. She was to be married next March; nine months from March – she knew it took nine months for a baby to be born – was October, November, December. Next December: another one year and two months and perhaps she would be lying as Shanta was lying now, and the baby in the cot would be hers. Not just a sister's child or a brother's child but her own. The thought made her very happy and she took another sweetmeat. As she chewed it, she wondered how babies came to be born. But she did not wonder very much; she had a vague idea that there was something strange there, something which one should not think about. So she did not think about it: only sat and looked at the baby. When it stirred, she nudged her sister Nimmi and said in a tense delighted whisper, 'See, see, she is moving, she is waking up, oh soon she will open her eyes!'

But Nimmi was by this time rather bored with the baby and was amusing herself by making a critical survey of the women sitting round the bed. 'How fat they all are!' she thought with disdain; and if not fat, then thin and dry and meagre like Phuphiji. And how badly dressed they were; of course, they were old women but, Nimmi thought, even if she were old, she would still take care to be always beautifully dressed. She looked at her eldest sister. Rani wore expensive clothes but she did not have much taste; her sari and her blouse did not match, for one thing, and she was wearing too much jewellery, and her lipstick was the wrong shade. Rani would have been good-looking, in a big-boned coarse way, if she had not accumulated so much fat. Nimmi looked at her own long slender arms and thanked God she was not fat; and she resolved, as she often did, that she would always remain slim and small and lovely, even in old age. And what bad manners they all have, she thought, looking at her female relations. One scratched under her armpit, another wiped the perspiration from her face with the end of her sari, another blew her nose between her fingers, and even Rani made a noise and opened her mouth too wide while chewing sweetmeats. Nimmi would always have perfect manners: she would always eat with knife and fork and never make a noise when she chewed; she would always have a dainty little silk handkerchief with her and turn away her face when she blew her nose; she would never scratch in public. She thought of Kanta: yes, she would be like Kanta, only of course she would be more beautiful than Kanta, and lead an even more fashionable life; and her husband would be better looking than Chandra Prakash.

More people came in, friends and distant relations. All of them pressed money into the baby's hands, and Shanta's mother started an account of her own in rivalry to Phuphiji. Lalaji was very happy: he slapped the men on the back, laughed heartily and pressed them to eat sweetmeats. Nimmi, Usha and two of Shanta's younger sisters passed round with the fruit. The room was so crowded that they had to open the doors and overflow into the passage and veranda. The children played games in the bathroom, splashing one another with water and flushing the lavatory. Shanta woke up again and lay there, quite still and placid; sometimes she groaned and then all the women clucked their tongues and said, 'Poor girl,' and her mother fanned her with the hand-fan. Lalaji's wife recounted how she had felt after each of her eight confinements.

A passage was cleared and the Lady Doctor came in, accompanied by two nurses. The Lady Doctor said there were too many people and too much noise; but as there were a number of prospective patients in the room and the expenses of the nursing-home were heavy, she could not say anything more. After she had gone, the men started to leave, having run out of jokes and insults and being anxious about business. Lalaji also went, with Om Prakash, for he had to see his lawyer and meet various people. The women stayed behind and spent the rest of the morning in agreeable, if pointed, conversation.

After leaving the nursing-home, Viddi went straight to the Rendezvous. This was his favourite place ever since it had been redecorated; before that he had gone to the Swiss Miss, but now he liked the Rendezvous because it had a chromium-plated bar and expressionistic murals, and the sort of people he liked went there. It was almost empty now, for it was still early in the morning; but Tivari was already sitting at a table by himself, drinking whisky and staring in front of him in a melancholy fashion. He was not very pleased to see Viddi because he knew that Viddi could not stand him any drinks. Viddi was painfully aware of this and felt ashamed. He ordered coffee for himself but, to excuse himself for not taking a drink (which anyway he would not have wanted), he said, 'What can I do? My father will not give me money.'

Tivari laughed and turned sideways on his seat to look at him. 'But he gives you enough to eat,' he said, making a gesture with his hand to suggest Viddi's bulky outline.

Viddi looked down at his stomach and felt more miserable. 'Sometimes

I feel I will go mad,' he said. 'You do not know what it is like in my father's house.'

Tivari did not look very interested; he cleaned his nails with an old train-ticket and yawned. But Viddi was determined to confide: 'They understand nothing, they know nothing, only money.'

'That is not a bad thing to know about,' Tivari said, digging the edge of the ticket deep under his thumbnail.

'How can I live with people like that?' Viddi appealed. He wanted some response from the other, sympathy, agreement, comfort, suggestion, anything. He admired Tivari very much, for Tivari was a journalist and had been to England and smoked cigars. He had a well-paid Government post, but no one had ever known him to go to any office. Most of the time he sat about in restaurants and let other people buy drinks for him.

'They are killing my soul,' Viddi declared passionately. He did not realize that this sounded odd, because he looked so well fed, so comfortable in body.

Tivari took out a cigar and lit it. He did not offer one to Viddi, who looked on enviously. 'What am I to do?' Viddi asked. 'I want to go away, to Europe, to England. I want to see things, I want to speak with intelligent people, I want to *live*.' Uniformed waiters stood about clustered in corners, waiting for customers.

'But what have you to worry about?' Tivari said. 'Your father is a very rich man. Beyond that you need not look. All your problems are solved.'

'No!' Viddi cried. 'What do I care about money? I hate money, it is horrible –'

'It is beautiful,' Tivari said emphatically.

'You would not think so if you had to live with it every day as I have to. My father, my elder brother – it is all they know, all they can think of – money. More and more and more money. It is the only thing they understand.' Huge trays of pastries were carried out from the kitchens; in the rear, on a plate by itself, came a cake in the form of a fish with silver icing. 'But all the things *I* want,' Viddi said, 'they do not understand. They only laugh and look like animals when I speak of them.'

'What are the things you want?' Tivari asked with an air of bored patience. But he did not wait for an answer; he went to speak with the Manager, who stood surveying the silver fish.

Viddi was left thinking about what were the things he wanted. He knew very well, but it was difficult to state them precisely. He looked round the restaurant – yes, he wanted to sit in places like that, places with many waiters and a bar and grill-work lamps and expressionistic murals on the wall. He wanted to sit there and talk with interesting people, with journalists and painters and post-graduate students who had been abroad. But first he wanted to go abroad himself, to England or America, and lead a very gay life there, drinking and ballroom dancing and sleeping with English girls. Perhaps also he would go to a University and study some more. He would learn about modern art and literature, and then when he came back he would be able to speak about these things with authority, while he treated his companions to whisky and cigars. He would have a beautifully furnished flat all to himself, with books and pictures and a gramophone, and throw late night parties to his friends; they would sit and listen to western music on the gramophone and sometimes they would dance. All the girls present would be beautiful and artistic and very modern. 'I want to go abroad and study at the University,' he told Tivari, who came to sit beside him again.

'The Manager sends you his compliments,' Tivari said. Viddi turned round and the Manager greeted him very deferentially, with his palms joined together and his head bent low. Viddi was delighted.

'He sends his regards to your father,' Tivari said.

Viddi stopped being delighted. Always his father: the Manager was only polite to him because his father was a rich man, who often threw expensive parties in restaurants for business purposes. That was all people could think of – his father's money and how they could get a share of it. Viddi felt that his own personality was swamped by his father's wealth, and that all people saw in him was the reflection of formidable investments.

'I would like to meet your father,' Tivari said. 'He must be a very interesting man.'

'How you would hate him,' Viddi said, his own hate brimming in his voice. 'You do not know what he is like. He is so crude. He is crude in his manners and his ideas also are crude. He does not know anything except eating and sleeping and making money. When I speak of anything else, he laughs and picks his teeth. He is quite uneducated; even reading and writing he cannot do easily, and he speaks very bad English.'

'But what need has he,' Tivari pointed out, 'to read and write and speak English? He pays people like us to do it for him.'

The restaurant was beginning to fill up now. Foreign ladies from the Embassies came in for morning coffee, wearing low-cut summer dresses and high-heeled sandals, their legs naked and very bold and white. Viddi stared at these ladies, wondered about them and admired the way they smoked cigarettes. Tivari also looked at them, puffing at his cigar. They were very lively and talked volubly among themselves, but they never looked round, which was a disappointment.

'In my family,' Viddi said with a sneer, 'it is thought that all European women are prostitutes. My mother and aunts are quite sure of it, and when they see a woman with a white skin they gape at her with their mouths open and think terrible thoughts. Of course they have never spoken with one.'

'Have you?' Tivari disconcertingly asked.

'No,' Viddi said, 'but I would like to. That is why I want so much to go to Europe. I want to study them closely and observe their ways. Perhaps I will even write a thesis about them, comparing and contrasting them with our own women. It will be very interesting, a sort of anthropological study. Do you not think that is a good idea, Tivari? I shall go everywhere and take notes.'

Zahir-ud-din joined them. He wore a pale green bush-shirt and a signet ring and he walked languorously. He was an artist and very handsome. It was he who was responsible for the murals on the walls of the restaurant; he now sat looking at them with one eye critically closed. He said: 'They have depth and vision.' He opened his eye: 'Who will buy me a drink today?' Tivari continued to stare at the European ladies, while Viddi looked down into his coffee and felt ashamed all over again. He wished fervently that he could buy Zahir-ud-din a drink; he even felt that it was his duty to do so. But he could not, and for this he hated his father. Zahir-ud-din philosophically ordered a coffee.

Several business men had come in, fat and prosperous, and sat talking to one another and scribbling figures on the menu. Zahir-ud-din looked at them in fascination and said: 'How rich they must be.'

'They are busy bribing one another,' Tivari said.

Zahir-ud-din laughed, showing many beautiful teeth. 'You have been following the T— bribery and corruption case? Oh, it is a wonderful case. Mister T— was Director of Government Purchases – a very useful post and he made the most of it. His purchases were all at 250 per cent normal cost and in return the suppliers gave him a house, cars, liquor, furniture, clothes and untold sums in cash. He made a fortune.'

'He is not the only one,' Tivari said with a shrug. 'Only he was stupid enough to get caught.'

'Hundreds of people are involved,' Zahir-ud-din said. 'All the richest business men in the country sold things to him. Is your father not involved too?' he asked Viddi.

'How should I know?' Viddi asked listlessly. This talk bored him; it was not for this he came to the Rendezvous. He did not know that his father was fighting and bribing hard to keep out of the case: Lalaji did not believe in sharing his worries with his family.

'He must have been,' Tavari said. 'Men like your father do not miss such opportunities. Only they are too clever. Therefore we do not hear their names mentioned.'

'Clever!' Viddi said disdainfully. 'It is animal cunning.'

Zahir-ud-din threw another look at the business men and assumed an ostentatious expression of pain. 'What is worst for me,' he said, 'is that they should sit here with my murals and not even look at them. Perhaps I would not mind so much if at least I had been paid for them. But the proprietor has paid me almost nothing. He has robbed me and cheated me.' From the business men he looked at the European ladies, speculatively. 'Let us send a note by the bearer – please will you sleep with me tonight,' he suggested. Viddi thought this was very good and laughed heartily.

Tivari said, 'Why do you not introduce us to your father? He could do so much for us, only let us speak with him. We will persuade him what a good business proposition we are.'

'Please,' Viddi said, 'do not talk to me about my father.'

But Zahir-ud-din entered into the idea with enthusiasm. 'Yes, we will make him richer, and not only richer but also great and famous. Does he not want to be a great patron of the arts? Only let him send me to Paris for two years, I will come back famous and everybody will say it was Lala Narayan Dass Verma who first set this man on the path of fame, it is to him that we owe this world-renowned artist who so enhances our national prestige.' He rapped his knuckles on his fine chest and smiled brilliantly.

'Or perhaps,' Tivari said, 'he would like to finance a magazine. I will edit it for him. After the first two issues it will be self-supporting. I will get overseas subscribers, and after four issues it will show a handsome profit.'

'In return for the fare to Paris and guaranteed support for two years,' Zahir-ud-din said, 'I will give him the first five pictures I paint there. *Free* I will give them and no conditions attached. After a few years these pictures will be worth ten times his initial outlay on me. Tell him like that. I am sure he is too clever not to know the worth of such a proposition.'

'What are you talking,' Viddi said. 'He does not even know what a picture is, and a mazagine he cannot read. He reads only business letters and advertisements in the newspaper.'

'That does not matter,' Tivari said. 'Only tell him we are offering good investment and he will listen.'

'He never listens to me. For months I have been begging him to send me to Europe, to let me study at an English University, but he does not hear me. You do not know how I suffer at home. Not one of them

32

understands me. They cannot understand what it is I want, for they think that the only thing one can want is money.'

Zahir-ud-din sighed wistfully: he wanted money very badly. It was true that he wanted to be a famous artist, but above all he wanted to be a rich one. This was understandable; for though he was young and gay and spent a lot of time in expensive restaurants, he had sitting at home, never seen and never heard of, a wife and three small children.

'We have a radiogram,' Viddi went on, seizing this opportunity to confide at least some of his grievances. 'It is very big, in a walnut case, and of course, like everything in our house, it cost a lot of money. Nobody ever listens to the radio, though sometimes they put it on when there is film music. Several times I have tried to listen to a concert of classical western music, but each time they have told me that such noises they cannot bear, turn it off. So I turn it off, I am only the youngest son.' He swallowed a lump in his throat and stirred his coffee furiously. 'If I had money,' he said in a trembling voice, 'I would buy records of classical music. But I have no money, and even if I had and could buy them, they would not allow me to put them on.'

He stopped, afraid lest his voice should break and tears gush from his eyes. The others were not listening, they were looking at the European ladies. 'Also there are no books in our house, only the Gita and a few Commercial Registers. When I want books to read I have to beg people to lend them to me, for of course I have no money, my father will not give me ...' His voice had become loud and high-pitched and several people looked at him. He knew that the business men noisily drinking coffee were acquaintances of his father's, but he did not care ... 'He will not give me anything, he will not send me to Europe or to America, he will not let me study further. Do you know what he wants me to do?' He paused for a second for effect: 'He wants me,' he said slowly and clearly and with a laugh that was half mocking and half tearful, 'he wants me to go into his business.'

Both Tivari and Zahir-ud-din became attentive. 'He wants you to go into his business?'

'Yes,' Viddi said with the same laugh. 'Can you imagine it? *I* to go into his business!'

Zahir-ud-din laid his hand on Viddi's and said enthusiastically: 'But what a wonderful idea. Why are you waiting? He will make you a partner, you will have all the money you want.'

'But I do not want it!'

'Of course you want it,' Tivari said. 'Is it not better than to sit here for the rest of your life and drink coffee because you cannot afford to buy yourself whisky? And all these books and gramophone records you speak of – go into your father's business and you will be able to buy as many as you like. What more can you want?'

'And you will be able to buy my pictures,' Zahir-ud-din said, only half joking.

'I want to go abroad,' Viddi said passionately. 'I want to study, I want to learn things, I want to meet people. I want to get away from home, from my father and my eldest brother and all the women in our house.'

'That will come later,' Tivari said. 'In your father's business you will become rich and then you will be independent and able to do what you like.'

'Independent!' Viddi laughed bitterly. 'When once he has got me into his business, the next thing will be he will find a wife for me, the cross-eyed stupid black daughter of some other rich contractor. She will bring me a great dowry and we will live in my father's house, like my brother Om Prakash and his wife. We will have many children. My charming wife will sit gossiping with my mother and aunt and sisters and I will talk with my father and my brother about business. That is the life my father wishes for me.'

The other two thought how it would be if they had millionaire fathers who offered to make them partners. They looked at Viddi, and Zahir-ud-din said wistfully: 'At least think of us. Think of your friends.'

Viddi was flattered that they regarded themselves as his friends; but he said: 'If I went into business, you would not want to be my friends any more.' When the other two made no comment, he added: 'And your friendship is worth more to me than any money my father could give me.'

At this they gave him up. Zahir-ud-din said sadly: 'At least, ask your father if he would not like his portrait painted. Tell him I will give him a beautiful picture of which he will be very proud.'

Nimmi missed the lecture on Keats, but at lunchtime in the College canteen she copied out the notes her friends had made, which was just as good. In between nibbling biscuits she wrote, 'John Keats was born in 1796 and died of consumption in Rome in 1821.' Her friends were talking about one of the lecturers, and she listened as she wrote.

'She would not be bad looking,' Rajen was saying, 'if she dressed better and did something with her hair.' She fingered her own hair, cut short and set very fashionably.

'She has no style,' Indira said. 'It is easy to see she has not been abroad but has studied only at a College in Madras. Not like Mrs Bose.'

'Mrs Bose has been to America,' Rajen said. 'That is why she is so modern and knows how to dress. My sister says that she has heard Mrs Bose fell in love with an American and wanted to marry him, but her family quickly called her back and made her marry Mr Bose.'

Nimmi stopped writing: 'Really? She has had an unhappy love affair?'

'So my sister says. She says the American was very handsome and also very much in love with Mrs Bose. Nimmi, will you come and play tennis at the Club this evening?'

'I can't,' Nimmi said sadly, though she would have loved to go. She adored going to the Club: it was there, she felt, that the life she wanted was lived. Rajen's parents were members, and now that Rajen was eighteen they had allowed her to become a member independently, so that she could go whenever she liked and take her friends as guests.

'Oh why not?' Rajen said, very disappointed. 'We could have a swim after tennis and then sit on the lawn and drink pineapple juice. Please come.' Indira talked hard with one of the other girls, pretending not to notice that Rajen was not inviting her.

Nimmi shook her head. 'I have to go to the nursing-home because of the new baby. Mummy would be very angry if I did not go.' At home she never called her mother 'Mummy', but among her friends she did, because that was what they called their mothers.

'Oh!' Rajen said impatiently, 'you always have new babies in your family.' She did not mean it as an insult, she was only disappointed that Nimmi would not come. But Nimmi did not take it well: she felt that there was something not quite nice about having too many babies in one's family; only lower-class people, people who were not modern and did not go to Clubs, had a lot of babies.

'Will you come?' Rajen asked Indira, but not very graciously, so that Indira felt it to be more dignified to refuse.

'Do go with her, Indira,' Nimmi said. 'You will like it; it is so nice there and you do not have to play tennis if you do not want to. Please, Rajen, ask her very nicely and she will go. But please go this evening, I want very much that you should go this evening.'

'Why?' Rajen asked.

Nimmi threw a significant glance towards the others: 'I will tell you later,' and then ostentatiously busied herself with her notes.

'My parents do not like me to go,' Indira said primly. 'They say it is not right for a young girl who is not married to go to a Club.'

'What nonsense,' Rajen responded indignantly. 'I did not know your parents were so old-fashioned. Of course everybody goes to Club nowadays. It does not matter how old they are or whether they are married or not. Tara Mehta goes and she is only seventeen and her father is a

Minister, and Neena often came before her father was sent as Ambassador to Indonesia, and now I am sure she goes to Clubs in Indonesia.' She could have said a lot more, but because Nimmi was so anxious for her to go in the evening and she could not very well go alone, she only added, 'If you like, I will ask Mummy to telephone your parents and then it will be all right.' To which Indira agreed, because she was far too keen to go to be able to hold out any longer.

'What does sensuous mean?' Nimmi asked, looking up from her notes.

'It means when someone likes to feel things, like John Keats did,' Rajen answered; she had listened very carefully to that bit in the lecture, for she too had been anxious to know what it meant.

'How do you mean feel things?' Nimmi said. The word interested her and she was not satisfied with Rajen's explanation. 'I thought it meant something else.'

'What did you think it meant?' asked Rajen, who had also thought it meant something else.

Nimmi continued writing, saying: 'Please do not ask me stupid questions,' but she made a mental note to find out more about the word.

Rajen was impatient to know why Nimmi so particularly wanted her to go to the Club in the evening; and since the other girls gave no signs of moving, she suggested, 'Nimmi, shall we go to the Library?'

Nimmi, who was also anxious to be alone with Rajen, agreed at once. She gave the notes she had been copying back to Indira, saying very politely, 'Thank you. May I have them again later please; I have not quite finished yet,' and went out with Rajen. She was well aware that Indira was hurt because they were excluding her from their company, but she could not help that now. She had to talk with Rajen very particularly. But she would make it up to Indira some other time. She was very proud of her friendship with both of them. It had not at first been easy to make them accept her, for they came from the best Delhi families – Indira's grandfather had been a very prominent Congress leader and Rajen's uncle was president of a United Nations sub-committee – while Nimmi was only the daughter of a newly rich Punjabi contractor. But she was charming and pretty and very well mannered, so that she had soon managed to make them forget her defective family background. They now regarded her as quite one of themselves.

Nimmi and Rajen walked along the corridor, proud and graceful, their heads in the air. Nimmi wore a sari of pale blue chiffon and Rajen a white Kashmiri silk with a pattern of tiny green squares. Sometimes they nodded to a group of girls, but they kept themselves aloof, for they were very conscious of their position as the prettiest and most fashionable girls of their year. They walked up the stairs and stopped on the first landing by the long staircase window. They looked out into the garden, trees, lawn and tennis-court flooded with white sun, quite empty except for a gardener in a loincloth. Rajen said, 'Why do you want me to go to the Club this evening?'

Nimmi smiled a little to herself, and then she said in a low voice, 'You cannot guess?' looking away from the other and drawing her finger along the window. Rajen looked puzzled and shook her head. 'Try,' Nimmi said, her eyes fixed on the big banyan tree under which they often sat in the cooler weather and talked or tried to study. 'Please tell me,' Rajen said.

'I think,' said Nimmi, still with the same half-smile, 'Pheroze Batliwala will perhaps be there this evening.'

Rajen at once became pleasantly excited. 'You want to send a message to him?'

Nimmi shook her head vehemently. She had not yet reached the stage of sending messages to Pheroze Batliwala and the suggestion embarrassed her. 'No,' she said, 'not a message.'

'What then?'

Nimmi laughed and swung round, away from the window. She took a pin out of her hair, adjusted the coil on top of her head and then put the pin back again. 'I only want you to see if he is there and then tell me.'

'And?'

'And,' Nimmi echoed, laughing again, 'and nothing. Just tell me if he is there and what he is doing and who he talks with. That is all.'

'Shall I talk with him about you?' Rajen asked, also smiling and watching her friend's face.

'Oh no!' Nimmi cried, putting up her arm and shielding her eyes.

'I will tell him: "Nimmi is dying of love for you."'

Nimmi flung her arm round the other's neck and with a little giggle buried her face in Rajen's shoulder. Rajen also giggled: 'You want me to tell him so?'

'Please do not tease me,' Nimmi said, squirming and laughing. Then she sobered up and raised her head again and added: 'No, I am not so very interested in him.'

'But he is nice?' Rajen suggested in the same teasing tone.

'Hm-m,' Nimmi said, 'he is not so bad.' She opened the little suede handbag which dangled from her wrist, and taking out lipstick and mirror began to touch up her lips. Midway she stopped and lowered the lipstick to ask earnestly: 'Rajen, do you think he is good-looking?'

'Oh yes, he is very good-looking. Most Parsis are.'

Nimmi did not respond to this but continued to paint her lips. Some girls coming down the stairs stared at her disapprovingly; but she did not care. She despised these girls, for their manners were not very refined and they spoke English badly. And she knew that they were jealous of her because she was friends with Rajen and Indira: they expected her to be friends with them, because they were of the same community and their families were acquainted.

Rajen stared after them disdainfully: 'What horrible clothes they wear.'

'Horrible,' Nimmi said, wrinkling her nose, trying to forget that these were the things her own sisters liked to wear – gaudy saris sparkling with sequins and little gold hoop earrings and even – oh horrible – diamonds at the side of their noses.

'I do not think,' Rajen smiled, 'that Pheroze Batliwala would be very interested in such girls.'

Nimmi laughed out loud at the idea of associating Pheroze – so elegant, so well bred, so well spoken, England-returned – with these crude Punjabi girls. 'Poor Pheroze, he would not even know how to speak with them.'

That reminded Rajen to ask with great interest: 'Last time we were at the Club you spoke with him a long time. What did you talk about?'

'Oh,' Nimmi said, feeling superior, 'we only made conversation.' Actually she had found it rather difficult making conversation with Pheroze. She kept having to think up new topics, and he was so very refined that she had been constantly afraid she might say something wrong, something which would reveal to him that she did not come from a high-class family. But she had been very flattered that he should have chosen to sit and talk to her.

'But what about?' Rajen pressed her. Naturally she was very interested; it had been at the Club and in her company that Nimmi had first become acquainted with Pheroze. 'What did he say to you?'

Nimmi thought back, but she could not remember anything very outstanding that he had said. 'He said he liked the way I did my hair.'

Rajen looked at Nimmi's hair: yes, she made the most of it and it looked quite attractive, piled up like that on her head and wound about with jasmine; when the sun shone on it, one could see that it was not really black but a very rich dark brown. But what a pity it was that she kept her hair long; it was so much more fashionable to have it cut short. Rajen fingered her own clipped curls. 'What else?' she asked.

'I cannot remember anything very particular. Rajen, do you like the way I do my hair?'

'Ye-es. It is nice.'

'I love the way you do yours ... Oh, how I wish I could have my hair cut short, I would so much like to wear it like you do. It looks very attractive.'

'I will take you to my hairdresser. He is quite good; he does the hair of all the ladies from the Embassies, so he knows what are the styles in Europe.'

Nimmi sighed and looked out into the garden. A green parrot flashed across the sun-white air and buried itself in the leaves of the banyan tree. She wished very much to go with Rajen to her hairdresser and have her hair cut short and styled in European fashion, but she knew it was impossible. But she did not quite know how to tell Rajen that it was impossible.

'I will telephone and make an appointment. You must have it cut and washed and set, and I will come and sit with you and keep you company.'

Nimmi smiled in a self-conscious manner. 'Daddy would be very angry,' she said. She did not mention that not only her father but her whole family would be very angry. There would be an uproar – Rani would be summoned, Phuphiji would pray, Om Prakash remark upon the results of sending girls to College, and her mother would weep and wring her hands and think only of what Shanta's mother would say.

'What nonsense!' Rajen cried. 'Why should he be angry? Everybody has their hair cut nowadays! Neena had hers cut before she went to Indonesia.'

'I am going to the Library. I have work to do.' Nimmi began to walk up the stairs.

Rajen followed her, saying: 'I am sure Pheroze Batliwala would like you even more if you had your hair cut short. He is the type of man who likes women to be fashionable.'

Nimmi did not even turn round. She walked up the stairs, one hand at her knee to lift the sari a little above the ground. 'I do not care,' she said, and looked proud, 'what Pheroze Batliwala likes and what he does not like. It is a matter of great indifference to me.'

Lalaji sat in his New Delhi office. It was not much of an office, only a small square room with a high ceiling in which stood two old wooden tables, three chairs and several cane-stools. There was a tiny closet leading off it, with a wash-basin and a towel, and here the typist sat, rather uncomfortably. Lalaji had another office in Old Delhi, in the heart of the city, more comfortable than this one, where he transacted all his private business. The New Delhi office was chiefly a place where people could come to see him and, being very central, it was ideally situated for this purpose. Its only drawback was that it was stiflingly hot all through the summer. Lalaji had been intending for a long time to install an air-conditioner, but somehow he always forgot. For this office was not very important to him, and he ceased to think about it the moment he was out of it. Om Prakash, who sat here almost all the time (his father did not encourage him to come to the Old Delhi office) reminded him practically every day about the air-conditioner, but still he forgot.

Om Prakash was sitting at one of the little tables, perspiring profusely. He asked, 'When will you get the air-conditioner, Pitaji?' and looked cross.

'Yes,' Lalaji said, 'we will get air-conditioner. You go and order it, son.' This was only a manner of speaking; Om knew very well that his father would not allow him to order anything. Once, years ago, he had had a new desk made on his own initiative; but when Lalaji had found out about it, he had asked, 'Am I dead already?' and had cancelled the order.

'It is a little hot,' said one of the men sitting in the office. There were many people sitting in the office. Lalaji did not know who some of them were, though on their first entrance he had greeted them all very cordially. By and by they would tell him their business. Meanwhile he looked at his letters. Most of them were from distressed Punjabis who implored him for work, money, letters of recommendation, houses to live in '... I come from very respectable family in Lahore. I have two daughters now it is my duty to marry them but I cannot give dowry. All know what is the goodness of heart of Lala Narayan Dass Verma and also how he spends his time in prayer and helps poor people from his own community ...' Lalaji had had many letters like this since 1947, when the stream of Hindu refugees had come pouring into Delhi from the Punjab. It was natural that these refugees who had lost everything should turn to him for help, for he was himself a Punjabi and never forgot it, though he had been settled in Delhi for many years. His heart throbbed with sympathy for his people and – so he often told himself – if he had been a richer man, he would have done a great deal to help them.

He pushed aside the letters with his elbow and turned to one of the men sitting patiently waiting. 'Please command me,' he said, and they went through the preliminary formula of disinterested affection. The visitor declared that his sole purpose in coming was to regale his eyes on Lalaji; Lalaji said that it was too long a time since he had had the pleasure of seeing his visitor (though as far as he could remember he had never seen him before). The visitor solicitously enquired after Lalaji's health and after the health of his family; Lalaji equally solicitously enquired after that of his visitor and his visitor's family. They continued in this strain for some five minutes, both very cordial and both thinking of something else. The man was a Sikh and not very clean; he wore a collarless striped shirt over grimy white pyjama trousers and his turban was a faded pink. His face was lined and weather-beaten, his beard straggled with grey; but his eyes were still very bright, gleaming shrewdly and warily out of wrinkles. Lalaji took all this in as he talked and thought of other things, and knew that the man had started off as a skilled labourer who had worked his way up to overseer and from there, bitterly, stubbornly and ruthlessly, with many setbacks, much hardship and a very few very small triumphs, to a position of precarious independence.

'This is the matter,' said the visitor at last and Lalaji listened with more attention. All the other people in the room also listened. It appeared there was some small Government work to be given out – some very small work, the visitor said, not worth the attention of such a man as Lalaji – some sweepers' hutments to be erected. He felt ashamed even to mention such a trifle. But he was a poor man, he had four daughters to be married, he had a son whom he wanted to send to College, whom he wanted to become a Sahib, to sit all day on an office-chair and never work with his hands. He was such a very poor man and Lalaji such a very great one. Everywhere Lalaji's name was spoken, he was so good, so religious and he had so much influence, one word from him and all would be settled . . .

Lalaji listened and nodded and made encouraging noises. He asked some more details about the work and declared, without irony, that he was the man's servant, that he sat here only to serve him. More courtesies were exchanged and then the visitor took his leave, joining his palms together and walking backwards for a few steps. Lalaji knew that he would see him every day till the disposal of the work was settled. The man would come to the office and, the preliminary courtesies having been exchanged, would sit and patiently listen to whatever conversation was going on; after half an hour he would go away without saying another word. Most of the people sitting in the room – contractors, sub-contractors, carpenters, locksmiths, electricians, sanitary fitters – had been there before, had stated their requests and now sat there only as a reminder. Sometimes they made some veiled reference to their business, spoke of daughters to be married and sons to be sent to College, but mostly they only sat and let Lalaji see them. He accepted this: it was the way things were done, and one day he might find some of them useful. He himself in his beginnings had sat just so in great men's offices, meeting with much courtesy and very little help. Still, he had known how to make the most of the little and in the end it had been worth it. It was a necessary step to progress: without it he would never have been able to sit himself like this, receiving suppliants.

He greeted another visitor whom he did not remember seeing before. This man was very long and thin and looked mournful; his clothes, though clean, were frayed and had been washed too often. He touched Lalaji's feet and spoke in a whine. After the first few sentences, Lalaji no longer bothered to listen. He knew the man's story already too well, had heard it too often – a refugee from the Punjab, his family had been rich and respected, he had had a house and servants and had consorted with lawyers and engineers. But he had lost everything, his son had been killed in the riots, his house, furniture, ancestral land all gone, he could not get compensation from the Government. His voice rose higher and shriller, sentences became confused; he spoke incoherently of his poverty, his son killed in the riots, Lalaji's goodness, lawyers, engineers, a house with furniture: Lalaji sat there, courteous but discouraging.

'You are my father and my mother!' cried the man.

Om Prakash got up with a sigh of resignation and said mechanically, 'My father is a very busy man, please state your request in writing.' The man touched Om's feet, his voice became more desperate, his sentences more confused; Om towered above him. The other people in the room looked on and listened with interest; only the typist in his little closet continued to type undisturbed. Om raised the man and edged him towards the door. Out on the stairs the voice could still be heard.

Lalaji wiped his hand down his face and sighed, 'Ah! poor people, how are we to help them,' although in reality he did not feel much sympathy. It was seven years now since the refugees had come to Delhi, and he considered that any Punjabi worth the name should by this time have re-established himself. As indeed most of them had. Those that were left – there was nothing much one could do for them; they were finished, and the sooner they accepted the fact the better. Big disasters must always leave small wrecks behind. He sighed again and sent the peon out for Coca-Cola.

All the time he was thinking of that small job the contractor had mentioned. A row of sweepers' hutments: it was a very small job, not the sort he would ever bother himself about, but just now it might do for Viddi. A kind of token job for the boy to cut his teeth on, to introduce him into the business. He thought about it as he telephoned his lawyer: certainly the boy must be brought into the business and quickly too, he could not be allowed to drift about doing nothing but sit in restaurants and consort with undesirable people . . .

'I am not satisfied!' he shouted down the telephone; 'I will change my lawyer! For months I have been paying out large sums and still nothing is settled!' The lawyer protested from the other end – 'the Deputy Minister,' came the remote worried voice – and Lalaji shouted, 'Always the same! He is a man only! I give you four days then I will change my lawyer!' and slammed down the receiver. The people sitting in the office thought, 'Lalaji is angry,' and wondered if it would be better for them to go or stay.

Lalaji really was angry; not with the lawyer but with the Deputy Minister. Ever since this man had come into office there had been trouble. Before that everything had gone quite smoothly, he had tactfully passed on little gratifications to the officers and things got done. But now everyone was frightened of the new Deputy Minister who had launched an offensive against what he called bribery and corruption. It was he who had first instigated proceedings against T—. That was how he had climbed into office, Lalaji bitterly thought: by stirring up untold trouble for respectable business men. Lalaji himself had already paid out enormous sums, patiently pursued prosecutors and witnesses, in order to avoid being caught up in the case; and still he was not sure whether he would in the end succeed in keeping out of it. And all because this new Deputy Minister had ideas about bribery and corruption.

Bribery and corruption! These were foreign words, it seemed to him, and the ideas behind them were also foreign. Here in India, he thought, one did not know such words. Giving presents and gratifications to Government officers was an indispensable courtesy and a respectable, civilized way of carrying on business.

It was a custom, a tradition even, and hence should be respected; not tampered with by upstart Deputy Ministers who had been abroad and brought home unsuitable ideas.

That was the worst about sending sons out to study in foreign countries: they invariably came back with unorthodox ideas and tried to upset the old order at home. If he had his way, no man who had studied abroad would ever be allowed into office. They only did harm, for they always failed to understand the spirit in which things were transacted. They falsified and vulgarized it by attaching words like bribery and corruption to acts of common courtesy.

He had had experience in his own family of the evils of sending sons abroad. There was his son Chandra Prakash, who had come back entirely changed, had refused to come into the business, had refused to be purified after consorting with beef-eaters, had married a girl outside his own community and against the wishes of his family. He was quite lost to them; he failed to understand his own people and they failed to understand him; that was what came of sending sons abroad.

'Please command me,' he said to yet another new visitor who edged forward with an ingratiating smile on his face. No, Lalaji thought, he was not going to make the same mistake again: there would be no foreign studies for Viddi. He assumed an expression of great sympathy as his visitor began to tell him about a dead brother's family – a widow and five children – whom he, a poor man, had to support in addition to his own. Lalaji thought about the sweepers' hutments and about Viddi.

'How hot it is,' said Om and looked crossly at his father.

Shanta was awake now, looking weak but complacent. All the women were grouped round her, massaging her legs, settling her pillows, wiping the perspiration from her face. The baby screamed in a high-pitched voice while an old aunt rocked it on the palms of her hands and made soothing noises. Servants from Lalaji's family and servants from Dev Raj's passed in and out and cooked on the veranda: the smell of clarified butter and horseradish mingled with the smell of hospital disinfectant.

Phuphiji sat cross-legged on a charpai. Her lips were drawn in tight and her eyes, very large and round above jutting cheekbones, darted sharply round the room. She was looking for misdemeanours on the part of Shanta's family, and found much to displease her. But the worst offence – and this was galling – lay on the side of her own family. She whispered fiercely to Rani, 'Go telephone again. Still they have not come. We will be shamed for ever in the eyes of that family.'

'But three times already I have telephoned,' said Rani in despair. 'All day she was not at home and now she says they will come in the evening.'

Phuphiji threw a warning look round the room and said: 'Shsh, not so loud, you know what those people are.'

Rani shrugged. 'But everybody knows. They have all noticed.' Indeed, everybody – especially those from Shanta's side – had commented upon the absence of Chandra Prakash and his wife Kanta; from time to time they made polite enquiries.

'It is a disgrace,' Phuphiji said severely. 'They have no sense of the honour of their family.' She beckoned to Lalaji's wife, who came over looking very miserable. 'I know,' she said before Phuphiji could begin, 'but what can I do? So many times Rani has telephoned and still they do not come. It is terrible.'

'I knew such things would happen,' Phuphiji accused her. 'I know very well what happens when people marry outside their own community. I have lived long enough in the world. But you were all too weak.' Lalaji's wife said nothing. She had heard this so often, ever since Chandra Prakash had married Kanta, and she had never been able to find an adequate reply. In her own heart she had amply forgiven her son; but this did not prevent her from bitterly knowing the truth of Phuphiji's indictment.

'Now it is too late,' Phuphiji said. 'Now we can only sit and bear the reproaches of that family.' Lalaji's wife instinctively looked towards Shanta's mother, who sat smoothly smiling by the bed.

'Now at least see to that one,' Phuphiji said, thrusting her sharp chin in the direction of Viddi. He sat listlessly in a corner, scratching his chin. 'If you do not watch him, we will have the same trouble there.'

'He will always be a good son,' Lalaji's wife said, sounding neither convinced nor convincing.

Phuphiji snorted. 'Tomorrow, if I had my way, my brother would make a match for him. Today even. Or it will be too late and then another one will be lost to us.'

'His father will not allow him to go abroad,' Lalaji's wife said. 'He will stay here with us and go to office with Om Prakash and his father. There is no danger.'

'I warn you,' Phuphiji said. 'You have heard me.'

'No danger,' her sister-in-law repeated miserably. 'He is a good son.' She glanced at him and was worried because he looked discontented and would not speak with anyone.

Nimmi came up and said: 'Can I go home now? I have so much work to do.'

'Go home!' Phuphiji exclaimed. 'What sort of talk is this?'

'Why not? I was here this morning and now I have been here nearly two hours. And I have very important work to do for my examinations.'

'Your important work is here,' Phuphiji said. 'It is bad enough that your elder brother and his wife are not to be seen, the rest of us at least must sit here and show ourselves.'

Nimmi looked for help towards her mother, but she also said, 'You must stay; already they are asking: "Where are Chandra Prakash and Kanta?" How can we let them ask where is Nimmi also?'

'But the Doctor and all the nurses say there are too many people in the room,' Nimmi protested. 'They say Shanta must have rest. How can she have rest when we are all sitting here?'

'Doctors, nurses,' Phuphiji said scornfully. 'I know no doctors, nurses. Only I know a child has been born into our family and it is our duty to be here.' Nimmi sighed and gave it up. It was never any use arguing with Phuphiji, especially when she spoke of duty.

Lalaji's wife began to worry again whether she should stay the night in the nursing-home or go home to her own house. She had almost decided to go home, because she was quite sure that everything was being mismanaged and the servants breaking into her store of sugar; but now that Phuphiji had spoken about their duty, she wavered again. 'Shall I go home tonight? I want to see to my house,' she said in self-defence. 'I can trust nobody.'

Phuphiji said, 'You can go. I will be here to see to everything.'

But Lalaji's wife did not like that either; she did not think it was right for only the aunt to stay and the mother-in-law to go home. People might blame her and say that she did not love her daughter-in-law sufficiently. 'Shanta's mother will say bad things about me. And if I go away, perhaps it will happen like that first time and we will lose another child. She is very neglectful; all morning she was asleep while her daughter was lying there. If I had not stayed awake to guard everyone, I do not know what could not have happened.'

'I will be here,' Phuphiji repeated. Lalaji's wife did not like to point out that Phuphiji had also been asleep. 'Yes,' she said doubtfully, 'but still she will say I am not doing my duty by her daughter. You know how she talks.'

'As long as I am here she will say nothing.'

'But she will *think*.'

'We also have our thoughts about her,' Rani said scornfully.

Nimmi, listening, wondered why her mother and her sister and her aunt should feel so bitterly towards Shanta's family. She had heard the women of that family abused by the women of hers for almost as long as she could remember, but lately she had begun to question this. For it was not as if Shanta's relations were such bad people or had done anything really outrageous. Of course, they were not modern or fashionable or anything, but they were not on the whole so bad. And every day almost they came to the house and everyone talked with them in a very friendly manner. Why should one do that – be friendly with people and afterwards, after they had gone, abuse them? Nimmi frowned and made another resolution (nowadays she was always making resolutions to be different from the other women in her family): never to say anything bad about anybody with whom she was keeping up friendly relations. If she did not like people, she would have nothing to do with them. She looked up and saw Shanta's cousin, Lakshmi. Yes, she would treat everyone she did not like in the same way as she treated Lakshmi: by turning her back, as she did now, unceremoniously.

Lakshmi came straight up to her and said, 'Hallo Nimmi.' She returned the greeting coldly. Lakshmi went to the same College as she did and was one of the girls who dressed in gaudy saris and spoke English badly. Nimmi took good care to avoid her at all family functions. This she did instinctively, because she did not like her, and also deliberately because she did not want to encourage her. Lakshmi was just the sort of girl who,

46

on the strength of one polite word, would come and claim intimacy with her at College.

'I saw you today,' Lakshmi said, looking Nimmi up and down, taking in her sari, her choli, her sandals, the way she did her hair. 'You were standing on the stairs.'

Nimmi made no reply; but to her annoyance her mother came in with, 'You two girls must know one another very well, you are both College girls.' Shanta's mother also came over and said, 'Lakshmi and Nimmi have much to talk.'

'I am taking Honours course, she is taking General,' Nimmi said brusquely. She realized that this meant nothing to the two women, but Lakshmi would know that a girl taking a General degree was inferior to a girl taking an Honours degree; and the tone of her voice was not polite.

'They are very great friends,' said Lalaji's wife, and all the women sitting round looked at them and smiled.

Lakshmi fostered the impression of intimacy by saying: 'You were with Rajen Mathur.'

Again Nimmi did not answer. She was not prepared to discuss a girl like Rajen Mathur with a girl like Lakshmi. But Lakshmi carried on obliviously: 'I often see you with her and also that other girl, Indira Malik. I think you must be great friends.'

'Yes, they are my friends,' Nimmi replied coldly.

'You go to visit in their houses also?'

Such unashamed curiosity, coming from a girl like Lakshmi, was most distasteful, but Nimmi was too proud of her great friendships not to be able to answer 'Of course,' in a haughty manner.

'What is it like there?' the shameless girl eagerly continued. 'You have met their families? I think they are very rich people.'

Nimmi knew what the other girl meant by rich. Their own families were rich too, in terms of money, probably a good deal more so than those of Rajen and Indira – but only in terms of money. What Lakshmi meant was that the parents of Rajen and Indira were very modern and advanced, had been educated in England, gave dinners to exclusive people and went to garden-parties at Rashtrapati Bhavan. But because she was a crude uncultured girl she used the word 'rich'. 'No,' Nimmi said, disdainfully turning her head away, 'not very.'

'But Rajen Mathur and Indira Malik always wear nice clothes, and I know Rajen's sister has been sent to England to study, so they must be rich. Next time you go to their house, please take me with you. I would like to see.'

Nimmi was so indignant that she could not even speak. But her mother

said, 'Yes, you must go everywhere with Lakshmi, you two are sisters';
and Shanta's mother put in, 'It is better for girls who are related to be
friends, then at least their families will know that they do not go into bad
company.' Perhaps they would have said more, but just then Chandra
Prakash and Kanta came in, and their attention was diverted.

All the women of Shanta's family noticed that Kanta did not touch her
mother-in-law's feet, nor her elder sister-in-law's. They were pleasantly
horrified at such disrespectfulness and told themselves, with an inward
knowing nod of the head, that this was only what was to be expected from
a girl like Kanta, a girl from a different community. They watched her
with great attention, for they did not see her often and were much
interested in her. She was quite bold and self-confident, walked straight
up to the baby and looked at it appraisingly; Chandra Prakash followed
her, very much less confidently. They were all curious to know how much
money she would press into the baby's hand, and were shocked when she
took out only a five-rupee note. She placed a perfunctory kiss on Shanta's
forehead and asked in a matter-of-fact tone, 'How are you feeling.' Not
a word of explanation, not a word of apology, for not having come earlier:
Phuphiji's lips were drawn in tight and Lalaji's wife smiled uneasily.

Shanta answered Kanta with a groan and her mother said: 'Naturally
she is very weak. I hope your child is better, what did the Doctor say?'

Kanta looked puzzled. Rani bit her lip and interposed hastily, 'So how
do you like our new baby, Kanta?' which successfully deflected Shanta's
mother, who said: 'Of course she likes it, why should she not? Such a child
is not born every day.'

Kanta laughed and said, not very tactfully: 'It is what all proud
grandmothers say.'

Nimmi looked at Kanta's clothes very carefully. She was wearing a red
sari with a red blouse to match: Nimmi did not like red very much, but
Kanta looked quite nice, certainly better than any of the other women
present. She was also the only one who had her hair cut short. Seeing
Kanta always made Nimmi think of the Club; and thinking of the Club
made her think of Pheroze Batliwala; and thinking of Pheroze Batliwala
made her want to be alone to think more intently. So she was not very
pleased when Lakshmi interrupted her by whispering: 'Kanta is very
fashionable.'

Lalaji slapped Chandra Prakash on the back, saying, 'Now it is your
turn, son,' and laughed cordially. But actually he was not quite at ease;
ever since his second son had come back from England, and especially
since his marriage, he had not been quite at his ease with him.

The other men also laughed and said: 'Your sons are both very productive, Lalaji, but now the eldest is leading.' This brought forth roars of laughter and much hearty back-slapping. Chandra smiled weakly and adjusted his spectacles.

In his embarrassment Lalaji seized a bowl of sweetmeats and thrust it into Chandra's face. 'Eat, son, eat,' he urged. 'Sweeten your mouth in honour of your eldest brother.'

'Also it will give you strength to emulate him!' one of the other men put in to another burst of laughter. Chandra, who hated sweets, took the smallest he could find. He would like to have said something humorous in reply, but could not think of anything. Usually he was fond of a joke and carried on banter with his colleagues very successfully, but theirs was a different, more refined kind of humour from that indulged in by his own family.

'How is your office, son?' his father asked him.

Chandra, embarrassed by the question, blinked three times very rapidly behind his spectacles and then answered, reluctantly, that it was all right. He looked towards his wife, but she was sitting in the midst of the women and could not come to his support. He wondered how soon they would be able to go without causing offence.

'Ah yes,' said Dev Raj; 'we are very fortunate to have a Government officer in our family. Soon he will be Head of his Department and then there will be nothing we cannot get done.' He stretched out his palm and Lalaji, laughing, brought his slap down on it, in appreciation of the humour. But Chandra felt more uneasy than ever. He did not like to have his office discussed in these circles; he felt it to be highly compromising. Especially the reference to Head of the Department: he knew he still had many years of service before him until he could aspire to such a rank in the hierarchy of Government servants.

'It will save us a lot of money,' said Lalaji, winking, and thinking of all the many subordinate officers who had to be gratified before one could begin to speak of gratification to a Head of Department.

'And also much time and whisky,' Dev Raj continued the joke. Chandra took off his spectacles and wiped them.

Om Prakash took no part in this conversation. He had not been on speaking terms with his brother Chandra Prakash for seven years. Besides, he was very tired and wanted to go home and sleep. He stretched out his legs far in front of him and yawned widely.

Lalaji continued to joke and laugh with the other men. But he was not happy: he never was when, at these family gatherings, he was brought face to face with the oddities of his three sons. There was Om who would not speak with Chandra; there was Chandra who did not know how to speak with anybody; there was Viddi who sat apart and looked supercilious. Wistfully he glanced at the sons of Dev Raj, who took a hearty part in all the jokes, laughed uproariously, slapped one another on the back, supplemented each other's humour, and stood as a tower of strength behind their father. His own three sons, Lalaji sadly reflected, did not stand behind him as a tower of strength. Not that he needed any such tower: but it would have been pleasant to know one could depend on them. It seemed to Lalaji that he could never be sure of his sons; they were strange boys, and sometimes he even suspected that they did not like him, though all he did he did only for them. He sorrowfully thought how it would have been if he had been a poor man and dependent in his old age on their earnings, and could not help feeling that it would not have been pleasant. Yet he himself had done his duty and more by his father, had seen to it that the old man's last years were years of prosperity and comfort. Why then should he be so punished in his own sons?

Whenever she had to give a dinner Kanta felt nervous the whole day. Not that she did not enjoy giving dinners; she did, very much. But there was always the fear that something might go wrong: not enough salt in the rice, the vegetables too watery, the pudding not set – in which case she would appear in a very bad light before the wives of the other Government officers. She knew they would be on the look-out for things to criticize (as she was when she went to their homes), especially since her house was so much grander than their own. They all envied her the possession of this house, for they had to make do with uncomfortable Government quarters – utility flats or, worse, furnished rooms in Government hostels. But she and Chandra Prakash had their own house, a beautiful one in the best New Delhi district, seven rooms, three bathrooms, kitchen, servant-quarters, garage, a big lawn and garden.

Kanta loved her house. Perhaps it was the house that had decided her that she could really love Chandra and be happy married to him. It had been given to them by Chandra's father who, though he strongly disapproved of the marriage, did not wish to miss this opportunity of showing the world with what munificence Lala Narayan Dass Verma established his children. Kanta's parents, who had objected even more strongly to the match, were finally won over by the house: Chandra's family might be wholly undesirable, but at least they would enable their daughter Kanta to live like a lady.

And Kanta made the most of her chances. She lavished much care on the furnishing of her house, studied copies of Bombay women's magazines and learnt there how to arrange armchairs and settees round a fireplace,

place little lace doilies on occasional tables, serve drinks from a cocktail cabinet, polish her dining-table and decorate it with cork mats and a candelabra. She also derived many other valuable hints from these magazines. It was there, for instance, that she learnt there how to style her hair, take care of her skin and make casual conversation. She began to wear nylon lingerie and acquired social self-confidence. She joined the best Club, did ballroom dancing and gave informal little dinners. Twice a week she attended a ladies' committee and knitted winter pullovers for the poor. Her social life was thus quite satisfactory; especially since it was above the level of that of her sisters.

True, her sisters had married into better families than Chandra's, into professional families of their own community; but then, their husbands, not having had Chandra's educational opportunities, were Civil Servants of a somewhat lower grade and moved in less distinguished circles. And of course they had no houses of their own, no modern furniture, no doilies or candelabras. On the whole Kanta regarded herself as happy. Chandra's family were unfortunate, but Chandra himself was undoubtedly a gentleman. And there was Lalaji's money. Kanta had never dreamt that she would be connected with so much money. Her own father was a doctor with a practice something less than distinguished; he had been able to give his daughters a College education, but could not settle any very great dowry on them. Kanta had become a teacher in a Girls College and had been quite content to stay there till her parents found as good a husband for her as they could afford. Her meeting with and attachment to Chandra had been a surprise as much to herself as to her family; but it had, on the whole, turned out a pleasant one.

But keeping up her social position was really sometimes a strain. She felt this every time she had to give a dinner-party, especially when Chandra's superior officer was expected, as he was tonight. She sat on the settee in the lounge, sipping a cup of tea while her exhausted mind went over the preparations. Everything should be all right; she had worked hard enough, God knows! She had supervised the polishing of all the cutlery and glasses herself, had impressed upon the bearer a hundred times to keep the tray quite still while the guests were serving themselves, had with her own hands trimmed the roast chicken and made a sauce for the vegetables. For tonight she was going to serve English food, having found several interesting new recipes in her woman's weekly. She narrowed her eyes and looked round the room. As far as she could see everything was in perfect order: not a speck of dust, each doily and each cushion exactly in position, and the modernistic Swiss clock on the mantelpiece nicely polished. The children had strict orders to play in their own room, and she had inspected the bearer's uniform to make sure that it was spotlessly clean and all the buttons on. Everything should be all right, but one could never tell; somehow something always managed to happen – like the last time, when Mrs Kannekraj's coffee-cup had borne faint traces of old lipstick and she had seen Mrs Kannekraj noticing. The memory was painful to her, and she quickly called for another cup of tea.

Then Chandra came home – ten to six already! She had not realized it was so late – and said he was tired. But she soon talked him out of that. 'Please remember, darling,' she told him, 'that you have to play host tonight and have to be quite fresh and smart.'

They went off into the bedroom where she laid out his clothes for him while he had a shower. She put on one of her best saris and looked in the mirror long and hard, trying to decide which necklace looked best. Chandra, rubbing himself with a towel, told her about the exhausting day he had had in the office, to which she made absent-minded noises of sympathy. In the middle of this they heard someone arrive, and Kanta's heart beat faster, for she feared it might already be one of the guests. But it was only Nimmi, who made herself comfortable in the lounge and admired the furniture.

When Kanta came in, all dressed up, Nimmi transferred her admiration from the furniture to her sister-in-law's sari and jewels. In return Kanta said some nice things about Nimmi's own clothes. She was pleased with Nimmi: the girl looked very nice, very fashionable and as if she came from a good family. Kanta thought it suitable for a married woman to take a young unmarried girl under her patronage, and Nimmi – pretty, charming, lively – was just the sort of girl she wanted for this purpose.

'Please tell me who will come,' Nimmi said; 'I am feeling nervous.'

'Nonsense,' Kanta said, sitting herself down in a manner that was slightly matronly, as a contrast to Nimmi's. 'There is nothing to feel nervous about. You must learn how to behave with ease when you go into society.'

'It is so difficult. But I love meeting people. Kanta, you are sure I look all right?'

Kanta surveyed her carefully – the pale green georgette sari, the short red choli shot with gold, the filigree silver necklace and earrings to match, jasmine wound around the hair, open sandles with high platform soles, toenails painted a neat plum red – 'Yes, you look nice.'

'You are sure? You think your friends will like me?'

Kanta turned to Chandra who was reading the newspaper and said, 'Please, Chandra, when our guests come, do not just crumple up the newspaper and throw it on the floor, it looks so bad.' To Nimmi she added: 'Of course they will like you, you look very nice.' Chandra obediently folded his newspaper and called to the bearer to take it away.

'But tell me who is coming,' Nimmi said. 'Then I will know how to behave.'

Kanta arranged her sari to fall gracefully over her feet. 'They are all colleagues from Chandra's office with their wives. The Head of Department is also coming.'

'He is nice? Is he very clever?'

Chandra smiled: 'He is Head of Department,' he said, which explained everything.

'You reminded him in the office?' Kanta anxiously asked. 'He will not forget?'

'A Government officer never forgets,' Chandra answered, only half joking.

'And who else is coming?' Nimmi asked.

'There are S. C. K. Ghosh and his wife,' Kanta said. 'They are Bengalis. Last year S.C.K. was sent to England by the Government for further training and because of this his wife thinks they are very grand. She brought back a pressure-cooker and all day we hear about nothing but her English pressure-cooker. But I have not noticed that it makes her cooking very much better. Last time we went there she gave us something she thought was a soufflé and Chandra had indigestion all night.'

'I think it was the vegetable rissoles we had for lunch that gave me indigestion.'

'And the food was very badly served. Of course, she has no proper dining-room and only a very cheap dinner-service, so it is difficult for her to entertain. The Head of Department did not come.'

Nimmi decided that Mrs Ghosh could not be very nice. 'And who else?'

'There is also Mr and Mrs SankarLingam. Mrs SankarLingam is very jealous of her husband's position. She is always telling me how soon he will be promoted and that he will be Deputy Head of Department in five years, but of course this is nonsense. SankarLingam will never become Deputy Head of Department as long as Chandra is there.'

'I think we ought not to speak about that,' Chandra said. 'Nobody can know what will be and it is not right to talk too much about these Government matters.'

'But everybody knows that you will be Deputy Head of Department!' Kanta heatedly replied. 'There can be no question about it, and that is why it annoys me so to hear Mrs SankarLingam giving people wrong impressions. She does it only to make herself seem more important, but it does her no good at all. Quite the contrary; it will prejudice the Head of Department and all the officers against poor Mr SankarLingam, who is such a nice man.'

She called the bearer, for she wanted to make sure again that everything was in order. 'And when you strike the gong for dinner,' she told him, 'strike it only three times. Do not forget yourself like last time. We do not want to hear a concert. You are sure they have not forgotten?' she asked her husband and looked anxiously at the clock. 'You spoke to them in the office?'

She knew that the guests would arrive at least half an hour after the stated time. She herself always made a point of being at least half an hour late when she was invited out, and she would not have thought much of people who were exactly on time. But when one was the hostess and had spent the whole day in arduous preparations, waiting for guests and wondering whether they had not, by some terrible misfortune, forgotten, did become a strain.

'They will come,' Chandra said. 'Please remember that they also will have had to change their clothes and rest after a tiring day in the office.'

'I do hope they have not forgotten,' said Kanta, biting her lip. 'It would be so terrible after I have worked so hard and who is to eat all the food that has been prepared?'

But they did come, all of them, and almost all together, at the regulation half-hour late. Nimmi was rather confused at first because suddenly there were so many strangers in the room. When Kanta introduced her, she instinctively greeted the visitors with her palms joined together in Indian style; and only realized how unsuitable this was when the other ladies shook hands with her and tolerantly smiled. She felt so embarrassed by this blunder that for five minutes she did not dare look up again; but after that she recovered and took great pleasure in studying the guests. The gentlemen, she saw, were dressed in black trousers, white jacket and black bow-tie; only the Head of Department wore Indian evening-dress, white leggings and a long white coat buttoned right up to the neck. But she concentrated more on the ladies, for she was always anxious to learn how ladies dressed and behaved in society. She admired Mrs Ghosh very much, although Kanta had given her an unfavourable impression of her. For Mrs Ghosh was good-looking and fashionable; she wore a sari which was ornate without being over-ornate and just the right amount of jewellery. Mrs SankarLingam also looked nice, though she was dressed a little less fashionably and had a dark complexion.

After the first greetings were over, there might have been an awkward pause, but Mrs Ghosh, who was a very lively – even vivacious – lady, said, 'Again today it has been too hot,' comically turning her eyes up to the ceiling while she fanned her face with her hand and pouted. So then they discussed the weather, each one adding a contribution, and when this subject had been exhausted, Kanta got up and brightly asked, 'What will everybody drink?' opening the cocktail cabinet of which she was very proud. She and Chandra handed the drinks round themselves, which created a charming impression of informality. The gentlemen drank whisky and soda and Kanta and Mrs Ghosh had sherry; only Mrs SankarLingam sipped pineapple juice, since she was not quite modern enough to take to alcohol. Nimmi was very thrilled when Kanta gave her sherry, and as she drank, she wondered with a little inward giggle, what they would say at home if they knew.

'Nowadays the sherry in the Club is not of very good quality,' said Mrs Ghosh. 'I think it is from South America.'

'But they have very good Scotch whisky in the Club,' said Mr Ghosh. 'It is difficult to buy such whisky in the shops.'

'I get all our drinks from the Club,' said Chandra. 'The prices there are more reasonable and that is something we Civil Servants have to consider.' Everybody was very pleased with this little joke. Chandra threw a look at the Head of Department and was gratified to find that he too was smiling.

'I often wish,' said Mr SankarLingam, 'that our salaries would be a little more elastic. Perhaps if we submitted our budget to the Government, they would see what poor fellows we all are and take a little pity on us.' This was followed by more appreciative laughter and the Head of Department himself said, 'Or perhaps they would say we are too wasteful and cut our salaries for us.' Everybody was delighted. Mrs Ghosh threw back her head and gave a very modern giggle.

'Then we will have a strike, sir,' said Chandra.

'A hunger strike,' said Mr Ghosh. 'We will all sit and fast outside the Prime Minister's residence.'

Nimmi joined in the general amusement though she did not quite get the point of the jokes. But it was wonderful sitting there, listening and looking and sipping her sherry, which she tried to persuade herself she liked.

The Head of Department said smilingly, 'Perhaps instead of having strikes, we ought to try and persuade our ladies to cut down their budgets a little.' The ladies very charmingly put on an air of mock indignation. 'Now, now! Please!' said Kanta. 'We lead very simple lives. It is you men who are so extravagant.'

The men laughed heartily at this. 'Certainly,' said Mr Ghosh, 'it is we who wear lipstick and gold necklaces and have tea-parties every afternoon.'

55

'Tea-parties every afternoon!' the ladies cried as with one voice, and Mrs SankarLingam said: 'Perhaps you would like to come and see me one afternoon when I am trying to keep the children quiet and supervising the cooking of the dinner.'

The Head of Department smiled appreciatively; his smile looked odd on him, because he had very severe features and sat in a position of rigid ease with the right ankle placed precisely on the left knee. But Kanta was pleased to see him smile. Her little party was going well.

'I often wonder,' said Mrs Ghosh, 'what you men do in office all day. I am sure you do no work, you only sit and drink tea.' But nobody laughed; this was going a little too far, especially with the Head of Department present. So, to take his mind off Mrs Ghosh's tactlessness, Kanta asked him, 'I hope your wife is quite well?' It was a purely formal question for nobody cared about his wife. She was never seen, he never took her anywhere and never talked about her; she was one of those old-fashioned women who sat all day in the house and gossiped with the servants. She was socially a great drawback; really one had to feel sorry for the Head.

'And how are the children?' asked Mrs SankarLingam, which was Kanta's cue to go and get them. They stayed in the room for five minutes, quiet and well-behaved, only speaking when they were spoken to and then very prettily. Kanta was proud of her children. They were well brought up – she had not been a teacher for nothing – had exquisite little manners and spoke English perfectly. She had been very particular about the children's English; they could speak in Hindustani with the servants, but with their parents and with one another they had to speak in English. After they had gone, the ladies fell to discussing children and how difficult it was to find good schools nowadays, while the gentlemen talked office affairs. Nimmi took no part in either discussion, but sat silent and looked round with bright eager eyes.

The dinner itself was a great success. Everybody praised the food and looked impressed by the handsome way in which it was served. Kanta had spent much time thinking how to seat the diners. Her problem revolved round the Head of Department, for she was reluctant to place either Mrs Ghosh or Mrs SankarLingam next to him. She herself would of course sit on one side of him and, after long reflection, she decided to place Nimmi on the other. She knew that she was thus throwing a weight of responsibility on the girl and she felt a little uneasy about it; but then, she had faith in Nimmi and this occasion would be something of a test.

And she was not disappointed. Nimmi behaved really admirably, answered in a clear sweet voice whatever questions the Head chose to put to her, laughed when he made a joke, and listened to him with a flattering expression of interest. She looked so very pretty, so very young, that even one as strict and correct as the Head must enjoy the company of such a neighbour. Mr Ghosh, who sat on the other side of Nimmi, seemed to be enjoying her company too; he was very attentive and spoke to her whenever she was not speaking with the Head. Nimmi liked Mr Ghosh, she thought him witty and charming and quite nice-looking; and she liked the way he passed the dishes and held them for her and recommended her to take a little more of this, just a taste more of that. He was so charmingly domesticated, and she thought it was nice for men to be domesticated; not like her father and her brothers and all the other men in her family, except Chandra, who were rough and clumsy and had no idea how to be polite to ladies. She liked the Head too, though she felt a little nervous with him; he was so stiff and formal, and when he asked her a question it was like being cross-examined. Still, she did not underestimate the privilege of sitting next to him, even though it was always a relief to turn back to Mr Ghosh whose little jokes were really funny.

In the afternoon, at tea-time, the Rendezvous was more crowded than in the mornings. There was a band playing at that time and there were coffee and cakes and a cosy cosmopolitan atmosphere. People came in from the Embassies, and also radio-artistes and playwrights and freelance artists and journalists. Viddi liked to sit and hear them talk, and eat cakes when he could afford to. Usually he squeezed in at whatever table there was a spare chair; for being neither a radio-artiste nor a playwright nor an artist nor a journalist, he could not expect a clique and a position of his own. But today he was surprised to hear Tivari and Zahir-ud-din calling him over to their table the moment he came in. Zahir-ud-din even shouted to the waiter to bring an extra chair. Viddi was greatly flattered, though he tried to look nonchalant, as if all this were a matter of every day.

'You know Bahwa?' Zahir-ud-din asked, lightly tapping that person on the chest with the back of his hand. Viddi knew him to be a playwright who produced his own plays and acted the chief role; he dealt only with profound social problems. Viddi had never before been thought worthy of being introduced to him.

'We have been telling Bahwa what we were saying yesterday,' said Zahir-ud-din, 'and he is interested.' Bahwa nodded his large head up and down.

'What we were saying?' Viddi innocently enquired.

'About you and your father financing us.'

Before Viddi could disclaim anything, Bahwa had leant across the table and explained himself forcefully. His forefinger bored the air on a level with Viddi's chest. 'I have in mind,' he said, 'that we form a professional company of actors to tour the country. That is the only way to establish ourselves. I have had much experience with non-professional companies here in Delhi, and perhaps you will not believe me when I tell you that, through bad publicity and organization, none of my plays has made profit and several of them have even run at loss. So now I think a professional company must be formed.'

Zahir-ud-din nodded earnestly at this and looked at Viddi, who felt uncomfortable. 'We have all the talent for such an enterprise,' Bahwa said. 'I will write the plays and produce and act the dramatic parts. Zahir-ud-din will paint scenery and Tivari will be our Publicity Manager and Press Representative.'

Tivari puffed at his cigar and looked at Viddi with an expression of amusement on his face. This amusement embarrassed Viddi even more than Bahwa's bland assumption. 'You cannot disappoint him,' said Tivari.

'Listen,' said Zahir-ud-din. 'I will give you beautiful stage designs and costumes, we will have lavish dance-dramas, so that people will think the Mogul Emperors have come back after a visit to Paris.'

'Dance-dramas,' said Bahwa contemptuously. 'We will leave these outdated hybrid forms to people from Calcutta who can think of nothing better. No, we will have problem plays, dealing with all the evils of our Society. You must have seen some of my plays?'

Viddi had, but was not quite sure what to think of them. Bahwa, it was true, wrote problem plays, but he was inclined to overstate the problem and, having overstated it, attempt to balance it on the dramatic side with comic and romantic relief. The result was bewildering. Viddi remembered one social drama which, he gathered, had been a plea for the domestic servant. It had included a rich landowner falling in love with his wife's maid, and consequently causing the maid's husband to lose his job and starve to death, the maid and her baby also starving but refusing to give in to the solicitations of the landowner, the landowner's brother getting drunk and making a comic exhibition of himself, the landowner's daughter falling in love with her husband's clerk, the clerk secretly loving the maid, the maid finally succumbing to starvation and falling down dead, the clerk spurning the landowner's daughter, and the landowner poisoning himself in a fit of bitter remorse. Bahwa himself had played the landowner, very wickedly and very loudly.

'Your plays are all nonsense,' Tivari said. 'Even you know it.'

Bahwa was not in the least disturbed. 'Please do not try to tease me. I know your type of humour very well,' he said.

'But even a bad play can be made a good one with beautiful scenery and costumes,' Zahir-ud-din urged. 'Really I like a bad play better, because it does not take the attention of the audience away from my designs.'

'There!' cried Bahwa, shooting out his forefinger at Zahir-ud-din. 'That is just the kind of selfishness we have to avoid. What we want in our professional company is team-spirit, everybody being equal and all work of equal importance, even if it is only tidying the stage after the actors have gone.'

'This sort of talk will not get you far with Ved Prakash's father,' said Tivari. 'You cannot expect him to build up a communist company for you.'

Viddi laughed and said: 'My father is so afraid of Communism that he keeps some old and ragged clothes in his trunk to wear when it comes.'

'Quite right,' Tivari gravely agreed. 'The people who are not wearing such clothes will be strung up on lamp-posts at once. It is a well-known fact.' He looked at Bahwa and added, 'And the first will be those wearing bush-shirts.'

'Please do not be flippant,' Bahwa said. 'I am speaking seriously with Shri Ved Prakash.'

Viddi turned appealing eyes on Zahir-ud-din: 'But I told you . . .'

Zahir-ud-din smiled brilliantly; he looked very handsome when he smiled. 'Listen, you are a cultured man and you care about Art. We need men like you. We need patrons. But how can you be our patron if you have no money? Listen, Ved Prakash, what is so bad about going into your father's business? If I had such a father, I would give up everything and at once go into his business so that I could do good to my fellow-artists.'

'And if you do not like the idea of a company of actors,' Bahwa said, 'then we will form a film company. Much good work can be done through films. I have a scenario already, based on a very profound idea and dealing with many evils in our society. There is also singing and dancing. I have composed several romantic lyrics which will be very popular and can be reproduced on gramophone records.'

'Or if you do not like a film company,' said Tivari, 'then at least buy a ticket for his play.'

'Yes,' said Bahwa, promptly bringing out a book of tickets. 'Take ten-rupee ones. I will give you the first row. How many?'

'But I have no money,' Viddi said.

'You can pay me tomorrow. I will trust a friend. Six shall I give you, seven?'

'Tomorrow also I will have no money.'

Bahwa smiled tolerantly. 'When you have you can give me. But I would very much like that you bring your father. I wish him to see what sort of work we do.'

'I have told you,' Viddi said unhappily, appealing to Zahir-ud-din and Tivari, 'my father does not care for such things. He does not know what a play is. If I tell him play, he will think it is all prostitutes and he will be very angry with me.'

'But at least he will come,' Bahwa urged.

'I think you underestimate your father,' said Tivari, whereupon Viddi laughed bitterly. At the next table a radio-artiste sucked chocolate milk-shake through a straw. Viddi felt even more bitter. Chocolate milkshake – his favourite; and he, the son – as they were pointing out to him – of a millionaire, had no money.

'And you have asked him about the portrait?' Zahir-ud-din asked.

'What portrait?'

'The one I will paint of him. Arrange the times when he can sit for me. The terms we will settle later. I am sure your father will not be a mean man. Not like the proprietor of this restaurant, who has dealt so badly with me and refuses to pay me the rest of my money or to let me take it in kind. People only come here to look at my murals, and still he will not pay me, though he is making a fortune from my work.'

He pointed at the band, each member of which sat in front of a rectangular box painted bright orange and scrawled over with the outlines of Indian musical instruments: a veena in blue, a sitar in yellow, a sarengi in green, a tabla in black. At the back of the band was a huge mural, stretching from ceiling to floor and repeating the colours of orange, blue, yellow, green and black. It was difficult to make out the subject-matter of this mural, but glimpses could be caught of girls in saris, musical notes, palm-trees, lotuses and fish under water. 'The band can play for three days without stopping,' Zahir-ud-din said, 'and still no one will listen to them. People are interested only in the setting I have given them.'

'You may please come to our rehearsals,' Bahwa told Viddi. 'It will be very interesting for you, and you will see me produce.'

Viddi was flattered. He had never before been appealed to in this manner by people he admired, and he found it very pleasant. At the same time he was uneasy because they were assuming that he had a share in his father's money. This he wanted to disclaim, since he had a revulsion against anything to do with his father.

'I wish very much to help you,' he said. 'But I have told you, I am very poor. I have no money at all and my father will not listen to one word I say.'

'If you go into his business,' Tivari said, 'he will listen and you will no longer be poor.'

'But I have told you!' Viddi cried desperately. 'I want nothing to do with his business; it will kill me!'

'I have wonderful ideas for film décor,' Zahir-ud-din said. 'Listen, how do you like this? The heroine sings; she is sitting on a little golden chair by the side of a lake. It is night and there is a moon and everything is silver. In the middle of the lake is a lotus; as the heroine sings, the lotus spreads and grows and grows and as it spreads and grows, slowly there come out of the petals beautiful girls wearing only gauze scarves, and all these beautiful girls will dance. The lotus will grow so high that it is level with the moon and the girls will dance against the moon. Then as the heroine ends her song, the lotus will get smaller again and fold up and all the girls will disappear within it, and then there is silence again and the lake is very still, with the lotus floating on it and the reflection of the moon. Is it not beautiful?'

'First class,' said Bahwa. 'I have a lyric all ready, which will suit this theme very well.'

'Do you not know,' Tivari asked Viddi, 'that all the big film magnates are really business men who have made their money elsewhere and then invested it in films? You can do the same: first you get money by entering into your father's business, then you sponsor our film company. Of course you will be the most important person in it and your word will be final on all productions. Also you will be our Business Manager and I will be the Press Representative. I will edit a special film magazine to boost our productions.'

'I do not want to be Business Manager or magnate,' Viddi replied. 'I want nothing to do with business. I hate this word.'

'You like to act?' Bahwa asked. 'I will produce you, you can play romantic parts. If you are not able to sing, you only have to learn how to open and shut your mouth. We will have a voice recorded. All the leading stars do that; none of them sing themselves.'

Viddi thought of himself in romantic roles; but the idea did not particularly please him. He knew he was too plump and might look ridiculous. 'No,' he said, 'I do not want to act.' He liked being coaxed like this, it was almost as good as really having money and sponsoring artists.

'You can help me produce,' Bahwa offered.

'No. I am not interested in making films. I do not like films. I like literature and art.'

'But our films will be full of literature and art!'

Viddi shook his head. 'No, I want first to go to Europe.'

'What do you think you will be doing when you are sponsor of a film company?' said Tivari. 'You will be flying to Europe once a month and to America to make all arrangements.'

'All big film people do that,' Zahir-ud-din said, drumming his hands on the table in time with the band which had now struck up a Hungarian rhapsody.

'Yes,' said Tivari. 'They meet all the biggest people in Europe and America, directors and producers and actors and writers and artists. If you went only as a student or a tourist, you would never meet such people.' This sounded very agreeable, but Viddi could never be sure whether Tivari was serious. There was always an expression of amusement on his face which made Viddi feel uncomfortable. He did not like being laughed at, even though Tivari was clever and educated and England-returned.

However, the other two were serious enough. 'You will be a great man, a patron of all the arts,' Zahir-ud-din said. To which Bahwa added: 'I will write such scenarios, our films will become internationally famous.'

'We will call our company International Films Limited,' said Tivari, taking out another cigar. Viddi watched him light it and wished he would offer him one; but this was not done.

'We will have mostly historical films,' said Zahir-ud-din, 'because they give more scope for décor and costumes. Or film fantasies; they also are very good, with dream interludes.'

'I have been reading about Mahmud of Ghazni,' said Bahwa, 'and I have been thinking of writing a play about those times. But a film would be even better.'

'We will show him smashing the great Lingam in the temple of Somnath with one blow of his mighty sword,' said Zahir-ud-din, his eyes shining, 'and as it breaks up the treasure within will come tumbling out, rubies and diamonds and great golden goblets.'

'And out of each goblet will come a dancing girl,' said Tivari, which made Zahir-ud-din look at him and enquire dubiously, 'Are you making fun of us?'

'Also we will show the Court at Ghazni,' said Bahwa, 'with poets and artists and historians and slaves.'

It all sounded very exciting, and Viddi wished it were real. But he could not help comparing it with reality, his existing poverty which would not allow him even to drink a chocolate milkshake, and his father at home wanting him to enter into the contractors' business.

Lalaji received his lawyer at home. He always liked to see him either at home or in his Old Delhi office. The New Delhi office was not private enough, and what he and his lawyer had to say to one another was always very private. The lawyer was a small, quick and able little man. He was accompanied by his clerk, who stood in the background holding files and a briefcase. An excellent man, this clerk, who knew everything but gave the impression of hearing and knowing nothing. Lalaji himself sat in an armchair with his feet up on a little stool. His eyes were half shut and his hands folded over his stomach: this was his usual attitude for listening intently.

The Lawyer gingerly broached the subject of the Deputy Minister, glancing at his client sideways. But Lalaji did not stir, not even when the lawyer, growing bolder, told him how the Deputy Minister had been heard to declare his intention of ruining and ousting Lalaji and all men like him. Lalaji heaved a staccato but very round and rich laugh from the stomach and then ran the tip of his tongue quickly over his lower lip. The lawyer nodded: he quite understood his client's contempt for the Deputy Minister and shared it. But he said: 'There is only one thing.'

'What?' Lalaji lazily asked.

'The letter.'

Lalaji knew about this letter. It had been written not by himself – he never wrote letters if he could help it; he knew too well what trouble they could get one into – but by Om Prakash. Five years ago, when Om was still fairly new to the business and acted on his own initiative (he had learnt better since), he had written this letter to T—. In itself the letter was innocent enough. It referred to one of Lalaji's many transactions with T—, but stated nothing directly; a bland, innocent, routine letter. But seen in connection with the evidence which the committee of inquiry had since accumulated, it could be wrested out of innocence, could be made incriminating. That the letter had been written and, having been written, had been filed and preserved in Government records, was one of those slips that could happen in the best organizations. Lalaji wasted no time in recrimination – he had not even mentioned the existence of the letter to Om – but took his usual attitude of what has been has been: now the only thing left was to take steps to eliminate the consequences. The committee of inquiry had not yet found out about the letter. But this, Lalaji knew, was only a matter of time. Official bodies moved slowly, more slowly than his own organization, but equally surely.

So the letter had to be destroyed, and quickly too. If only it could be found. For to say that it was in a certain Government office in a certain file was not to say much; Government files had a way of never being where they were expected to be. It might have been lying on some officer's desk for months (perhaps it was even lying, unnoticed, unthought of, on the Deputy Minister's desk – a grimly amusing thought). Or it might, at the very moment, be circulating from one Government department to the other, marked 'For immediate attention' and with a long and ever-growing list of illegible initials. The elusiveness of Government files and the general innocence of one department as to what the other was doing had often been useful to Lalaji: but one could not rely on it indefinitely. The existence of the letter was a terrible risk, and he could not rest easy until it had been found and destroyed. All other steps, the destruction of evidence, the friendly arrangements with prosecution witnesses, were useless until this one letter was found. He said as much to the lawyer, who agreed, as he usually did.

'You must find it,' Lalaji said, opening his eyes and unfolding his hands from his stomach. 'I do not care how much it costs.'

The lawyer nodded again, his lips wisely pursed, and then gave a sign to the clerk. It was a surprise to see this clerk, who all the time had seemed lost in thoughts of his own, instantly open the briefcase and extract, without a moment's hesitation, a sheet of paper which the lawyer handed to Lalaji. 'Expenses,' murmured the lawyer, drumming his hand on his thigh and looking the other way.

Lalaji ran his eyes down the items. But he did not study them very thoroughly: he trusted his lawyer. He knew the man took a professional pride in his skill at this kind of business, and would have been ashamed to present his client with an expenditure account out of proportion with the services rendered. It was his boast that he knew the price of everyone, high or low, on whom a price could conceivably be fixed, and he prided himself that he would never make the mistake of either under or overestimating this price.

Although all more orthodox payments went through Lalaji's accountant, secret expenditure accounts such as this one were settled from a store of ready cash which he always kept in the house. He left the lawyer and went to his bedroom, fumbling under his kurta for the little key which he wore tied to his pyjama-cord. The bedroom had built-in walnut wardrobes with sliding doors which had cost a lot of money. But they were almost empty, for both Lalaji and his wife preferred to keep their belongings – their clothes, their valuables – in the huge old family-trunks which stood pushed against the wall. These peasant coffers, heavily padlocked and iron-bound, spelt more security to them than any safe or any bank.

Opening the topmost trunk, Lalaji thrust his hand in surely and confidently, and drawing out an old jacket which had once belonged to Om, extracted the required amount from inside the lining. It always pleased him to feel this ready cash of his. He had properties, securities, bank accounts, shares – but none of these was quite real to him. It was only the hard crackle of paper-money under his fingers or the sight of heavy gold and silver ornaments which could convince him that his wealth was real, was there, was tangible, was his.

Afterwards he sat thinking. He thought about the letter, long and hard, and tried to devise various complicated plans for recovering it. But after some time he gave it up. It was no use thinking too much about a thing; it was bad for the nerves and anyway, could do no good. Somehow a solution would come, whether he thought about it or not. He switched his mind on to something else; and there were enough problems for him to ponder. There was, for instance, the problem of the new building of the Happy Hindustan Trading Company. This was becoming really urgent, for rumours had begun to reach him that the Directors were inclined to favour a rival firm of contractors. Yesterday in the nursing-home he had met Dev Raj and had managed to remind him. It would do no harm to give him a ring in his office now, enquire after his health.

He put his hand on the telephone but just then he was disturbed by a commotion outside. Something heavy was being carried indoors and servants shouted instructions at one another. Above this, giving conflicting instructions of their own, he heard the voices of his wife and his sister. 'So they have come,' he thought.

'Be careful with my charpai!' Phuphiji shouted, and his wife cried, 'You are trying to break it? You have learnt some bad ways while I have been away!' The children were very excited; Lalaji could hear them jumping up and down and asking their grandmother what she had brought for them from the nursing-home.

He picked up the telephone again, but instead of calling Dev Raj he called his own office. Om said there was nothing to report; only that it was very hot.

'We will get air-conditioner,' Lalaji said. 'Your mother and aunt have come home.' Om made no comment. 'You have seen your brother Viddi?'

'That one,' Om snorted down the telephone. 'He will be sitting now in a restaurant like a great Sahib.'

Lalaji hung up. He sighed, thinking of Viddi sitting in a restaurant. Bad reports constantly reached him about the boy – how he had been seen in this restaurant, in that restaurant, conversing with drinkers and loafers and irreligious anarchists. But after a while he got up and went into the women's quarter. Out of habit he coughed before entering, and the women, hearing this male sound, automatically pulled their saris over their heads. Maee was kneeling on the floor, unpacking the boxes, and servants ran about with cups of tea and fritters and betel-leaves. His wife, sitting cross-legged on a grassmat, stirred her tea and gave directions to Maee. Phuphiji lay stretched on her charpai and groaned while Usha massaged her legs.

'You have come home very quickly,' Lalaji said.

'And what are we to do there?' his wife replied with spirit. 'When that woman will not let us come near our own children?'

Lalaji ignored this reference to Shanta's mother. He always did. He lowered himself on to a charpai and sat rubbing one knee.

'And it is good that we have come home,' his wife said. 'Everything here is in disorder, already I can see. Your clothes have not gone to the washerman and the steps are dirty and one week's sugar and tea has been drunk in two days. I will throw all the servants out of the house, not one of them can be trusted.' The servants continued to walk about the room, with an air of great preoccupation.

'And what have you been doing – cutting grass?' Lalaji's wife turned on her daughter Usha. 'Two grown-up daughters I have living in the house, and still I cannot leave from here one minute even. When I was your age, I was married and had children and my mother-in-law and elder sisters-in-law could sit at their ease all day in the courtyard because I was there to see to everything.'

Usha massaged her aunt's legs. Her face usually wore a calm and satisfied expression and this could not easily be disturbed. Her father defended her. 'She is a good girl,' he said, though not very energetically.

'She is lazy and thoughtless,' her mother retorted emphatically. 'All she knows to do is to sit quietly on a charpai and eat sweetmeats.' This was not altogether incorrect: Usha was a placid girl, and like eating. 'What will you do when you are married in two–three months?' her mother demanded. 'I pity your husband and also your poor mother-in-law. They will think they have got a very bad bargain, and they will blame us for sending such a girl into their house. I feel ashamed when I think how they will speak about us because we have not taught you better.'

Lalaji chuckled. 'They will be content enough when they think of the dowry they have got with her.'

'Dowry-showry,' his wife said contemptuously. 'They will wish they had had half the dowry and twice the better girl.'

Phuphiji opened her eyes to contribute: 'Have I not told you, have I not warned you? I know what sending girls to College leads to; I have lived long enough in the world.'

'If I had had my way,' Lalaji's wife said, looking at her husband, 'there would have been no such College. Both of them would have stayed at home and learnt what it is right for a girl to learn.'

'You would have had *my* daughters brought up like a poor man's?' asked Lalaji, smiling.

'Poor man, rich man,' his wife replied, 'a daughter is a daughter and there is only one way.'

'In my time,' Phuphiji said, 'a father would have killed himself before letting his daughters become eighteen or twenty years old without finding good husbands for them.'

'*She* is settled,' Lalaji protested, pointing at Usha. 'Wait two–three months, then you will see what sort of marriage celebrations I am arranging for her.'

'However great the marriage celebrations,' his sister replied, 'this will not blind people to the fact that the bride is twenty years old and knows nothing of household matters. Not even massage can she do properly. Leave off!' she shouted at Usha, 'you are putting more pain into my leg than there was before.' Usha contentedly left off and called to the servant for tea and fritters.

Widely yawning and stretching his arms above his head, Lalaji got ready to leave. He never stayed long in the women's quarter. But they had not finished with him yet. 'Where are you going?' his wife demanded.

'To office,' he said, idly twisting his finger in his ear.

'An old man like you, why do you not stay at home and rest and eat some proper food which I will prepare for you.'

'What is the use of always going to office?' Phuphiji asked. 'It would be better for you to stay at home and think about settling your children in a proper manner.'

'Why do you think I go to office?' Lalaji said. 'Will I earn money for my children by sitting at home only?'

Phuphiji assumed an expression of contempt. 'I do not see what great things you have done with money.'

'No,' said his wife. 'On the contrary, when you had less you did better by your children. Without money you did not think of College and such things for them.' The two eldest, Rani and Om, had had little education and marriage had been arranged for them at an early age. Which was as it should be.

'Then you still knew what a father's duty was,' Phuphiji said.

Lalaji heaved himself up from the charpai. 'You understand nothing of these things.'

Without troubling to rebut this insult – which at another time she would have done, very forcefully and at great length – Phuphiji cried, as loudly and quickly as she could, for she knew that once her brother was set on going, it would take much to hold him back, 'See to your Viddi and your Nimmi – if anything happens, please do not say we have not warned you!'

Lalaji stopped short. It was not the reference to Viddi that arrested him – he knew all about that, and was taking steps – but Nimmi. That anything should be hinted against his Nimmi!

Phuphiji, seeing her advantage, continued quickly, 'He is twenty-one and she is eighteen, and what have you done about settling them?'

'Yes, what?' cried Lalaji's wife, though she was busy supervising Maee unpack the clothes.

'To College you have sent them,' Phuphiji said in deep disdain. 'That a boy should be sent to such a place to unlearn all the good and religious things he has been taught at home, that is bad enough, but a *girl*! *We* would not care to marry one of our sons to a girl who has been to a College.' This, with its implied reference to Kanta, was an effective double-hit.

But Lalaji merely shrugged. 'It does no harm. Let the child enjoy herself.'

'Enjoy herself!' Phuphiji cried. 'A girl of that age has no right to *enjoy* herself! She should be managing a household and bearing children and looking after a husband. That was thought good enough in our time.'

'It will come to her soon enough,' Lalaji said.

His wife, hearing this, looked up sharply to ask: 'You are arranging for her? You have not told me.'

'When the time comes I will tell you,' Lalaji said.

'It has come!' Phuphiji cried. 'It has come and more! Eighteen years old she is. Is that an age for her to go and play at a College and show her face to all the world?'

'Yesterday she went to Kanta's house,' his wife said. 'She would not come to the nursing-home to be with Shanta and the new-born baby, because she said there was a party at Kanta's house. I do not know what sort of people Kanta asks to her house, but I do not think they are *our* sort of people.' She compressed her lips very primly, but had to release them again at once to say to Maee: 'Just see how you are handling my things. They will all have to be pressed again.'

'A hundred times I have told you,' Phuphiji said. 'She must not go to that Kanta's house. I know very well what sort of people go there, all without morals or religion, people who have been abroad and have eaten beef. It is not a house for a young unmarried girl to visit.'

But Lalaji's wife bridled up at that: 'It is also my son Chandra Prakash's house,' she said. 'He will not allow his sister to sit with such people.'

Phuphiji passed this over. It was a theme she would take up another time, at more leisure; for the moment she did not wish to confuse the issue, especially as Lalaji was making off again. 'She should be kept at home,' she said. 'Arrangements should be made for a good marriage, and in the meantime we should teach her all she has to learn. It is a disgrace to us that she does not even know to cook.'

'My daughter Nimmi,' Lalaji proudly said, 'will never need to know how to cook. She will have so many servants that all day she can wear her jewellery and drive about in a motor car.'

'Servants!' his wife shouted. 'You do not know what you are saying. The more servants you have in the house, the more work there is for you to look to. This is a lesson I have learnt very well in this house!' But he was already on his way out. He moved his great bulk forward with remarkable agility and, hunching up his shoulders to his ears, gave himself a conspiratorial little smile as he pretended not to hear.

# Part Two

Nimmi and Rajen played tennis on the Club courts. They did not play well, but they looked nice. Long slim brown legs stretched out from their brief pleated shorts, and they wore silk jerseys which were tight and revealing. Rajen was quite at home in her tennis-costume, but Nimmi still felt a little self-conscious. It was so strange, showing bare legs in public. She felt uncomfortable every time she thought what her family would say if they could see her, so she did her best not to think about it. Her tennis-costume was a great secret. She had bought it out of her own money – her father gave her a liberal allowance – and Rajen had ordered it for her from Bombay. Of course, she never took it home, it always stayed in Rajen's locker at the Club. Sometimes, while she was sitting with the other women of her family, she thought about it and the thought always made her giggle; then they would all look at her and Phuphiji would be very cross.

'Fifteen–thirty!' Rajen announced over the net. Nimmi took up her position for service; she stood there, very straight and graceful, and pretended not to notice the two young men who were watching her. She was not at all put out when both her services failed. Rajen called, 'Fifteen–forty!' and Nimmi said, 'I don't know what is the matter with me today,' though she did not usually play any better than this.

After they had completed the set, they walked off the courts and went to change in the dressing-room. They took a long time over putting on their saris and doing their hair and applying lipstick. There were several other ladies in the dressing-room who talked about clothes and parties; they spoke mostly in English, only sometimes, in their asides, they broke into Hindustani. Rajen had to change a book for her father in the library, so Nimmi went with her and, standing there, idly looking round, she saw a dictionary and that reminded her and she looked up 'sensuous'. It said 'of, derived from, affecting the senses', which did not mean much to her. But then her eyes travelled upwards and she saw 'sensual: self-indulgent in regard to food and sexual enjoyment', and she quickly shut the dictionary and put it back on the shelf.

She had been thinking of Pheroze Batliwala all evening but now she thought about him more urgently. She wondered whether he was sensuous or sensual, and felt a little ashamed of her thoughts, especially when she imagined him finding out about them.

They walked through the lounge, marbled and pillared and empty, out on to the lawn where they sat at a little table in green and white wicker armchairs. A bearer in white with a huge red turban served pineapple juice to them from a silver tray. Rajen had to sign the bill, since she was the member, but she and Nimmi had come to an arrangement by which Nimmi always paid her own share afterwards, when the monthly account came, and sometimes also some of Rajen's. For Rajen's parents could not afford to give her as big an allowance as Lalaji gave his daughter.

'How lucky you are,' said Rajen, thinking of this, 'to have so much money of your own. Of course, Mummy and Daddy would like to give me a bigger allowance but they have so many expenses, especially now that Amita is studying in Cambridge.'

Nimmi thought that she would willingly sacrifice half her allowance if only she could say that she had a sister studying in Cambridge, England. 'And when I go next year,' Rajen said, 'they will be poorer still. Nimmi, you must tell your parents to let you come with me, we will have such fun together there.'

Nimmi smiled but made no answer. She knew there was no hope of that, absolutely none, so it was no use talking about it.

'I am sure they can afford it,' Rajen persisted. 'If they can give you so much money every month, they can also send you to Cambridge.'

'It is not the money,' Nimmi was forced to reply. She wished Rajen would stop nagging her about this. It was painful enough thinking about how she would have to stay behind when Rajen and Indira went off to England, and Neena far away in Indonesia. 'Who is that lady over there in the white dress?' she asked, indicating a group of Europeans at a neighbouring table.

'She is the wife of someone from the German Embassy,' said Rajen. 'She is called Frau Kunz. But Nimmi, Indira is also going – '

'She is pretty,' said Nimmi. 'Do you know her?' She studied Frau Kunz's solid bare shoulders and marvelled at their whiteness.

'Mummy and Daddy met her at a party at the German Embassy,' Rajen said. 'Nimmi, we will have such jolly times together. Amita writes to say how wonderful it is in Cambridge and how everybody, the boy-students and also the girls, can do just what they want . . .'

But Nimmi was thinking of Pheroze Batliwala. She thought: 'Well, even though Rajen's sister is at Cambridge and her parents go to parties at the German Embassy, still it is to me Pheroze Batliwala likes to talk.' She said, 'Do you think he will come this evening?' and Rajen, successfully deflected, said, 'Who, Pheroze Batliwala? I think so: every evening he likes to play at least one game of tennis.'

Nimmi knew this very well, but she had wanted to hear Rajen's confirmation. She was quite excited now, because she thought she might see him any minute. The tables out on the lawn were beginning to fill up. There were little groups of men in white tennis-shorts, their rackets laid across their knees, and there were girls in fresh pastel saris, and ladies from the Embassies like Frau Kunz in fashionable shoulder-free frocks. Waiters were already laying tables on the veranda for people who would want an open-air dinner, and at a discreet distance cooks, picturesque in tall white hats, were busy at the barbecues. It was almost dark and shaded lamps had been lit on the lawn. Rajen pointed out her parents' acquaintances to Nimmi, and sometimes people came up to her and asked after her parents, or she went herself and was polite to middle-aged couples. If she had not been waiting so tensely for Pheroze, Nimmi might have felt her own anonymity more sharply.

At last he came. He stood near a lamp so that she was quite sure it was he, although she thought she would have been sure anyway, even in the dark. He seemed to be looking for someone and tapped his tennis-racket against his legs as he stood and looked around. His legs, protruding nakedly out of short shorts, had from the first been a surprise to Nimmi, because they were strong and muscular, whereas the rest of him was so thin; they were also rather hairy. She wondered whom he could be looking for, and her heart beat faster when she thought that it might be herself. Any moment his slowly turning eyes would rest on her table, and as she did not wish to appear to be waiting for his attention, she began to talk with Rajen. She said, 'Your parents have many friends,' this being the first topic that occurred to her, and Rajen, sounding superior, replied, 'They go out a lot. Every day there is some party – Oh! look, there he is, Pheroze Batliwala.'

Nimmi kept her eyes intently lowered. How clumsy Rajen was, to speak his name so loudly! He might have heard and then he would think they were sitting there waiting for him. She plucked at the canework binding the edge of the table, and then she saw his legs and neat white ankle-socks, and she looked up as he said, 'Good evening,' in his slow voice. Feeling herself grow hot, she smiled at him, successfully assuming an expression of casual politeness.

'May I sit down?' Pheroze Batliwala asked. With the same polite smile, Nimmi graciously gave permission, thinking triumphantly: so he *was* looking for me. The thought gave her confidence.

Pheroze drummed his fingers on the table. 'It is hot this evening.'

'Yes,' said Rajen, 'but I think the cool weather will be coming soon.'

'I love very much the really cold weather,' Nimmi said. 'In December and January, it is my favourite season.'

'You must go to Simla for winter-sports,' said Pheroze. 'I go every year for one week, mainly for skating.'

'My sister who is in England will go to Switzerland this year,' said Rajen. 'She will learn to ski.' Nimmi thought that this was unnecessary; Rajen was only showing off. She wondered what to ski was, and made a note to look it up in the dictionary at the first possible opportunity. She was reminded of 'sensuous' and 'sensual', and her self-confidence wavered.

Pheroze continued to drum his fingers on the table. There was an awkward pause. Nimmi felt Rajen looking at her with a faint expression of amusement, and this annoyed her. She flung back her head and tried to look unconcerned.

'What will you drink?' Pheroze asked. Rajen and Nimmi looked at one another, and Rajen said, 'We have just drunk pineapple juice.'

'Have a proper drink,' said Pheroze, looking at Nimmi.

On an impulse of daring Nimmi asked, 'May I have a French sherry please?' She hoped this was correct. Authoritatively gesturing the bearer, Pheroze asked, 'Dry or sweet?' and Nimmi plunged again to say, 'Sweet please.'

'Dry for me,' said Rajen, fingering her short curls. Nimmi wondered whether this was more correct or whether Rajen was only trying to be different.

Pheroze cleared his throat, crossed and uncrossed his legs and drummed his fingers. Nimmi covertly studied him and admired his handsome appearance. He had a long thin face with a big nose and a very pale yellow skin. It was his fair complexion that attracted her most. She watched him taking out a long silver cigarette-case and was taken aback for a moment when he offered it to her. She shook her head, sweetly smiling, but she wished she did smoke: how impressed he would have been if she had nonchalantly taken a cigarette and said, 'thanks,' as she let him light it for her. He lit his own cigarette, flicking his silver lighter with a practised gesture which she admired. He had such elegant, worldly ways. She thought: 'Parsis are not allowed by their religion to smoke,' but of course Pheroze was England-returned and very modern and emancipated.

Rajen said, 'This sherry is good; I like a dry sherry.' Nimmi thought hers tasted like petrol, but she hoped she looked as if she liked it.

'It is a good lady's drink,' said Pheroze, drinking whisky and soda. His large melancholy eyes were fixed on Nimmi over the rim of the glass. She was very conscious of this, and wondered whether he was thinking she was pretty. She tried to imagine herself as he saw her but could only visualize a dim slim shape. However, she drew confidence from the fact that she was wearing an attractive sari, a flowered georgette, and a white blouse of Swiss lace through which the straps of her pink brassière could be seen. She had taken even greater care than usual over dressing, and also over her hair, because she had known that she would meet him.

'Please excuse me for one minute,' said Rajen, and got up to speak to a well-dressed middle-aged lady, another friend of her parents. Nimmi's heart beat a little faster at being left alone with Pheroze; and she quickly tried to make casual conversation.

'Do you come here every evening?' she asked, but was sorry the moment she had done so because it might lead him to suspect that she was interested in him.

She need not have worried, for he did not take her up on it. Instead he said: 'I have not seen you for several days. I have been looking out for you.'

She did not answer. She really did not know what to say. Was he telling her that he liked her and wanted to see more of her? And if so, should she meet him halfway or only sit there modestly listening to him? Or should she ignore it altogether and quickly change the subject? She wished she had more experience in these matters; and wishing so, she kept quiet, looking down into her glass.

Pheroze cleared his throat, but when he spoke his voice was still hoarse. 'I wanted to ask you,' he said; 'will you have dinner with me one night?'

'Where?' Nimmi promptly asked.

'Here in the Club, or anywhere you like. Please will you meet me here next Sunday at seven thirty?'

There was no time for thought, for here was Rajen back again, and Nimmi had to say quickly before the opportunity was lost, 'All right,' and to Rajen: 'Was that another friend of your parents?'

Rajen made a face. 'It is awful to have to be polite to so many old people, only because they know your parents.' But neither Nimmi nor Pheroze heard her. Pheroze got up and beat his racket against his shins, 'I have to go home to change for dinner,' he said and then he went.

Rajen stared after him and asked, 'Why is he in such a hurry?' Nimmi smiled and put up a hand to arrange her hair, which did not need it.

'What did he say to you when I was gone?'

'Shall we go home now?'

'Did he say I love you, I love you, I love you?' asked Rajen, flinging wide her arms.

'You are an owl,' Nimmi replied, still secretively smiling.

'He said so to you?'

Because she could hold it no longer, Nimmi said: 'He asked me to have dinner with him.'

Rajen was properly impressed. She drew up her eyebrows and looked at Nimmi, waiting for more. When no more came, she asked: 'And then? What did you say?'

Nimmi began to wonder whether she had been right in accepting so promptly. But there had been no time to pretend that she was busy or reluctant; and she had not wanted to lose the opportunity – he might never have asked her again. She asked, 'What would you have said?' and Rajen replied without hesitation: 'Of course, I would have said "yes", what else. It is nice to be taken out to dinner.'

This answer was a relief. And Rajen was right: it was nice to be taken out to dinner, especially by someone like Pheroze. 'Do you think he is very handsome?' she enquired, for she wanted confirmation on this point again and again.

'Ye-es,' said Rajen, slowly and as if not very convinced. Nimmi looked at her sharply. She was surprised, for Rajen had always assented to this question so vigorously before. 'What do you mean "ye-es"?' she asked quite indignantly.

'What do you mean, what do I mean?' Rajen countered; and changed the subject. 'Shall we have another pineapple juice?'

'Do you think I am a bucket? First juice, then sherry, now you want me to drink more juice.'

'Why did you say *French* sherry? It sounded silly.'

'Because I did not want South American sherry.' Nimmi remembered Kanta's party and felt almost sure of herself. 'Perhaps you think there is only one type of sherry?'

'*I* think ...!' cried Rajen, who among her friends had always been considered the expert on these subjects.

Nimmi said, 'Why do you think he is *not* handsome?'

'I did not say he was *not* handsome.'

'But you meant he was not very handsome. Well, I think he is very handsome; very handsome indeed. I do not know one man who is more handsome than he is.' She looked at Rajen with defiance.

'But he does not know how to make conversation. He sits there and does not say anything interesting. The men my parents know and who come to our house always have something interesting to say. Every gentleman in society must know how to make conversation, especially with ladies.'

'Oh,' Nimmi cried, 'he makes conversation very well! *I* know, I have talked with him; and he has many interesting things to say. Only he is very intelligent and very dignified, so he does not like to sit and chatter about stupid things. He is quiet and reserved. I like men who are quiet and reserved. I do not like men who sit and chatter; they are like monkeys.'

Rajen only shrugged in reply to this. For the rest of the evening the two friends were rather cool with one another.

Early in the morning Viddi lay on his bed and smoked a cigarette. His own room was the only place in the house where he could smoke, and even there he had to be careful. If he should hear his mother coming, he would have to extinguish the cigarette very quickly and hope she would not notice the smoke. As he smoked, he composed poetry. He had had so much practice at this that the verses came to him almost instinctively: 'In the morning, there is song; at midday, toil; in the evening, sorrow comes upon us: so life passes.' All his verses were like that; all about how life passes, philosophical and melancholy. But sometimes he composed a lewd verse: 'Until I came, she sat all day among women, sifting rice; she did not know what men can do; until I came.' This struck him as being very witty and meaningful, and he looked forward to repeating it to Tivari and Zahir-ud-din.

When he had composed enough poetry, he began to think about what he was going to tell his father. He was determined to talk with his father, now, today, soon; but he did not know how. It would be different, he thought bitterly, if we lived in a civilized way. Then at least his father would have some place where he could be seen alone; Viddi would go to him and say, 'Please may I speak with you, Pitaji,' and Lalaji would sit quietly and listen. But as things were, how and when would he sit quietly and listen? Even when he was at home, downstairs in the sitting-room, he was never alone. There would be Usha massaging his legs, Nimmi curled up on the settee, Mataji serving tea and food, servants bringing his shoes, his letters, the telephone ringing, and – worst – Om grunting in an armchair.

It was the thought of Om, scornfully listening, impatiently and imperially interrupting, that was the greatest hindrance. Viddi hated his eldest brother even more than he hated his father. For it was Om, more than Lalaji himself, more than the women, who was set against his being sent abroad for further studies. As it was, he resented Viddi's College education, because he himself had not had one; instead, he had had to go into the business and marry Shanta. He had never forgiven his brother Chandra for having been abroad and married a wife and taken a job of his own choice; and he was determined that Viddi should not be allowed to go the same way. Because he is a brute, Viddi thought, he wants me to be a brute too. Without Om, perhaps he could have made some impression on his father: if only – and it always came back to the same thing – he could make him listen. But Lalaji would be thinking of a hundred different things, talking with three people at once, giving directions over the telephone, reading his mail and the advertisements in the newspaper, drinking tea, cursing a servant. And even if, under these unfavourable conditions, Viddi could somehow begin to talk to him, he would listen only superficially and draw his own conclusions and prepare his own decisions before Viddi had stated even half his case. Perhaps the best time to catch him was in the very early morning: Lalaji was always the first to get up, and then at least he was alone. Viddi had been meaning to go to him at that early hour for a long time now; but somehow he had always overslept.

When he went downstairs, it was just as he had thought. The telephone was ringing and his father shouting that he would not speak with anyone unless it was someone important. Om was quarrelling with Nimmi and the children were playing hide-and-seek among the furniture. Everybody was eating puris and potatoes, and the moment Viddi came in his mother shouted for more puris and potatoes. He was glad that his mother was home again. She saw to it that his food was always punctual and hot, and hovered over him while he ate. And when Om said, 'This great Sahib likes to sleep late and then sit all day and eat,' she turned round very sharply to answer, 'Let him then, he is a boy only, he needs sleep and food.' Lalaji laughed and said, 'He has no worries, he has a rich father,' which made Viddi furious, though he did not say anything. But his mother defended him again, told the father, 'What else are you here for, if not to provide for your sons?' and to Viddi, 'Eat, son, eat, do not listen to them.' Lalaji laughed again and shook his head, thinking of the things *he* had been doing at Viddi's age.

Nimmi also came to Viddi's defence, mainly because she had been quarrelling with Om. She told her eldest brother, 'I do not see that you go hungry or without your sleep,' and indeed no one looked better fed than Om.

'Be quiet,' the mother told Nimmi. 'This is not the way to speak to your eldest brother.'

'She has no respect,' Om said, enjoying himself. 'We have not taught her right. Why is she allowed to sit here? Because she goes to a College? Girls who go to a College can sit with the men?'

Successfully infuriated, 'I am not in purdah!' Nimmi cried.

'But you should be,' Om promptly replied. 'We do not want to see our women sitting around us. Soon you will make yourselves masters of the house and *we* will have to sit quiet behind a screen and cover our heads.' Lalaji was vastly amused; he slapped his thighs and roared and then threw a handkerchief over his head and looked demure. The children also laughed, in high-pitched voices.

'Enough now,' the mother said crossly, but when Nimmi shouted at Om, 'This house would be better if you were not seen!' she rebuked her: 'Have I not told you to speak with respect with your elder brother. And he says quite right, you should not be sitting here – often enough I have told you, and Phuphiji also has told you. Except only to serve your father and brother, you must not be seen here.'

'What,' said Lalaji, looking fondly at Nimmi, 'you would deprive me of the sight of my pearl?'

'Pearl-shearl,' his wife said. 'Leave off such talk and let the women of your house manage your daughters. When no one will take them for wives because they are spoilt and immodest, then you will know.'

'Only the whole of Delhi is standing on my doorstep with hands joined together, begging for my daughters,' said Lalaji with a fat pleased smile.

Viddi fed the children. They sat on the floor while he ate his breakfast and from time to time he popped bits into their mouths. He was very fond of children, and did not hold it against these that they were Om's. But his thoughts were on other things. He was thinking how it was quite impossible to say what he wanted to say. Yet he had to speak, now, soon. He could not go on like this, with nothing to look forward to and nothing to do except sit in the Rendezvous and feel unhappy because he could not treat the others to drinks. He must go away, go abroad and study and lead a cosmopolitan and emancipated life. He must be given the opportunity to become a finer man than his father and his eldest brother. He *was* a finer man already, he knew it: he did not think only of money as they did, he thought a lot about other things, such as art and literature. He was a B.A. (true, he had only got a pass degree, but he was a B.A. and he had read books and also he composed poetry). But now he needed opportunity to study and learn more, and it was so easy for his father to give him that opportunity. If only he would listen and let himself be persuaded; if only there was a chance of making him listen. He watched Lalaji reading a letter, his lips moving to form the words. Then he ate a hardboiled egg and with his mouth full said: 'Today the big car must go for servicing.' He took the telephone receiver which a servant held out to him and bellowed into it, 'Yes, please Sahib, command me!' No, there never was a chance of really and truly making him listen; and even if there had been,

Viddi pessimistically concluded, wiping the last piece of puri round his empty plate, talking to him would do no good. His father understood nothing but money.

Two men came into the room, deferentially smiling, their hands joined together, and Lalaji hastily finished off his telephone conversation and cried out, 'Please come, please come!' Lalaji's wife covered her head and hurried from the room. Viddi also got up; he did not want to stay there and hear his father talking complicated and unsavoury business. Only – and this was the trouble every morning, ever since he had left College a few months ago – he did not know where to go nor what to do. It was still too early for the Rendezvous and besides, he did not want to go to the Rendezvous. There was nothing to be done with his father, and less with his eldest brother; so he decided to go and see his second brother. He knew Chandra had very regular habits and was sure to be found at home at this time in the morning. At quarter to ten he would take the car out and go to office; so Viddi could have about half an hour with him. It was not much, but at least it was something: more time than he would ever get with his father.

As was to be expected, Chandra was having his breakfast. The whole family was seated in orderly fashion round the dining-table, eating scrambled eggs and toast. Chandra was reading the newspaper and from time to time he read a bit aloud to Kanta, who was keeping an eye on the children to make sure that they handled their knives and forks properly and did not make noises when they drank. Nobody was very pleased to see Viddi. The children chorused politely, 'Good morning, Uncle,' in English, and Chandra said straightaway, 'I am just going to office.'

'I know,' said Viddi, sitting down at the table uninvited.

'You will have some breakfast?' Kanta asked, though not very graciously. She did not care to see any member of her husband's family, except Nimmi, in her house.

Because he liked the smell of the eggs, Viddi said yes, though he had already eaten very plentifully at home. Kanta was annoyed because there were not enough eggs to go round; but Viddi did not notice this. He said, 'Listen, Chandra, I must go abroad. I want to study in England.'

Chandra neatly folded his newspaper. 'Then please speak with Pitaji about it.'

'Speak with Pitaji,' Viddi repeated contemptuously. 'You know very well he will never listen, and then also there is Om and he will never allow it.'

Kanta asked: 'But what can *we* do?' Then she clapped her hands and cried, 'Now then, you kids, off you go, get ready for school.'

Chandra looked at his wristwatch and said, 'It is getting late, I must go to office.' He was all ready, his hair was oiled, his spectacles gleamed; he wore a stiffly laundered white shirt and white drill trousers.

'You have time till quarter to ten,' Viddi said. 'Please help me. I must go to England, I cannot stay here. You went yourself, why can you not help me to go too?'

'How can I help you,' Chandra said, not offering but pointing out the impossibility of it. He looked uncomfortably at his wife, who came to his support: 'Chandra has no influence with your father or with your eldest brother.'

'But you can try at least!' Viddi cried. 'Talk with Pitaji, go and see him and tell him that it is important for my future that I go and study abroad. Tell him that afterwards, after I come back, I will be able to earn more money. That is the sort of argument he can understand.'

'It will be better if you tell him yourself,' Kanta said. 'He will not like it if Chandra goes and speaks with him about it. He will think he is meddling, and then he will only do the opposite of what Chandra asks.' She called to the servant to clear away the breakfast-things, although Viddi had not yet finished.

'But he will not listen to me at all!' Viddi cried.

'What can *I* do?' Chandra asked miserably.

'It is your duty to help me. You are my elder brother and you have had all the opportunities which I want. Now it is your duty to see that I get them too. Why should you be the only one to study abroad and choose your own career? I have the same rights as you have.'

'Chandra was sent abroad,' Kanta replied acidly, 'because he was a brilliant student and did very well at College. His professor at College recommended your father to send him abroad.' But no professor's recommendation could have had much weight with Lalaji if his mind had been inclined otherwise. At the time, fourteen years ago, he had not been a rich man for very long and so had wanted all the things a rich man traditionally has – including an England-returned son.

'I also went to College,' Viddi retorted. 'I am B.A. too.'

'But you only got a pass degree,' Kanta pointed out. 'Chandra got a second-class degree, and he would have had a first-class degree if the examiner had not set such a difficult paper.'

'I also would have got a better degree,' Viddi said, 'but my professor was very prejudiced against me, so he told the examiner to mark me down. Everybody knows this, and if my father took more interest in these matters, he would have filed a suit against the professor.'

Chandra put a hand over his spectacles and adjusted them on the bridge of his nose – a gesture he had picked up from the Head of his Department. 'My dear brother,' he said, 'all this is beside the point.'

'I know,' said Viddi. 'Is that my fault? The point is that I want you to speak with Pitaji and persuade him to send me to England. It is not very much I am asking you. Considering all the advantages you have had, you should be glad to do this little thing for me.'

'I would do it, but I know it is of no use. If Pitaji does not want to send you to England, he will not listen to anything I say to persuade him.'

Viddi knew this was true; but Chandra was his only hope now, so he insisted. 'At least try,' he said. 'Do not simply sit there and say it is of no use.'

'We do not like to ask your father for favours,' Kanta said primly. It hurt her that they so often had to do so, for Chandra's salary was sufficient only for their daily needs. Household and entertaining expenses were heavy, not to mention clothes bills and the children's school; so anything extra, like the cocktail cabinet and the yearly holiday in the hills, had to come out of Lalaji's pocket.

'But I do not ask you to ask him for favours! I ask only that you tell him to give me the same chance that he gave Chandra. This is only right. If he sends one son to study abroad, then also he must send the other.'

'The case is quite different,' said Kanta. 'You cannot compare yourself with Chandra.' And before Viddi could protest, she switched on to, 'Darling, today I have an appointment with the hairdresser. Will you pick me up from there in the car at one o'clock and we will come home together for lunch.'

Chandra looked at his wristwatch again and got up. 'Now I must really go,' he said. It was still five minutes early, but he would be able to finish reading the paper in the office and perhaps send out for a cup of coffee.

Viddi also got up. 'Please give me a lift in your car,' he asked his brother and Chandra could not very well refuse, though he would have liked to.

In the car Viddi returned to the attack. 'You must help me,' he told his brother. 'You are older than I am and also you are married and independent, so Pitaji will listen to you. And you know very well it is necessary for me to go. If I stay here, Pitaji will make me go into the business and he will marry me to someone like Shanta and then perhaps, God forbid! I will become like Om.'

'Om is quite uneducated,' Chandra said. 'He has not been to College at all and he speaks bad English. You have been to College and you are B.A., so you can never become like him.'

'But I want to study more,' Viddi said. 'And I do not want to go into the business. I want to enter a profession – perhaps I will become a

University professor or an art critic and write books, or perhaps edit a magazine.'

'If you go with Pitaji and Om into the business,' Chandra said, 'you will earn more money than in any profession. You do not know how difficult it is to manage on a fixed monthly salary. Of course you have a pension to look forward to, but it is not a very big pension, and you can never hope to become rich.'

'I do not want to become rich! I have seen enough of rich men. I do not want to be one of them.'

Chandra sighed as he steered and said, 'It is easy to talk. But when you have a family to support, then you will think differently. The life of a gazetted Government officer is not always easy.' He gave another sigh.

'At least you are independent, and you do not have to mix with crude and uneducated people. Chandra, I am surprised, I did not think you thought so much of money. You speak like Pitaji and Om.'

Chandra became almost angry. 'It is quite different!' he said and forcefully changed gear. 'They think of money because it is money, but I am only thinking of my family and my position. As a gazetted Government officer, I have to keep up a certain standard. I have to do a lot of entertaining and my children must go to good schools, and we must keep at least three servants. It is not easy to manage all this on a salary of 950 rupees a month. You have no idea how expensive these private schools are, and servants cannot be had cheaply today. Then there is my life-insurance; I have to think of the future. Supposing something happens to me – I owe it to Kanta and the children.'

Viddi said: 'But you will talk with Pitaji?'

'What is the use.'

'At least try!' Viddi cried vehemently, and Chandra, less firm without the support of his wife, had to promise, 'If the opportunity arises, I will speak with him, but of course I cannot –' he drew up outside the office and said in a voice from which he could not keep the tone of relief: 'Here we are, this is where I must drop you. You will take the bus?'

Shanta was home again. She was still weak and of course would not be able to leave the house for another forty days. But oh! she was glad to be home. She squatted on the floor and sifted rice. After the week's enforced idleness in the nursing-home, it was good to go again through the familiar motion of tossing the grains of rice from the sieve. But her mother said, 'Be careful, my daughter; do not strain yourself. There are others to do this work.' She came to see her daughter every day now, to make sure that the girl was given proper food and rest; for as she always said with a sigh and a look at Lalaji's wife, 'there is no heart like a mother's heart: no one else can take her place'.

But Shanta only laughed. 'I must do something,' she said. 'I cannot sit like a Memsahib with my hands in my lap.' The bangles on her arms jingled with enjoyment as she vigorously shook the sieve.

Lalaji's wife nodded. 'And it is said that women must work after childbirth. It exercises the muscles and restores us quickly back to full health. Take, child, take,' she sweetly said to Lakshmi, Shanta's cousin, who sat eating a great many pistachio nuts. She had come to see Nimmi, whose friendship she wished to cultivate.

'Everybody must work,' said Phuphiji, sitting on her charpai, her legs tucked under her, drinking tea.

'Excuse me,' said Shanta's mother, 'but it is my belief that a mother must have rest. How else is she to have sufficient milk for her baby? Lakshmi,' she said, 'that is enough now, you will have no appetite left for your food.'

'I have so much milk,' said Shanta, 'I do not know what to do with it all. Often I am so full it is painful.'

'Exercise stimulates the milk-flow,' said Lalaji's wife with authority.

Shanta's mother did not answer. She only looked her contempt, and this was not lost on the women of Lalaji's family. Shanta felt the atmosphere around her thicken and was unhappy. All she wanted was a peaceful life with everybody loving one another. So, as always on such occasions, she attempted to turn the conversation: 'It is good,' she said, 'to be at home again.'

But this, it turned out, was the wrong thing. Her mother said sharply, 'What do you mean to be at home?'

'To be back,' Shanta said lamely.

'Perhaps you mean to be in your mother-in-law's home?' her mother said.

'Her own home,' said Lalaji's wife. She patted Shanta's hand. 'I have tried to make it her own home.' She really was fond of the girl. Shanta was all that a daughter-in-law should be – respectful, obedient, hardworking. Only at the beginning, when she had first come into the house as a bride, had there been any trouble; for whenever anything was said or hinted against her family, she would burst into tears and run away to sit in the bathroom. Afterwards she would go and tell Om. But he never listened to her: 'Leave me alone. You and your women's quarrels!' he would shout. 'I have enough troubles sitting on my head!' So she had given up complaining to him. Nowadays, when things were spoken against her family, she sat quiet and pretended not to hear. She was a very good girl.

Phuphiji said: 'A girl's home is in her husband's home, nowhere else.' Rani added: 'After marriage it becomes so,' though she herself, even after nineteen years of marriage, still thought of Lalaji's house as her real home, rather than the one in which she lived with her husband and her children and her husband's parents and unmarried sisters.

Lakshmi asked, 'But where is Nimmi?' – not in any attempt to turn the conversation, but because she was getting very bored.

'She is at College,' said Lalaji's wife, rather hastily because she saw that Shanta's mother was on the alert.

'Today is a holiday,' said Lakshmi and chewed a handful of nuts.

Phuphiji and Lalaji's wife looked at one another. Nimmi had not told them that today was a holiday in the College. Shanta's mother took a hairpin out of her hair and put it back again with an air of preoccupation. 'She is with a friend,' said Lalaji's wife. 'She has many friends, always she goes to their houses.'

'Is she at the house of Rajen Mathur?' Lakshmi asked with interest.

'You know Nimmi's friends?' Shanta's mother asked her, also with interest.

Lakshmi nodded and took some more nuts. 'I have met them at the College. All Nimmi's friends are girls from other communities.'

Shanta's mother looked at Lalaji's wife and probed deeper: 'She does not like to make friends with girls from her own community?'

'She is Lakshmi's friend,' Lalaji's wife pointed out.

'But at the College,' said Lakshmi, complacently chewing, 'she does not like to speak with me; nor with the other girls from our community. We say to her, "Nimmi, please come and sit with us," but she always goes away with Rajen Mathur and Indira Malik and they speak together in English.'

Shanta's mother politely made no comment; she only looked down at her hands and played with her bangles. Rani said, 'It is always useful for a girl to speak good English,' but this sounded feeble, as they all realized. Maee, who was sorting the laundry, held up a sheet to the light and frowned furiously. 'It is my belief,' said Shanta's mother after a while, in a gentle voice, 'that it is not good for our girls to mix too much with other communities. Some of these people lead very free lives; for instance, the women sit together with the men and do not cover their heads . . .'

'Oh no!' Lalaji's wife quickly said. 'I am very well acquainted with the families where my Nimmi visits. They are all respectable people.'

'The family of Rajen Mathur,' said Lakshmi, 'is very modern.'

Shanta's mother sorrowfully shook her head. 'I know too well what is meant by modern,' she said, and sighed. 'Such people think nothing of letting a young girl sit and talk together with men – oh, it is very dangerous, especially for a girl like Nimmi, who is not yet provided for . . .' She trailed off significantly, for this was another point she wished to emphasize.

And it went home. Lalaji's wife could do nothing except sit and inwardly curse her husband. Because a hundred times she had told him, day in day out she told him, that Nimmi must be provided for. Until she was settled, they were constantly open to insinuation, and it was difficult to be always on the defensive, especially when one had no true weapon of defence. 'Of course,' she said, not very confidently, 'we only allow her to go to houses where we are acquainted. And then also she is very young, no more than a child . . .'

'She is how old, our Nimmi?' Shanta's mother innocently enquired.

'Sixteen,' Phuphiji answered defiantly.

Lakshmi said, 'Oh but Nimmi must be at least eighteen. She is as old as I am. She could not be in B.A. class, second year, if she were not at least eighteen.'

They all looked at her in shocked amazement, for no one was ever as tactless, as crude as this. Even Shanta's mother said: 'Be quiet, Lakshmi, you do not know what you are saying,' and sounded very annoyed. Phuphiji, her lips drawn in tightly, commented: 'Young girls nowadays have loose tongues.'

'Usha,' said Lalaji's wife, to smooth this overt unpleasantness – Shanta's mother was a guest, one had to be polite and put her at her ease – 'Usha, daughter, go and prepare a sherbet for our guests.' Usha transferred the baby, over which she had been tenderly dreaming, to Shanta and got up in her placid manner.

Lalaji's wife looked after her and said eagerly: 'Ah! but our Usha, she is well provided for. Another two–three months, you will see what sort of a marriage we will make for her.' Usha concentrated on the sherbet bottle, her head bent very low.

'And she is how old?' asked Shanta's mother casually.

'Eighteen,' Phuphiji replied without blinking; and this time Lakshmi kept quiet.

'Eighteen,' Shanta's mother repeated, knowing perfectly well that Usha was twenty. 'Yes, at eighteen I already had two children and was expecting one more.'

'I also,' said Lalaji's wife. 'In those days we started very early, but nowadays, of course, in these modern times –'

Shanta's mother shook her head: 'The old customs were best – who can deny it? Look at Lakshmi here. College,' she said contemptuously, 'what is this College, why does she go there? But thank God, she will not be

86

there much longer. A few more months and she will be married' – Lakshmi sniggered and looked at the others out of the corner of her eye – 'already the boy's parents are very impatient, they ask why are we waiting? They will not be young forever.'

This was – as it was meant to be – mortifying. Lakshmi, who was four months younger than Nimmi and not nearly as beautiful, was to be married: and Nimmi not even betrothed yet, not even promised.

'In modern times –' Lalaji's wife suggested again, not very hopefully.

'Of course,' her daughter Rani came to her support, 'nowadays things are done very differently. We must all be modern, it is not good to keep only to the old customs.' Phuphiji, the most severe upholder of old customs, coughed over her tea; but she did not say anything on this occasion.

'And boys also,' said Shanta's mother, 'what is the use of sending boys to College? Let them go into their fathers' business, that is the best way.'

But that could be contradicted with perfect confidence. 'Oh but my Chandra Prakash,' cried Lalaji's wife, 'how many years he went to College, here and abroad, and see what a great Sahib he has become. A gazetted officer,' she said, patting the back of her left hand with the palm of her right in a complacent manner.

'Yes,' Shanta's mother said politely, 'that is very good position.'

'He is a gentleman,' Rani said, and Maee muttered over the laundry: 'A great Sahib.'

'But also one must think of salary,' Shanta's mother said. 'How much does a gazetted officer draw? Does he earn as much as a boy who has gone into his father's business? Does he earn as much as my son-in-law Om Prakash?'

At the mention of her husband's name, Shanta, who was suckling her baby, shifted it from the left breast to the right and wistfully, though inaudibly, sighed. For the next forty days she would not be allowed to go to him in their bedroom; she had to stay all the time down in the women's quarter, even in the nights. Om did not come often to the women's quarter; he felt bored there and uncomfortable. But she wanted so much to see him.

'Chandra Prakash earns very good salary,' Lalaji's wife said. She tried not to think of the many times he had had to come to his father for money, and the many times Lalaji had said a few more gazetted Government officers in his family and he would be a poor man.

'And your Viddi,' said Shanta's mother. 'How much he looks like Om Prakash, like his eldest brother. He is a good boy. His father will surely take him into the business?'

Lalaji's wife made a non-committal sound. Lalaji had not confided his plans for Viddi to her, though she made anxious inquiries every day.

'It is the best way,' Shanta's mother advised in an impersonal common-sense voice. 'These boys, it is best to settle them quickly, or they may perhaps mix with bad company and then one can never know what may not happen. They may even, God forbid! marry out of their own community and against their family's wishes.' Lalaji's wife decided to pass this over: she wanted to concentrate on defending Viddi, and would not be side-tracked to Chandra and Kanta.

'And if a boy is not settled,' Shanta's mother continued in the same impersonal voice, 'malicious people will say things about him. You know what bad tongues people have.'

'Nobody,' said Lalaji's wife anxiously, 'can have anything to say against my Viddi.'

'He is a good boy,' Shanta's mother said. 'I get very angry if I hear any word spoken against him, and of course I do not believe what is said.'

There was a moment's silence. Then Lalaji's wife called into the kitchen, 'Again you have put too much tamarind in the curry, I can smell it from here!'

'No,' said Shanta's mother, 'I do not believe it when people come to me and tell me that Viddi is sitting all day in restaurants with young men of bad morals. I do not believe it. I say to them, "Have you no shame to speak such things about a boy from our own community?" and I do not even listen when they say he sits and talks with loafers and people who eat beef and know foreign women. I say to them: "Why do you come to me with such lies?"'

Lalaji's wife said: 'Such people should have their tongues plucked from their mouths.' Phuphiji added: 'I know many people whose tongues should be plucked from their mouths.'

Shanta cried: 'Just see, Baby is smiling at me!'

'There is no religion left in the world,' said Phuphiji. 'People do not say their prayers and think on God. Instead they sit and think up lies about the sons of decent families. You are an owl,' she told Shanta. 'Eleven days old she is; how can she smile?'

'This is what I say to them,' Shanta's mother agreed with conviction. 'I say it would be better for you to go home and see to your duties than to come to my house with such tales.'

'She did smile,' Shanta said. 'She looked up into my face and smiled.'

'No religion,' Phuphiji said. 'Prayers and ceremonies are neglected, therefore people are bad.'

Shanta's mother sighed, 'That is how it is in the world nowadays,' and rose painfully to her feet, one hand on her thigh. 'Come, Lakshmi, child.'

'Why do you go so soon?' asked Lalaji's wife. 'Sit for one minute longer.'

'I must see to my house. I do not know what the servants are doing in my absence – only of stealing the food out of our mouths and the money out of our pockets they think; their work is nothing to them.' Phuphiji suddenly seemed to be asleep, so she could not return the farewell greetings.

'You heard?' Rani said as soon as they were alone.

Phuphiji opened her eyes and said, 'Is it true?'

'True!' Rani exclaimed. 'No word of truth has ever left that woman's mouth.' Shanta bent low over her baby and crooned, 'Butter, sugar, meat, sleep baby sleep.'

'My Viddi!' said Lalaji's wife. 'How dare she!'

'But is it true?'

'What do I know,' Lalaji's wife wailed. 'I sit here, I have to see to my household, to the comfort of my family. Can I run after them and see where they go and who they speak with? And that Nimmi too – she says she goes to the College and then I hear it is a holiday. How do I know where she goes, what unclean houses she visits, when she should be sitting here at home with us and learning household matters?'

'These are modern times,' Rani attempted to comfort her. 'Girls nowadays have more freedom, it is an accepted thing in all the best families –'

'Leave off!' Phuphiji cried. 'Such talk is all right when that woman is sitting here, but when we are alone we can speak out. Modern times! I do not know what this means; only I know a girl eighteen years old should not be allowed to run where she likes out of the house and no talk of a husband.'

'Is that my fault!' Lalaji's wife cried. 'Often enough I have told him: "See to your daughters." What a shame it is to me when that woman can say to me, "Why do you not provide for your daughter," and even that Lakshmi is to be married –'

'Such an ugly, black-faced crow,' Maee said; 'like a monkey she looks and her colour is like boot-polish. I pity the husband who has to take that one into his bed.'

'And my Viddi,' Lalaji's wife wailed, wiping a tear out of her eye with the end of her sari, 'how often also I have said to his father: "The boy is no longer a child; he must be settled in life. Find a good wife for him, take him into the business." But will he listen to me? And now what do I have to hear from that woman's lips about my son . . .'

'Pitaji will provide,' Rani soothed. 'See how he has provided for me and for Om – '

'In those days he knew his duty,' Phuphiji grimly said. 'Then he had less money and was still humble and did not neglect the proper customs and ceremonies. But now, because they call him Lala and come to him with hands joined together, he thinks he is greater than other men and can go his own obstinate ways, contrary to what has been laid down.'

'And it is his family who must suffer!' Lalaji's wife cried. 'His wife and his children, when people open their evil mouths to spit on them!'

'Why do you allow that woman into your house?' asked Rani, and Shanta sang a little louder.

'Cook!' Lalaji's wife screamed into the kitchen. 'Are the vegetables ready or do I have to come and do everything with my own hands! Yes,' she said, 'why do I allow her into my house when she only comes to speak such things about my children?'

'If you do not allow her,' Phuphiji said, 'still she will talk, in all the bazaars she will talk, and all the world will hear from her how Lala Narayan Dass Verma neglects to provide for his children.' Maee shook her head and said, 'hai hai hai,' in a pitying way.

'But what can we do,' Lalaji's wife moaned, and wiped away more tears with her sari. 'When he will not listen to one word we say.'

'He *must* listen,' Phuphiji replied. 'If he does not listen, our whole family will be brought to ruin, and all our prayers and good deeds will be unavailing.' She sat very stiff and straight on her charpai, and her sharp old nose twitched with anger.

In the morning Lalaji received a telephone call from his lawyer. The lawyer told him that he had located the letter to T—, that it was at that moment lying in a file on the desk of his son Chandra Prakash.

Afterwards Lalaji sat unusually pensive. He did not wonder how the lawyer had managed to obtain this information. Ways and means, he knew from his own experience, were always at hand. The cultivation of useful friendships, the tactful passing on of gratifications, the creation of unspoken obligations – a patient pursuit and accumulation of such methods, and it was surprising how far and into what unthought-of crannies one's interest could stretch. As the lawyer's had stretched into Chandra's office. That it should be Chandra's, this is what made Lalaji sit and think.

He had to admit it – he would have been happier if the file had been located in someone else's office. Because someone else could always be settled; past obligations, present cash or future promises could be conjured with. It was more difficult with Chandra: for what could he offer Chandra that he had not already given him or was paternally pledged to give him? It made him angry, that he had even to consider offering his son anything; that he could not implicitly rely on the boy's loyalty and his love and his gratitude. He thought of other sons and other fathers. He thought of Dev Raj. Dev Raj did not have to doubt the loyalty of his own sons. It grieved him that he alone – who had done more and planned to do more for his children than any other father – should be deprived of his paternal rights.

It was early in the morning and his family were sitting round him, Om and Viddi and Nimmi and Usha and Om's children, while his wife and the servants were walking about seeing to everyone's needs. As usual, there was a lot of noise, the children playing, Nimmi and Viddi quarrelling with Om, and his wife shrilly intervening. He frowned, annoyed not at the noise, which did not bother him, but at the lack of harmony in his family. Every day it was the same, every day there were these quarrels. It should not be so between brothers and sisters; it had not been so between him and his own brothers and sisters. It occurred to him that his children were spoilt: life was too easy for them, they had no worries, they knew their father would provide for them. Worse, they were ungrateful, they had no love for the father who did everything for them. When he needed their help they rejected him. He hit the flat of his hand on his thigh with great force and shouted, 'Be quiet! Is there no peace in this house?' There was a sudden silence. They all looked at him in surprise, for Lalaji did not often shout at his children.

But now that he had started, he could not stop. All his grievance was loaded on to his tongue. He told his children, in a loud angry roar, how they were worthless and shiftless and lazy and ungrateful, how they had neither heart nor brain, and how he was sorry that he had ever begotten them. His wife, seeing a good opportunity, put in and whose fault was all that if not his, since he would not provide for them as she had always been urging him to do...

'You too hold your tongue!' he shouted at her. 'Night and day she sits on my head, not one moment's peace will she give me!' His wife pulled her sari over her head and retreated with dignity. Lalaji continued to abuse his children, who sat silent and uncomfortable and avoided looking at him and at one another. With a sound of disgust he heaved himself to his feet, threw the newspaper on the floor and stamped on it and then screamed at the servant: 'Will you stand there for ever! Go and have the car taken out!' In the doorway he turned and shooting his finger out at

Om, shouted, 'I am going alone in the car. Today you can walk to office! Perhaps with a little exercise you will start to think of your father and what you owe to him!'

He swung out of the house and, while the driver with lowered head held the door open for him, he threw his vast bulk into the back of the car, so that he bounced from the leather seat and the whole car shook. But just as the driver, ostentatiously efficient, turned the key and pressed the accelerator, Viddi appeared in a supplicating attitude with hands joined together and spoke to his father through the car-window: 'Pitaji, you are right, we are all worthless and do not know how to work. That is why I want you to send me abroad so that I can improve myself and become independent and no longer be as a burden on your back.' For Viddi, with supreme miscalculation, had considered this the best opportunity of tackling his father he would ever get.

For a moment Lalaji only gaped at him. Viddi attempted a little smile, ingratiating, uncertain, but not unhopeful. Lalaji's face began to quiver, he opened his mouth and broke into a torrent of violent language. Viddi suffered a rather ridiculous change of face, the smile slipped off and he looked astonished. The driver held the wheel and stared straight in front of him with absent eyes. 'Drive on!' Lalaji roared and Viddi was left standing in the driveway, his hands still foolishly joined together.

Inside the car, spread out on the backseat, Lalaji shook with anger. His heavy hairy chest heaved within his kurta. It was to him as if Viddi had deliberately aimed to insult him. To suggest that he should send another son abroad! As if he had not brought enough trouble on himself by sending one! He did not know with whom he was more angry, with Chandra or with Viddi; but because Chandra was out of his reach, he concentrated on Viddi. He would soon show him. Now, straightaway, today, he would settle the business of the sweepers' hutments. Let Viddi work for his living, then he would have fewer thoughts of going abroad. Let him work as his father worked: though *he* had had no father to arrange sweepers' hutments for him.

'Where to, please, Babuji?' the driver respectfully enquired. Lalaji did not know where he wanted to go. He only wanted to sit there and brood upon his anger. 'To the old office,' he ordered, because he was not the man to indulge his moods at the expense of his business. It was a long way to the old office. He had plenty of time to sit back and think while the car threaded its way through dense shoplined streets, hooting hopelessly to clear the way of stray bullocks and tongas and coolies and overloaded pushcarts. He thought about his sons; he thought about them with anger, and felt his anger to be righteous. But, as always, he could not keep steadily on the one thought. There were too many other things clamouring for his attention. Thinking of Chandra, he glided into thoughts of the T— case; from there to the Deputy Minister; from there to various Government officers whom he had to contact for various purposes; from there to the Happy Hindustan Trading Building, and to Dev Raj whom he would have to telephone again today.

The car turned and slowly threaded its way through a narrow side-lane, hemmed in on one side by the old city-wall, on the other by a row of ragged but fertile little shops jutting out on to the road with earthenware pots and pomegranates and vats of dusty curds. Children played in front of the car and would not get out of the way till the driver stuck his head out of the window and forcefully cursed them. Lalaji said, 'Hold your tongue, they are children only.' He looked at them and was pleased. He was always pleased when he saw children, for they made him think of his own grandchildren, of the things he would do for them, the great marriages he would arrange for them, how all the world would gape at the costly celebrations in the house of Lala Narayan Dass Verma.

He walked up the stairs to his office. The house was old and narrow and crumbling; downstairs it was crammed with go-downs, upstairs with the offices of film companies, astrologers and wholesale manufacturers. Lalaji's own office was on the first floor, a surprisingly spacious room with a very high ceiling. The clerk sat on the floor, for there was no furniture, only carpets and an earthenware water-container and a telephone. Big dusty ledgers were piled against the wall. When Lalaji came in, the clerk got up and joined his hands and lowered his head over them with great respect. He was a frail old man and very clean in a while dhoti and a thin muslin shirt. He was known to be very religious; every day he said all the prescribed prayers and he lived only on vegetables and pulses. He was an active member of the 'Ban Cow-Slaughter' movement. Lalaji respected him highly and paid him a salary of seventy-five rupees a month.

Lalaji did not encourage suppliants to come to this office; only close associates or people with important and strictly confidential business were received there. It was a private and secluded place, yet set in the heart of business, so that always there were the thumps and shouts from the go-downs, the courtyard littered with crates and jute and men heaving, and from the street the noise and sense of crowds, the innumerable little shops wedged in haphazardly, the bicycle rickshaws, the pushcarts, the pavement-sellers. Lalaji would sit here on the carpet with his naked feet tucked under him. He chewed betel-leaves and sometimes he sent out for pomegranate juice, which was said to make a man potent and vigorous. The clerk sat very silently and wrote in a ledger. He never spoke, unless he was spoken to, and then in a soft and gentle voice, and always very wisely, quoting freely from the Upanishads and the Bhagavadgita. Lalaji loved to listen to him, and nod his head in appreciation and say, 'Ah, this is true.' But today, as he looked at him, he felt uneasy – because the man was so meek, so peaceful, and had so very obviously cast anger out of his heart. Lalaji remembered his own anger, which had now quite melted out of him, and he was ashamed. He shook his head: it was bad, very bad, to indulge in anger, especially against one's own children. Abruptly he said, 'Sohan Lal, I have a brother who is full of wrath: even his own children he curses.' In a very weak but very clear voice, finely distilled, strained of all roughness and imperfection, the clerk replied, 'In the Gita it is written that from anger arises delusion; by delusion, loss of memory is caused; by loss of memory, the discriminative faculty is ruined; and from the ruin of discrimination, he perishes.' Lalaji listened to the words; he silently repeated them after the clerk, moving only his lips. Then he picked up the telephone to call Om in the New Delhi office.

'You have arrived in the office?' he rather foolishly asked; and Om replied in a resigned voice, 'I came by taxi; it cost me one fourteen.' Lalaji grunted and hung up. He would put one hundred, no two hundred rupees, into Om's bank account: his son should not be sorry that he had had to spend one rupee fourteen annas on a taxi. He shifted his betel-leaf from one corner of his mouth to the other. There was also Viddi; something must be done for Viddi, something that would please him and make him think kindly of his father. He called the driver: 'Go to all the restaurants in Connaught Place, find my son Ved Prakash and bring him to me.'

When his father's message reached him, Viddi was sitting in the Rendez-vous, feeling disgruntled. He had been telling Tivari and Zahir-ud-din about that morning's occurrence; and had not met with the sympathy he expected. All Zahir-ud-din had said was: 'But we told you it is useless for you to go abroad, your father is quite right to refuse you.' Tivari had grinned and said: 'Your first duty is to us. Your father, because he is a clever man, realizes this better than you do.'

Viddi had protested, had pointed out the rightness of his cause as against the wrongness of his father's, but they refused to listen. 'No,' said Zahir-ud-din. 'You must stay here and be a patron of arts'; and Tivari nodded in amused agreement.

Viddi at that moment almost disliked them: Tivari squat and secret, drinking whisky and puffing at his cigar, and Zahir-ud-din with bright eyes and teeth and artistic hair, very sleek and very handsome. Much as he valued their friendship, Viddi began to doubt whether they felt as deeply for him as he did for them. It seemed almost as if the beauty of his friendship was of less consequence to them than his father's money. But then Zahir-ud-din said, 'You see, we think only of what is best for you.'

He was partly mollified. They were not to be blamed if they did not know what was best for him. He replied, 'It is best for me to go and study abroad; there I can become a scholar and a gentleman.'

'How obstinate you are,' said Tivari. 'After all we have told you.' And then Lalaji's driver came in, and told Viddi that his father wanted to see him.

Viddi was surprised and a little nervous: his father had never before had anything so important to say to him that he had had to send for him in business hours. He remembered very clearly Lalaji's angry quivering face and the stream of invective poured out of the car-window. But he said, with a brave sulk: 'I am not going.'

'What!' cried Zahir-ud-din. 'Have you gone mad?'

'Why,' asked Viddi, sulking still, 'am I mad if I refuse to run at the command of a man who has so insulted me.'

'Your own father,' said Tivari, virtuously shocked.

'If your father insults you and spurns you before servants, you do not take offence?' Viddi challenged him, though not very confidently, because he could not imagine Tivari with a father – certainly he had never heard him refer to one.

'It is a father's right,' said Tivari with lowered eyes. He seemed to be quite serious.

'Of course!' Zahir-ud-din cried. 'Especially when he is such a great man as your father.'

'A great man,' Viddi scornfully repeated. 'You do not know what you are saying.'

'It is perhaps not great,' Tivari demanded, 'to start with nothing and to end up as the owner of untold lakhs of rupees?'

'If you had heard the vile things he said to me,' Viddi said, 'you also would tell me not to go. You would tell me never to set foot into his house again. And that would be right. If I had any money or knew where to go, I really would not set foot in his house again.' But he wondered what his father wanted. It was so unprecedented for him to send for him. Perhaps he wanted to tell him that he would let him go abroad, after all. But this was doubtful.

'He spoke in a moment's anger,' Zahir-ud-din said. 'You told us he had been angry. Probably something was worrying him – you do not know how many worries these big business men have to carry . . .'

But when he arrived in the Old Delhi office, his father only stared at him and asked what he wanted.

'You sent the driver for me,' Viddi replied with a hurt air.

Lalaji then remembered that he had wanted to do good to Viddi. But what a nuisance that he should have to do it now; because now he had another, more important, problem to think over. He had in the meanwhile telephoned Dev Raj. The conversation had left him uneasy. It had been cordial enough – 'Hallo-hallo, Dev Raj Sahib! You have not melted yet in the heat?' he had shouted, and Dev Raj had shouted back, 'For a fat man like you it must be worse than for us meagre ones,' and bellowed with laughter.

But Lalaji had had enough dealings with men to recognize at once that embarrassment lay close behind the laughter. His mind, as he joked and laughed down the telephone, got busy: why should Dev Raj feel embarrassed before him? There was for him only one answer: that Dev Raj had already spoken to his relative, the Director of the Happy Hindustan, and had met with an unfavourable reply.

'Listen,' said Dev Raj, cutting short the humour, 'I have something to speak with you about.' Embarrassment fidgeted in his voice; it was undoubtedly a voice that had some difficult news to impart. Lalaji felt heavy with premonition. He had wanted to arrange the meeting immediately, but Dev Raj had excused himself: he had to attend the marriage celebrations of a distant relative of his wife's and would not be free till the next evening. Lalaji was now quite sure that Dev Raj had bad news for him. So he looked at Viddi with unwelcoming eyes and suddenly he barked at him, 'Take your shoes off! Why do you come in here with your shoes on.'

Viddi, feeling deeply humiliated, placed his shoes outside the door and came back to sit on the carpet. The clerk meekly copied figures into a ledger and did not seem to have heard Lalaji's rebuke to his son. Viddi hated this clerk: he is a hypocrite, he thought, he is so holy he washes only in Jumna water and yet he takes part in all Pitaji's dirty business.

Lalaji also looked at the clerk and at once felt ashamed of the harsh tone he had used to his son. From anger arises delusion, he recalled, and he asked Viddi: 'You will drink a sherbet? Or perhaps fresh pomegranate juice? I will send out for you.' But at the same time he was thinking that if nothing further could be done through Dev Raj, then he would have to look about him for some other method of approach.

'Listen, son,' he told Viddi, and tried hard to sound kind and concerned. 'Leave off talk of abroad and more studies-shudies. All this is only game.' Viddi began to protest, but he impatiently silenced him. This had to be got through as quickly as possible; he had not much time to spare. 'I will do much greater things for you,' he said. 'What will you gain by going abroad? Look at your elder brother Chandra Prakash: he is a Government officer, he has to go to office. When his superior officer calls him he must run and stand before him with lowered eyes. What sort of life is that for a man? It is not a life good enough for my son.'

'I do not want to be Government officer. I want to be art critic or write books.'

Lalaji ignored this; he did not understand what Viddi meant by art critic and writing books, and he had not the time to make himself understand. There was, he thought, the Ministry of Public Land Development. He had many friends there. If he could persuade his friends to issue a requisitioning order for the Happy Hindustan Company's plot of land ... the Directors of the Company would have to show themselves grateful to him if he used his influence to get the order revoked for them. He thoughtfully twisted his ear between his fingers and came back to Viddi. 'Stay here with me, son,' he said. 'Take over part of the business as your eldest brother has done. You will earn more money than your brother Chandra Prakash will ever see in his dreams; and when you clap your hands all the England-returned Government officers, Secretaries and Under-Secretaries and – yes – Deputy Ministers, will have to come to you and say, "Please command me." '

Viddi remained unimpressed; but all he could say, rather hopelessly, was, 'I want to be art critic or write books.'

His father was irritated. For here he was, in such a hurry, with so much important business to be seen to, and there was his son, who did nothing all day except sit about in restaurants and never earned any money, wasting his time with irrelevant interruptions. He would have given forcible expression to his irritation, had it not been for the anger-purged presence of his clerk. Anyway, he wanted to settle this business of Viddi, now, once and for all, and getting angry would only have meant a further waste of time. So he said in a patient voice, 'Listen, son. You do not even know what money is. I want to teach you. When you feel it in your hand and know that it will always be in your hand so, then you will know what it is.'

Viddi thought: 'Money, money, money, it is all he knows. Beauty, art, poetry, all this means nothing to him.'

'I will do like this,' Lalaji said. He wondered whether the threat of a requisitioning order could be fixed, and resolved to get in touch with one of his contact men the moment Viddi had gone. So Viddi had to be got rid of quickly. 'I will give you, to begin with, 500 rupees a month. For this

I will not ask you to do any work: it is only so that you may have some money in your hand.' Let him have his 500 rupees a month. After three months of it, he would start him on the sweepers' hutments and give him a salary of 800 rupees a month; and by that time he trusted Viddi would have learnt the value of money – how much better 800 rupees is than 500, 1,000 rupees than 800, 2,000 rupees than 1,000 – and would adjust his ideas accordingly.

Viddi thought: '500 rupees a month; he will give me 500 rupees a month.' He accepted the idea quite calmly and began at once to think of all the things he could do with 500 rupees a month: how many chocolate milkshakes and cigars and pastries he could stand treat for in the Rendez-vous; what beautiful clothes he could buy for himself, suits and shirts and shoes and a gold wristwatch. And of course, books and pictures and records of classical music.

'From today I will start,' Lalaji said. 'When I come home, at once I will give you your first 500 rupees.' Viddi thought from today life will start for me. He was pleased, but not unduly surprised; because, after all, this was his due, what he had always expected for himself.

Lalaji repeated absent-mindedly, 'Yes today, when I come home,' and thought about who were his best friends in the Ministry of Public Land Development.

Nimmi was nervous but very, very happy. This really was Life, was Society. She had never been to a Night Club before, and felt much impressed. The place was called The Sweet Spot and was extremely fashionable. The interior decorating had been done by a Bulgarian lady designer who lived in Bombay, and the most striking feature was the aquaria let into the wall with brilliant tropical fish dazzling through the water. One wall was completely of glass and through this could be seen chickens turning on a spit. Nimmi wondered whether the fish and the chickens were aware of one another but was immediately ashamed of indulging such childish thoughts. What would Pheroze think of her if he could read them? She gave him a covert glance, just in case he could, but was relieved to find that he suspected nothing.

She had given him many such covert glances in the course of the evening, for she was always afraid that he might guess something: might guess, for instance, that she had never been to a Night Club before or that she had never been asked to dine out with a young man, or – worst of all – that she did not come from a very good family. But if he did guess anything, he did not show it; his expression remained uniformly dignified, and all her covert glances did for her was to impress her again with the fact that he was very handsome. He was in evening-dress, black trousers, white coat, bow-tie, and it suited him well. She had never seen him look so handsome, so elegant. She was very proud to be seen with him, and wondered whether he was also proud to be seen with her. She felt quite confident, for she knew herself to be looking her best. No wonder, since she had spent three and a half hours over getting ready; which had made her sister Usha repeatedly exclaim, 'But where are you going? You are going to a wedding?' till Nimmi's patience had snapped – this was after she had had to take the pins out of her hair for the fourth time, because she could not, simply could not, get it right – and she had cried, 'Please leave me alone! Why must you nag me so, only because I like to wear nice clothes and look pretty?' But after those three and a half hours she really did look quite perfect. Her mother and her aunt had opened their eyes wide and demanded sternly, 'Where are you going?' She had answered, 'Today I have been invited to the house of my friend Rajen,' and then had quickly fled to the sitting-room, where her father was and where she was safe from further questioning. She had sighed a great sigh of relief when finally she got out of the house. But it had all been worth it, only to be sitting with Pheroze Batliwala in The Sweet Spot, knowing herself to be looking her best and seeing him look his. She felt that people were watching them and probably they were thinking what a beautiful couple they were. Perhaps she and Pheroze were even being taken for husband and wife.

Pheroze held his knife and fork in a very refined manner and when he chewed he hardly moved his jaws at all. Nimmi was thankful that she had been practising for such a long time how to eat like a lady; she was fairly confident of herself now, and did not think he would find anything wrong with her table-manners. In between mouthfuls of food – he never spoke with his mouth full – Pheroze made conversation. He said, 'This is quite a good place,' and Nimmi replied, 'Oh yes, it is very nice.' It was the third time they had said this – the first time had been when they had come in, the second time while they were waiting for their drinks. 'Later there will be a cabaret,' said Pheroze; this too he had said twice before, and as before Nimmi declared that she was looking forward to it.

She was so excited she could hardly eat. She kept looking round her with big brilliant eyes, and thought that it was even more fashionable than the Club. There were many Europeans and everybody, Indian as well as European, wore evening-dress. The European ladies wore strapless dresses, very flimsy and lacy, while the Indian ladies glittered in elaborate saris with heavy gold borders, and their necks and ears and arms sparkled with jewellery. Nimmi herself wore no jewellery at all, except for one bracelet; but she wore fresh white jasmine in her hair and behind her ears. The jasmine gave off a very sweet and pungent smell.

'I always think this is the best place in Delhi,' Pheroze was saying. 'The food is better than in the Pipal Tree and the cabaret and band better than in the Satin Slipper; and as for the Intimate, the tone has gone down so much, one cannot go there any more.'

Nimmi looked knowledgeable. She had never been to any of these places, though of course she had heard of them and always read their advertisements in the newspapers.

'Once the Intimate was quite a nice place,' Pheroze said, 'the people who went there were gentlemen and ladies. But now you cannot imagine what kind of people go there – they are all business men and are very loud and crude and have no manners.'

'How terrible,' Nimmi said. But she did not feel easy. She knew that Pheroze meant people like her family, and she wondered how he would feel about her if he knew her background. Her sister Rani, who always prided herself on the fashionable places she visited, had recently been to the Intimate and she had come back very enthusiastic and had told them what an exclusive place it was.

'But nowadays it is so everywhere,' Pheroze continued. 'These business men come into all the best places and spoil them for other people, and sometimes they even bring their uneducated wives. It is a great pity. I do not know why such people cannot stay at home or why rules cannot be made to keep them out.'

'Oh! look over there,' Nimmi cried, 'they are setting fire to a pudding!'

'It is an English custom,' said Pheroze, dabbing his table napkin against his upper lip, 'it is usually done at Christmas time.' Nimmi said quickly, 'Oh yes, of course; only it is not Christmas time so I was wondering why ...' She trailed off because he was not listening; he was frowning intently over the menu, choosing the dessert.

The cabaret singer was starred as 'Lisa, just arrived by air from Paris'. Lisa was not in her first youth, but she looked sleek and sang competently. She wore a very tight-fitting dress of crimson and grey which reached to her ankles and had one shoulder covered and the other bare, so that it looked as if it had slipped down. She smiled with large and beautiful teeth and sang American film songs. The lights were lowered while she sang, 'Darling, why do I feel so strange, so strange', standing in a pool of red spotlight. Everybody was silent and listened. Nimmi stole a look at Pheroze and felt almost jealous when she saw how hard he was staring at Lisa.

'She sings very well,' Nimmi said, when the lights went up again and they could return to their dessert. 'And she is so pretty.'

Pheroze looked supercilious. 'I do not believe she ever sang in Paris. Or if she did, only in a very small and cheap restaurant. If you had seen the cabaret artistes in Europe, you would not think she was good at all.'

'Of course,' Nimmi said. 'But for Delhi she is not so bad.' She felt ashamed for not having been to Europe and seen the cabaret artistes there. 'Daddy wants me to go to Cambridge in England for further studies.'

He nodded. 'Your family are Cambridge people?' he asked casually and she knew no reply. She said instead: 'My friend Rajen will also go, her elder sister is already there,' and then got off this dangerous ground, on to which she had mistakenly ventured: 'Just see how well that English couple is dancing.'

Coffee came in little gold cups; these Nimmi thought to be very sweet and much too nice only to drink from. But she tried to look as if it were nothing new to her to drink coffee out of gold cups, and both she and Pheroze held their little fingers crooked in the air as they drank. They watched the dancers, Nimmi very intently because she wanted to learn all she could from them. She had not often danced before, and never with a man: all she knew she had learnt from Rajen, who had learnt from her sister, and they practised in Rajen's house to a gramophone which played 'Waltzing in the Wind' and 'Just One More'. Nimmi was rather nervous. She was sure Pheroze was a very good dancer and he would expect her to be one too. How disgusted he would be if he found she did not know the steps properly! So she watched the dancers and tried to pick up all she could. Most of the European couples, she noticed, did very elaborate steps which she could never hope to imitate; and as they danced, they talked and laughed a lot. But the Indian couples danced more in the style favoured by herself and Rajen. They moved their feet rhythmically and correctly to the music, and kept their backs straight; they did not talk or smile while they danced, and they looked very respectable.

At last Pheroze said, 'Shall we?' and escorted her solemnly to the dance-floor. She managed to look at her ease as she arranged her sari over her left arm, though she was praying silently: 'Please make me dance well.' Pheroze touched her gingerly and his body was held well away from her; only his head was thrust forward, so that the cheek nestled against her hair. And to Nimmi's delight and surprise she found herself dancing quite fluently. Pheroze did no very elaborate steps but from time to time he swung her round and even then she followed him with ease and enjoyment. This was better than dancing with Rajen to the gramophone.

The dance-floor was rather small, so they were hemmed in on all sides by other elegant couples with whom they turned in a circle. Sometimes they collided, and then Pheroze and the gentleman-partner would say, 'I *beg* your pardon,' very stiff and correct, while Nimmi and the lady-partner exchanged smiles and looked at one another's clothes. Snatches of different quality perfumes came at regular intervals, and occasionally Nimmi's arm brushed against the cobweb chiffon of some other lady's sari. The band wore silver uniforms, which were made to look like fish-scales, and they played vigorously and very seriously.

Nimmi's eyes shone with happiness. She could not see much of Pheroze's face because it was held over her shoulder, only a smooth cheek and ear and hair. He smelt of an expensive brilliantine and of talcum powder, and she could feel his breath on her ear. She thought: 'I wonder if I am in love with him?' Certainly she was very happy and greatly aware of him, even though he held her so gingerly and did not speak at all. And all the time she was asking herself: 'What would they say at home if they could see me dancing in the arms of a young man?' She thought of Phuphiji and wanted to giggle. Fortunately there was no chance of meeting anyone acquainted with her family here: the furthest they ever got, she contemptuously reflected, was the Intimate. Except Kanta; and Kanta would not mind. On the contrary, she would approve of Pheroze, because he was so elegant and had beautiful manners.

When they got back to their table, Pheroze said: 'How about going for a drive in my car?' It was an exciting suggestion: to drive in the night with Pheroze, just the two of them side by side, like two lovers in a film . . . But she hesitated because it was late already and where would she tell her family she had been?

'We could take a spin down to Kutb Minar,' he said. 'It is a moonlight night, and the Kutb looks very nice by moonlight.'

Kutb and moonlight and Pheroze – it was irresistible. And it was so late already, they would be angry anyway. If she went later still, they would probably be asleep and then they might not even notice what time she came home. The watchman could unlock the door for her and she would give him eight annas not to say anything.

After all the noise and lights of the Sweet Spot, the silence outside was very romantic. The road to Kutb was deserted and white in moonlight. Pheroze told her about his car; he said, 'Last week I had to have the battery recharged, it was completely run down.' On either side of the road the land stretched away into vast empty distances, dry and flat and barren, sprouting only the scattered stumps of tombs and mosques and palaces, the dead remains of long-dead Delhis of the past. From time to time a jackal darted across the road in front of their headlights and Nimmi would cry, 'Oh look!' and Pheroze would say gravely, 'Jackals are to be found frequently in this area.' He drove very fast – 'good little car, this,' he said – and a pleasant wind rushed into their faces.

When they parked the car at Kutb, a whining ragged figure rose up from nowhere and begged for money. Pheroze gave two annas because he did not want to be pestered. The Kutb Minar sloped up a thick and solid silhouette into the jewelled sky. A forest of slender broken pillars stood blanched in moonlight like a forest of bones. Here and there a capital-stone lay abandoned on the ground. Nimmi looked round and tried to feel the right sensations. All this was so old, so historic, so ruined; and the moonlight so romantic – she tried to find a line of poetry to fit the occasion but all that came into her head was, 'I galloped, Dirk galloped, we galloped all three,' from the *Selections from Browning* which she was studying for her English exam. She did not want Pheroze to think her unfeeling, so she said, 'It is so beautiful, it makes one think of all the old times and the Mogul Emperors like Akbar and Jehangir and Shahjehan.'

Pheroze, elegant and modern and fashionable in his well-cut white evening suit and black bow-tie, said, 'The Kutb Minar was built in the thirteenth century AD by Altamsh.' The sweet and heavy scent of night-flowers floated over the warm air.

'There is the wishing pillar,' Nimmi said. 'It is said that if you can get your arms all the way round it, you can wish for something and your wish will come true.'

'Of course it is only a superstition,' Pheroze replied.

She cried, 'Let us wish for something!' and gaily ran to put her arms round the thick iron pillar. She could not get them quite round, but all the same she wished for something. 'Let me marry someone like Pheroze Batliwala,' she wished, and then laughed out loud and cried: 'I have wished, now it is your turn!' With a tolerant little smile, he put his arms round the pillar and then dropped them again almost at once. 'What did you wish?' she asked. But he only smiled and said: 'If you tell, it will not come true.' She blushed, thinking what would she have answered if he had asked her what *she* had wished.

They walked round pillars and marble tombs. The man to whom Pheroze had given two annas had merged again with the dry soil and withered bushes of the landscape outside. They were isolated amid green lawns and trees and marble and moonlight, like lovers in a miniature. Nimmi's silk sari gently rustled and the jasmine gleamed white in her hair. A bird stirred in a tree, and suddenly Pheroze turned round and took her into his arms and kissed her. It was sudden and not very successful. Ridiculous, but their noses got in the way; so he tried again and this time brought his mouth firmly down on hers. She kept her eyes wide open and thought: So this is how a man kisses – and next: What would they say at home? – and next: How excited Rajen will be when she hears!

He kept his mouth on hers for a long time and it was wet and warm, and also she felt hot from being so close to him. Pheroze thought: What would my mother say if she knew I was kissing a girl who is not a Parsi? He had kissed several girls in the course of his career, and this had always been his first thought. After a while he took his mouth away and they walked on and Nimmi rearranged her sari. She wanted to laugh but bit her lip because she thought he might be hurt. The Kutb Minar loomed up before them, its layers of sculpture dim through a veil of moonlight. She said, 'Shall we go up?' – not because she wanted to, but only for something to say.

'It is locked now,' he said. 'They always lock it in the night because of the many people who climb up to commit suicide.'

Nimmi thought of young girls like herself climbing up the steps of the Kutb, right up to the topmost balcony, and then throwing themselves down because they were in love. She wondered if she would have the courage to throw herself down for the sake of Pheroze. But she had never liked the Kutb Minar: it was too tall, too thick and its carvings too heavily ornate. She would go somewhere else to sacrifice herself for love. Perhaps she would drown herself in the Jumna. Only the Jumna had such a bad smell and washermen washed clothes in it and crowds of pilgrims bathed in it on festival days. Still, it was very holy; and it was even older than the Kutb and probably many lovers had drowned themselves in it.

'The Kutb is only 238 feet high,' Pheroze said. 'This is not so very tall. The Eiffel Tower in Paris, France, is 984 feet high. You can go up in a lift and on the top you can buy picture cards and curios.'

In the distance, out on the barren plains, a pack of jackals cried like inhuman children. Nimmi thought it must be nearly midnight; she hoped that they were all asleep at home and had not noticed her absence. She hardly heard the jackals, she was so used to them.

'I had my photograph taken on top of the Eiffel Tower,' Pheroze said. 'Next time I see you I will show you.'

They stood outside the mausoleum of Altamsh and Nimmi traced her finger along the delicate lattice-work of the windows. But it was thick with dirt and cobwebs and she quickly wiped her finger on her lace-trimmed handkerchief which she had drenched in rose scent: to go out with Pheroze, she had wanted everything about her to be sweet and dainty. He stood close beside her and she could hear him breathing rather heavily. She wondered if he was going to kiss her again and before she could stop herself, she had let out a little giggle. To cover this up, she took the jasmine out of her hair and said: 'These flowers fade so quickly,' and stood threading the wilting white blossoms soft as silk over her fingers. She could feel him looking down at her and tensely waited. But all he said was: 'Flowers remain fresh only if they are put in water.' She twisted her flowers round her fingers, and he kicked pebble stones with his elegant shoe.

It was only on the way home, while he told her about the carburettor of his car, that she got really excited about having been kissed.

The Ministry of Public Land Development proved to be a dead-end. His contact man had reported to him that at present nothing could be done, because everyone was still too much under the shadow of the T— case and of the new Deputy Minister. At the mention of the new Deputy Minister Lalaji's blood pressure rose. 'Only wait,' his contact man had attempted to comfort him, 'another six–seven months and we will hear a different story. Let him smell our money only, and we will hear a different story.' Lalaji's hopes also tended that way. If only they could get close enough to the Deputy Minister to confront him with temptation – actual, concrete, naked temptation, a pile of sweet crisp wonder-working bank-notes – he would soon know how to follow the proper instincts of man, however much these proper instincts may have been blurred by too close a contact with foreign ways. Lalaji looked forward to that day with pleasure. But until then, the man's presence in office had a paralysing effect on all decent business transactions. It was a great nuisance.

So there was only Dev Raj. Lalaji awaited his visit rather anxiously. He could not forget Dev Raj's tone of embarrassment over the telephone. He tried to convince himself that he might only have been imagining it, but he knew that he did not often imagine things.

However, there was no embarrassment when Dev Raj, at last, came. They greeted one another as heartily and as vigorously as ever and went to the women's quarter to admire Shanta's new baby. 'She is getting fat,' Dev Raj said, looking down with approval at his granddaughter. And Lalaji, also looking at her with a tender smile on his face, replied, 'What else, pure ghee we give her every day and chicken curry,' which made them laugh a lot. Afterwards deckchairs were put out for them on the lawn, where it was cool and pleasant, and they sat and drank sherbet. They bulged over the sides of the deckchairs, stretching the canvas tight with the weight of their backs and rumps. Both wore white kurta-pyjama, of finest muslin freshly laundered, which thinly veiled their immense amount of flesh. A servant crouched near them – not near enough to overhear their conversation, but within easy calling distance. Their voices droned soft and lazy in trivial conversation. From time to time they yawned and shifted their broad thighs. It would not have been possible to guess that their conversation was, very definitely and purposefully, drawing to a point.

When the proper moment was reached, Dev Raj said, 'I have spoken with my relative, the Director of the Happy Hindustan Trading Company.' Lalaji at once detected the same tone of embarrassment; but he only yawned and scratched the back of his neck and called to the servant for more sherbet.

'He is interested in your proposition,' Dev Raj said. Lalaji gave a vague indication of interest which, however, sounded indifferent enough to be almost another yawn. 'His influence is great,' Dev Raj said. 'Whichever way he decides, three of the other Directors who are related to his wife, will vote with him.'

'Please take,' Lalaji said, as the servant came up with more sherbet. 'In the hot weather such sherbet is refreshing.'

'It tastes very good. It is made in the house?' He took a few gulps, 'Yes, my relative is a man of great influence.'

'Of course,' said Lalaji. 'Who has not heard his name?' though he had never heard it before he became interested in the Happy Hindustan Trading Company.

'He tells me,' said Dev Raj, casually and smiling a little as if such an idea were rather ridiculous, 'that Chunni Lal is interested in the work. But we all know what sort of a contractor Chunni Lal is.'

Lalaji laughed, though not very easily. Chunni Lal was his greatest rival, and there were even people who said that he was a richer man than Lalaji himself.

'And then there is the new Deputy Minister,' Dev Raj said.

'Bring pān!' Lalaji shouted to the servant.

'The Company has to keep up good relations with the Ministry.'

'Naturally,' said Lalaji. 'Which one of us has not? It is Government, we all have to keep up good relations with Government.'

'The new Deputy Minister has strange ways.' Lalaji swatted a fly on his knee. 'Very strange ways,' Dev Raj continued. 'For instance, he does not like the gentlemen's agreement between contractors and other business men; and also he wants open tenders called for all big works. He is a great trouble to all of us.' Lalaji picked the squashed fly off his knee with his fingernail and proceeded to dismember it.

'But my relative is a man of great influence in his Company. He can bring all our worries in this direction to an end.' He helped himself to a betel-leaf, wrapped in silverfoil, which the servant offered him from a tray. 'And, as I have said, he is interested in your proposition.'

Lalaji waited. He knew that something more was coming. Meanwhile they chewed their pān and Dev Raj said, 'You have sufficient water to water your lawn? At my house there is this trouble, if the gardener turns on the tap, we cannot get water for a bath.'

'This difficulty is everywhere in Delhi. But of course the grass needs water. It is pleasant to sit on a lawn in the summer evenings.'

'I pity people who have no garden. For them the heat is hard to bear.' Dev Raj knew what he was talking about: his earlier years, like Lalaji's had been spent in close little rooms stuffed with relatives, and the only place to enjoy the night air was out in the street among the tattered little stalls, the smell of over-ripe fruit and pariah dogs stretched out like dead. 'My relative, the Director of the Happy Hindustan Trading Company, has beautiful garden; often I envy him, it is so large and spacious.'

Lalaji, his cheeks bulging with pān, nodded and continued to listen very intently, though he sat in an attitude of relaxation.

'His house also is very large and spacious. It belonged once to a Maharaja, who let it to an English colonel. In '47 my relative made a very good deal with the Maharaja; he paid two lakhs for the house, though today its value is at least four lakhs. He has had many offers.'

'Property is the best investment,' Lalaji said, chewing his pān.

'He also owns another house, on Prithviraj Road. It is a little smaller but also very valuable. He has let it to people of the American Embassy at a rent of 950 rupees a month.'

'That is very good rent.'

'These people, he tells me, will go back to America after six months, and then he is not quite sure what he will do.'

'There will be others. Foreigners from the Embassies pay high rent for good houses.'

'I will tell you the truth,' Dev Raj said. 'My relative is not very anxious to rent it out again. What need has he of the money? He is a rich man. As Director of the Happy Hindustan Trading Company he draws high salary every month, also he has his own house and some other investments, and he has married all his three daughters very respectably. Why should he let out his own house to foreigners?'

Lalaji knew they were drawing near the point. Soon he would hear what he was expected to do for Dev Raj's relative in return for his influence. He said, 'It is a pity to throw away 950 rupees a month. Perhaps next time he will get 1,050 rupees, especially if he lets it again to Americans.'

'950, 1,050, my relative is not anxious for this money. He has other plans.'

'Should I tell the servant to serve you with another pān? Perhaps this one was not to your taste?'

'It was exactly to my taste. I do not care for too much aniseed in a pān. No, he has no great need for 950 rupees a month. But perhaps he may need the house.'

'He has relatives who wish to live there? Perhaps one of his daughters?'

'No, not his daughters. They are all three, as I have said, very well settled in good families. One of them lives in Bombay; her husband is a great film magnate.'

'And he has no son?'

'He has one son,' Dev Raj replied, and there was a short pause which convinced Lalaji that whatever he was expected to do was connected with the son.

'Yes,' said Dev Raj. 'He has one son whom he desires now to settle. It is for him that he is thinking of the house in Prithviraj Road.' So that was it: Lalaji was to help in the settling of the son. Perhaps he was to initiate him into the contractors' business, find a suitable work for him to undertake, introduce him to a reliable sub-contractor. He was often approached by fathers in such matters, and though usually he avoided as much of the burden as possible – after all, he did not want to rear competition for his own sons – the securing of the Happy Hindustan contract was worth a lot to him. And this boy was the son of a relative of Dev Raj and therefore also related to himself. One must do all one could for one's relatives. 'Settling a son in life is always a great responsibility,' he said.

'A father's duty,' added Dev Raj. A sigh of sentiment heaved through his heavy frame, rippling under the flesh. 'But, thank God! so far my relative has been able to settle the boy very well. He is his only son, the youngest after three daughters, so naturally there is nothing that has not been done for him.'

'He has been sent abroad?' Lalaji asked with suspicion. But Dev Raj shook his head: 'His father told him: first you will start in business here; then you will take a wife; and then, if you like, you can go abroad for a short while to see how business is done in other countries. My relative is a wise man. Though of course,' he added hastily, 'for some boys it is best to go abroad even before they enter into business or are married, when they are very clever boys and good at their studies, like your son Chandra Prakash.' Lalaji thought it ironical that other people should find apologies for Chandra, when he himself could find none; but he made no comment, nor did he smile.

'And what business does your relative wish to settle him in?' he said, in order to help the request along. But to his surprise the other only laughed; he made noises in his throat and his shoulders shook. 'No,' said Dev Raj, laughing so, 'there is no question of settling him in any business. That has been done already. Thank God, the boy is very well settled in his father's business, already he has been made a junior Director in the Happy Hindustan Trading Company. All that a father can do for a son, my relative has done.' Lalaji was pleased to hear it, though a little put out. He did not often mistake people's meanings. Having had so much practice both in receiving and in placing supplications, he had learnt to recognize the particular nature a request would take, long before it was actually stated.

'He is earning very good salary,' Dev Raj said, 'although he is only twenty-two. He is a clever boy, the pride of our whole family. He is also B.A. His father sent him to a College for three years, but he has taste more for business than for study.' Lalaji nodded his approval. 'A very handsome boy, healthy and fair in complexion, and he is the only son, so there is nothing his parents will not do for him. Now only one thing remains.' He allowed a short pause, to let Lalaji grasp his meaning; but this was no longer necessary. 'Already there have been many very good offers,' Dev Raj said. 'For instance, six months ago the contractor Chunni Lal sent to my relative ...'

'Chunni Lal is a very rich man,' Lalaji said.

'And the dowry he offered was worthy of a very rich man. But my relative would not even hear him, and in the end Chunni Lal had to marry his daughter to the son of Munni Lal, who as everybody knows is only a small contractor and a man of little worth.'

Lalaji said, 'I knew Munni Lal when he had one shirt only, which his wife had to wash for him every night. He would come to my office and sit there with his hands joined together and eyes downcast.' And now Munni Lal was related to Chunni Lal and had three Government contracts and drove around in a Chevrolet car.

'These Munni Lals and Chunni Lals! My relative has no interest in such people. But,' he said and looked sideways at Lalaji, 'he has very great respect for Lala Narayan Dass Verma.'

For the first time Lalaji was sorry that he had betrothed his daughter Usha; though he had chosen an excellent family for her, a very rich family of military contractors with whom it would be both a privilege and an advantage to be connected. But if she had still been free, here would have been an excellent proposition and the shortest cut to the contract of the

Happy Hindustan twenty-five lakh building. Not that he would have sacrificed his daughter for a business deal: but there would have been no question of sacrifice – the family of Dev Raj's relative was unexceptionable and the son himself, by all accounts, a worthy handsome young man. It was really a great pity, but too late to draw back. He had already paid his 'deposit' for his future son-in-law – the short ceremony of paying it, though of course only a family affair, had been performed in very good style and had cost him 10,000 rupees – the date of the wedding was fixed, and the two young people had even been introduced to one another: (one lived, after all, in modern times, however much Phuphiji might protest). It was too late. He was sorry about it, and only hoped that the relative of Dev Raj might be induced to ask for some other favour in return for the contract. 'I too,' he said, 'have great respect for your relative. Naturally, he is a member of your family, what other recommendation need there be? I would like to serve him.'

Dev Raj shifted his thighs and cleared his throat. He held the end of his kurta and lifted it away from his body, to which it had begun to stick with perspiration. 'When we become older,' he said, 'the heat of the summer is hard to bear. When the end of the summer comes, we feel tired and exhausted and long for winter to come quickly. It is easier for young people, for our sons and daughters.'

'There is my daughter Nimmi,' Lalaji said complacently, 'like a flower, like a lotus she looks, so delicate; but in the worst days, when there were duststorms and hot winds, and in the rains with flies and mosquitos, always she sat and studied and did not complain.'

'She is a pearl,' said Dev Raj. 'I have heard many people speak in her praise. For instance, once she was seen at a wedding ceremony by the wife of my relative, the Director of the Happy Hindustan, and she said to my wife how beautiful is the youngest daughter of Lala Narayan Dass Verma, she is fair as a Kashmiri girl.'

Usually Lalaji revelled in every word spoken in praise of his daughter Nimmi, it was the sweetest music he knew. But this time he was not pleased. Because it was impossible – certainly impossible! He would not even think of it.

'Such a daughter,' said Dev Raj, 'is worth the greatest wealth a man can possess.'

Lalaji grunted non-committally – because he would not speak, would not commit himself. Dev Raj and his relative must be made to realize that it was impossible. He valued their good-will, he would do anything to serve them; and he really did want that contract very badly. But not his Nimmi! They could not, they should not, have her.

'She is how old now?'

'She is eighteen,' Lalaji replied with reluctant truth. Eighteen, he knew, was an advanced age. His wife and his sister told him so every day. Dev Raj would also think so; he would think it was a good time for her to be settled. So Lalaji said, 'I want her to have very good education; she must go to her College for several years more and she will learn to play the veena. She is very musical and I will place her under some famous pandit.' Nimmi was not musical, but he thought how beautiful she would look playing the veena. Everybody would say the daughter of Lala Narayan Dass Verma is not only very beautiful but also very talented. And it would be a great honour to have his daughter studying under a famous pandit.

Dev Raj flapped his kurta over his stomach to cool himself. He stared out over the garden with melancholy eyes. Then he said, 'What need is there for ceremony between relatives? If I wish to speak truth to Lala Narayan Dass Verma, I do not have to cloak it in formalities and lies and say only half my meaning. He and I have known one another many years, I have given my daughter into his family and our blood flows together in the veins of our grandchildren. We are as one, and his interest is my interest and mine his.'

Lalaji said, 'Please speak quite freely. You are my brother,' but reluctantly, for he could guess what was coming.

'You are a very wise man,' Dev Raj said. 'Everybody knows this. Your opinion is greatly respected and your words are listened to as the words of a sage. But there is one point – please forgive my impertinence – there is one point in which you are mistaken. I may speak?'

'You are my brother,' Lalaji said again and wiped his face with a handkerchief.

'I also have daughters. I know how a father's heart feels for a daughter and how he longs to do all he can to recompense her for having been born a girl. But I also know this,' he said.

Lalaji did not have to listen: he also knew: that a woman is a woman and her duties in life very different from the duties of a man. He had heard it so often, had himself said it so often. How it is a woman's fate to leave the house of her father and go to a husband's house, to bear his children, to look to the comforts of his family. These were all platitudes which Dev Raj was intoning so smoothly. Lalaji thought of the women in his father's house and in his grandfather's house and in his own house. His father had been poor, his grandfather poorer, he himself was now very rich: but it had always been the same. The women lived a life apart. They sat together in the inner courtyard and saw to the cooking and the children. This was right, this was as it should be. A family was not a family, a home not a home, unless there was a women's quarter in which the women could lead their own lives. Demure daughters-in-law, stern mothers-in-law, widowed aunts, all pounding spices, sifting rice, scolding servants, washing babies; the stone jars of rice and lentils, the vat of boiling milk, the barbecue, the pump in the courtyard; quarrels and recriminations and occasional songs, nostalgic peasant songs or plaintive hymns winding round the ceaseless kitchen noises – these constituted the necessary, if unconsidered, background to a man's life.

'In foreign countries,' Dev Raj said, and this also Lalaji knew. Who did not know it? In foreign countries this natural this God-given order had been subverted: women went out of the house, considered themselves equal with men in the most unsuitable spheres – equal with men! Of course they were equal with men, if only they kept to their own ground – neglected their households, did not care for their children: with the result that they lost the very character of women – were hard and bold, cut their hair short like a man's, smoked cigarettes, dressed themselves in immodest garments. And since the women were no longer women – no longer chaste, modest, home-keeping – and since they neglected their duties, which were bearing children and looking after them and teaching them all the old customs and ceremonies which had to be kept up; so it had come about in these foreign countries that the sanctity and the stability of the family, and with it that of the whole community, were destroyed. For, as Dev Raj was saying, 'It is only through the influence of the women in the home that the strength of a community and its religion are kept up.' Only too true; but Lalaji did not like the personal conclusion to which all this was tending.

Dev Raj came forcefully to his point. 'What, then, is the use of allowing a woman to go outside the home? Studies, music, these things are very well for a girl as playthings, but after she is sixteen, seventeen, eighteen, what is the use of them?'

No use, Lalaji knew it and had to say so. But he was very sad. Night had come on quickly. The margosa tree was almost black and alive with birds settling down to sleep; inside the house they would be melting the ghee now and browning the onions, and the first pungent smells would be creeping through the house. It was his favourite hour, but he was sad.

Dev Raj was saying: 'A daughter must be settled early in life. If we allow her to roam about too long, she will perhaps become discontented with her fate, and the sin of it will be on us.' Though this was only the echo of his own opinions, Lalaji refused to let himself be convinced that it applied in any way to the present case. It applied, he was very ready to admit, to his daughters Rani and Usha, to his daughter-in-law Shanta and to his daughter-in-law Kanta, to all the daughters of Dev Raj and all the daughters anyone had ever had: but no one had ever had a daughter like his Nimmi.

Kanta sat at her dressing-table and brushed her hair one hundred times. She brushed it very fiercely and said, 'How dare he suggest such a thing.'

Chandra paced up and down the bedroom. He looked worried and miserable and jangled his keys in his pocket. 'He does not understand,' he said.

'What is there to understand! It is only a question of right and wrong. Everyone can understand what is right and wrong. You are a gazetted Government officer; you are in a position of trust; you are highly respected by many people; when you walk along a corridor, all the peons salute and the clerks and typists pretend to be working hard. Also you have a social position to keep up. How dare he ask you?'

Chandra sat down on the edge of the bed and, stretching out his legs, looked down at his feet. He was wearing no shoes, though otherwise he was perfectly dressed in evening-clothes. 'It does not mean the same thing to him as it does to us,' he said, but did not sound happy about it.

'Because he has no morals, that means we also must have no morals?'

'He has different morals. We do not understand him and he does not understand us. You do not know what it is like in business.'

Kanta was applying lipstick, but at that she turned round from her mirror to ask: 'And what do you know about it?'

He continued to stare at his toes, wagging the big one and watching the effect. 'Only a little,' he said. 'Pitaji never talked much at home, but of course I know something of what goes on, if only from the papers. Look at the T—case.'

'The T—case,' Kanta said. 'That is the greatest shame for our national character. A Government officer to do such things, to mix with such people, to let himself be bribed by unscrupulous business men – do you know what I would do to T—?' She left a short pause for effect, her lipstick suspended in the air. 'I would give him the death penalty, this is what I would do, because he, a high Government officer, has betrayed his trust.'

Chandra looked very uncomfortable. He said, 'Sometimes there are circumstances ... it is not always easy to judge.'

Again she turned round from her mirror to say sharply, 'What do you mean? How can there be any circumstances to excuse such acts as he has done?' and then, as the children's voices were heard slightly raised in the next room, she shouted, 'Now then, you kids, quiet in there, do not let me hear one sound! I do not know,' she said, 'where they learn to be so loud and rowdy. It must be at the school. Nowadays even the best and most expensive schools take in children from not very good family. Really, I must speak to Mrs Dass about it. I do not want my children to become like those of your brother or your sister Rani or of other uneducated parents.'

Chandra had begun to pace the room again. Kanta could see him in the mirror, while she bent forward and studied the fine lines on her face, persuading herself that they were not very clearly visible. 'Why are you so nervous?' she said.

'Who would not be nervous!' he cried in a strained high-pitched voice. Kanta knew at once that this was serious and, putting everything aside, said to him: 'Now darling, I think we will go and sit in the lounge and drink a good cup of tea.' For all the books and magazines she read advocated tact and understanding on the part of the wife.

'You do not know,' said Chandra, sitting disconsolately on the settee in what they called the lounge while Kanta sat beside him and held his hand, 'you do not know how I felt when I saw him walking into the office.'

'I know, when you told me I also felt very bad. How could he do such a thing – has he no respect for your position? He must know that if he is seen in your office, it will be very compromising for you?'

'No,' said Chandra and he sounded more unhappy than ever, for this really was the worst, that his father should not even realize. 'No,' he said, 'he thinks it is quite all right for a man of his reputation and with his connections to be seen in the office of a gazetted officer in my position.' Chandra knew that his father walked freely in and out of the offices, and also sometimes in and out of the private houses, of Ministers and Secretaries and Deputies. But that was different. Ministers and Secretaries and Deputies did not have to be so very careful as a man in his position; their careers were made, his still to make.

'This is the worst about being related to such an uneducated man,' Kanta said. 'He does not understand the world in which you move so he does not know how people have to behave in that world, and always he embarrasses you.'

'I was so afraid,' Chandra said, 'that any moment Ghosh or SankarLingam may have come in – often they come in to consult with me on some point – and then what would they have thought if they had seen him sitting there.' Quite at ease, leaning back against the regulation office-chair, languidly scratching his chest, looking across the desk at his tense, embarrassed, rigid son just as if it were his own desk. Incongruous, in that official office atmosphere in his wide white homely kurta-pyjama. And he had asked for pān: Chandra had been so embarrassed when he had had to order his peon to go out for pān.

'And you are sure,' Kanta asked, as she had asked several times before, 'that nobody overheard what he said to you?'

'In that he was cautious enough. He has had enough experience in such things, he knows one must be cautious. Three times he asked me who sat in the next office and once I saw he tapped the wall – he pretended he was interested as a contractor in the thickness of the wall, but I knew.'

'He was cautious only for himself. For your position he does not care. If there had been only your position to think of, he would have shouted out loud.'

Chandra cried: 'And I did not know any such file was on my desk! How am I to know all the files that are brought to lie on my desk?'

'Of course not,' Kanta said. 'A busy man like you.'

'People who do not work in Government offices have no idea how much business we have to attend to. Always files are brought to us and they are all marked "Urgent" and every ten minutes there is a new departmental note. Often I do not know where to start, there is so much to attend to.' His father had laughed at him because he had not known that the file was lying on his desk (a glance at the date on which it had been sent to him revealed that it had been there for three weeks). 'You people lead a restful life,' Lalaji had said. This rankled. 'It is a well-known fact in all Government offices,' he told Kanta, 'that it takes time before a file or a note can be seen to and passed on.'

'Everybody with any sense in his head realizes this. One more cup of tea?'

'No. I think my stomach is upset.' And he clasped it and felt it. 'It is the worry. Always when I am worried, my stomach gets upset.'

'Do not eat too much at Mrs SankarLingam's house,' Kanta said. She put a hand to her hair, remembering that she had to look nice to go out to dinner.

'Please,' Chandra said, 'let us stay at home. I do not think I can see people this evening and talk, I am much too upset.'

'But she invited us and we promised!' Kanta cried. 'How can we not go?' She had been looking forward all day to a pleasant social evening; and also there was no dinner cooked at home.

'Please telephone and say I am not feeling well. I cannot go. All the time I will be thinking of that file.' The file now lay thrust at the back of his wardrobe, under his cellular vests. His father had not been able to persuade him to destroy the letter there and then, but he had judged it best himself to take the whole file out of the office and keep it, for the time being, at home.

'Darling,' Kanta said, 'please think for a moment how it will look if we do not go. Everybody will suspect there is something wrong, and you know how people are, at once they will think the worst.'

'They can think of nothing worse than the truth.'

'What nonsense! You have done nothing wrong, why should you feel like that? You are an honest, conscientious officer and no one can think a thought or speak a word against you. And you are not to be blamed for your father.'

Chandra cried: 'But what am I to do!' His face assumed a painful twist and his stomach rumbled. He really was very worried.

'Darling,' Kanta said and put her hand over his, 'of course you will do nothing. Only attend to the file first thing tomorrow morning and pass it on to the next officer as quickly as possible. That is the only way. Then your father will not be able to come and worry you any more: you will simply tell him I am sorry, I have had to pass the file on; the routine of a Government department cannot be upset.'

He groaned. 'If only I had passed it on before he came to speak with me about it. I could have told him at once that I know nothing about it and then there would have been no more talk.'

'There need also be no more talk now. Only do your duty in the normal way and no one will worry you. Because your father is dishonest, he cannot also make you dishonest.'

'He does not even know it is dishonest,' Chandra said. (Lalaji had talked about it so blandly: 'You will take this one letter out,' he had told him, 'and destroy it; more I do not ask. It is a very simple matter.')

'He has no shame,' Kanta replied with indignation. 'It is terrible to be related to such a man. I wish we need have nothing to do with him.' But this she knew was impossible. There were so many things they needed and which could not be managed on Chandra's salary. She especially looked forward to her holiday in the hills every summer. 'He is your father, we owe him some respect.'

'That is what he said,' Chandra said miserably. 'I am your father, your father.'

'And it is not altogether his fault. Much of the blame must also be given to the women of your family. It is the duty of wives and mothers to see to the morals of a family, that nothing shameful and dishonest is done. But the women in your father's house are too stupid and uneducated. They are,' she said with an intellectual air, 'victims of society. The society in which they were born does not believe that women also have a mind. They

116

think women must stay all day in the women's quarter and bear babies. Therefore they can give no intellectual companionship to their men.'

'How happy I am,' said Chandra, though he did not sound it, 'that I am married to you.'

'Darling,' she said and pressed his hand, 'we are quite different. Thank God I have had some education and also come from a class of society which is more advanced. Your father – just think – would have married you to someone like Om's Shanta.'

'You should have seen the letter,' he said. 'It was written by Om and it was in very bad English. There were three spelling mistakes and the grammar was quite wrong. How ashamed I feel that such a letter should have been written by my brother.' He had not shown it to Kanta and she had not asked to see it. It was something unclean which had to be thrust out of sight as quickly as possible.

'Please,' she said, and looked at the clock, 'do not worry any more. See, it is already twenty past eight. Mrs Sankar Lingam told us to come at eight. It is time to go.'

Chandra's stomach rumbled again. 'She will give us South Indian food. You know how I cannot digest South Indian food. They put so much spice in it, and all that rice.'

'I hope she will give us South Indian food. At least she knows how it is cooked!' Kanta said and laughed gaily.

Bahwa cried, 'No, no, no!' and ran up on to the stage. 'You must do like this.' And he strained his short plump body on to tiptoe and, holding his hand daintily in the air, spoke in a tripping high-pitched voice, ' "Why must we two, innocent as we are, be the victims of this moral evil? We are as two roses and the worm that eats our heart is the society we live in." Put passion into it,' he told the chief actress, returning to his natural voice, 'passion and conviction. Your heart is breaking and for this you are bitterly indicting society and its evil customs. It must be like a cry of anguish.' The chief actress, one Mrs Iqbal Singh, a married lady who had always been interested in acting, looked at him coldly and repeated the lines in the same way as she had said them before.

Bahwa returned to his friends who sat sleepily in the auditorium. 'How do you like my producing?' he asked. Tivari only yawned and Zahir-ud-din said: 'I am so thirsty.' But Viddi said: 'It is more fashionable to be restrained in acting.'

Bahwa looked at him for a moment in silence out of his big round eyes. Viddi shifted uneasily and wondered whether perhaps he had said the wrong thing; but then at once he reassured himself, thinking, 'So what, it is the truth.'

'No,' Bahwa said, and he was not angry after all, 'that is only for comedy. For tragedy you cannot have restrained acting, on the contrary you must be very dramatic and moving.'

'You must shout very loud and wave your arms,' said Tivari.

'A play like mine,' said Bahwa, 'calls for passionate acting and great feeling. Especially at the end when the two lovers decide to kill themselves. This is a very moving scene: Kamla says, "I will put an end to my existence. Not by one minute will I survive your marriage," and Ram Gopal throws himself at her feet, crying, "Such a marriage will never be, for when the wedding-party assembles the soul of the bridegroom will have abandoned the body it inhabited." ' Bahwa's voice quivered with emotion as he spoke these lines, and when he had finished he looked round at his three friends as if he wanted to hypnotize them.

'Very nice,' said Tivari. 'But is there any moral to your play?'

'Is there any moral to my play!' Bahwa shouted. But Mrs Iqbal Singh, who was still going through her lines on the stage, stopped in the middle of a speech and said, 'How can we have rehearsal if you shout so loud and disturb us?'

'Moral!' Bahwa said more quietly. 'It will be obvious to every right-thinking person, and it is also stated at the end by the uncle of Kamla, when the two lovers are found dead. He says to the father of Ram Gopal: "If you had relinquished your pride and your greed, today your son and also our daughter would have been alive. But you were rooted fast in pride and greed, you would not listen to your son when he pleaded to be married to Kamla whom he loved, even though her father could not give so great a dowry as the father of Padma, whom he did not love. But because the dowry given by the father of Padma was worth more to you than the wishes of your only son, therefore you must stand and weep today over his dead body. Thus you are as an example to all who think more of dowry than of the heart of their child." '

'Yes,' Viddi said, 'I can see the theme is very serious.'

'All my dramas have serious themes. I do not believe in writing for one hour's entertainment only. Always I take some social problem and make my drama out of that. Through my plays I want to make people realize what they do or think wrong, and so I will make society better. This is the true function of the dramatist, and also of every other artist. One of my plays taught that servants are also human beings, another threw scorn on people who took to drink and other vices, another was to make life better for widows.'

'A lively social conscience,' said Tivari.

'This play will teach parents that happiness is more important than big dowry. It is aimed against the whole dowry-system, which is pernicious and makes our women like slaves for sale. I do not admire people who marry a girl only for the money they get with her from her father.'

'I also do not admire them,' said Tivari. 'But I would like to be one of them.' At which Viddi laughed heartily. 'You would open your eyes wide,' he said, 'if you heard how much dowry my father gives with my sisters.'

'Is there a sister left for me?' Tivari enquired, but Viddi pretended not to hear. He admired his friend, but he would not have cared to see him married to Nimmi.

A slick German sports-car came driving right into the auditorium of the open-air theatre. At the wheel sat Captain Iqbal Singh, pressing the horn. 'He has come,' said Mrs Iqbal Singh. 'Rehearsal finished for today.' They all watched her getting into the car. She was pretty and well-groomed and when she walked her hips shook. Her husband started the car and she waved a slim and red-nailed hand out of the window. The other actors also came down from the stage and began to light cigarettes. 'All right,' Bahwa told them, 'tomorrow same time. And learn your lines. That is the trouble,' he told his friends. 'What is the use of writing good drama when the actors do not cooperate? They are lazy and careless, and most of them have no talent. They think more of going to Club and parties than of rehearsal. Just think, the play is to start next week, posters are being printed and I have booked the theatre, and they do not even know their lines.'

'How thirsty I am,' said Zahir-ud-din.

'And not one sketch have you showed me for the sets you promised. How is it all to be finished in time?'

Zahir-ud-din stretched himself and said, 'I will give you beautiful sets. They will be impressionistic. Realistic sets are very old-fashioned and quite inartistic.' He got up and climbed on to the stage; the others followed. 'You see,' he said, waving his arms in both directions, 'for the first scene which shows the lovers I will paint on one side a design which will suggest a lotus-bower and will give a romantic atmosphere. On the other side I will paint for you a patch of green which will suggest a cool pond. In the background will be a minaret.'

Viddi had never been on a stage before. He looked down into the auditorium and imagined it to be full of people. Perhaps, if he tried, he could be a good actor.

'The second scene, which will be the interior of Ram Gopal's house, will also be impressionistic. I will paint a huge figure of Lakshmi the

Goddess of Wealth, and also banknotes and piles of silver; this will suggest the greed of Ram Gopal's father.'

Though perhaps it would be even nicer, thought Viddi as he looked down into the auditorium, to sit there in the middle of the front row, opulent and critical, and languidly fan himself with the programme. The actors would act their hardest to impress him, and would be anxiously watching his face to discover his reactions. But he would look quite inscrutable. Only in the interval he might let fall some pregnant witticism which, in spite of the casual manner in which it was delivered, would devastatingly reveal his opinion of the play.

'Ah,' said Zahir-ud-din, 'what beautiful sets I could make if only you would give me a good stage, instead of –' he waved his hand '– this.' Indeed, the theatre left much to be desired. The proscenium arch, which had once been painted blue, was flaking and blistered, planks were coming loose, the rafters sagged. The hedge which surrounded the auditorium was full of gaps through which stray dogs and goats and children would make a delighted entrance during a performance. Beyond this hedge stretched a piece of ground which was used as a car-park when a play was being staged and for the rest of the time as an open space for the clerks' quarters grouped round it. The inhabitants of these quarters had many children and much tattered washing hung up on lines. Some of them also kept chickens and a cow.

'What else do I say every day?' cried Bahwa and struck his forehead with the flat of his hand in a dramatic manner. 'How many times have I said it? What we need most of all, more than any community projects or low-cost housing, is a real theatre. Why does Government not listen to our demands? Always they are telling us how we must preserve our cultural heritage and also make new culture so that we have something to show to foreign visitors. But they do not help us in any way.'

'Government,' said Tivari, 'what can you expect from Government? Only committees and sub-committees and reports which point out how culture must be run to a five-year plan. To get anything done, we must look for private patrons.' Viddi was not listening; he was still thinking of himself in the front row of the auditorium. Once he had seen an American film in which there had been a supercilious critic who went to all first-nights and sat there, a source of terror to actors and producer and playwright, in a coat with a fur-collar and chewing the top of a silver-headed cane.

'Yes,' said Zahir-ud-din, 'why do you not tell your father to build us a nice theatre.'

Viddi shut his eyes. 'I am tired of explaining to you.'

'Listen,' said Zahir-ud-din; 'your attitude is very selfish.'

'Only speak with your father,' said Tivari; 'you will see, he will understand better than you think.'

'Of course, a clever man like your father.'

'First bring him to my play,' said Bahwa. 'Let him get taste of the work we do. Then I will come to your house and I will read to him all the other plays I have written, and also my novel which I want to have published.'

'Or why do you not build a theatre yourself,' said Tivari, 'now that you are going into the contracting business? It will only mean an outlay of capital, with which your father will provide you, and afterwards you will get good interest on your money.'

'Please,' said Viddi. 'I have told you. I am not going into contracting business or any other business. I am going abroad, to study literature and art and perhaps also sociology.' Unfortunately this month he would not be able to save anything because his expenses had been so high; but he would definitely start next month.

'How ungrateful you are,' said Zahir-ud-din. 'After your father has been so kind to you.'

'He has not been kind to me. Only for the first time in his life he has done his duty by me. I think he was ashamed before other people that his son should go like a poor man's son. That is the only reason why he has decided to give me an allowance. He did not think of me, but only of his own good name.'

Tivari said: 'That was a nice party you gave for us yesterday. I like Chinese food.'

Bahwa said: 'Only next time let us go to the Intimate; the ice-cream there is much better.' He flapped his arms at some ragged children who had got into the auditorium and stood gaping up at them, and cried, 'Go away from here!'

'You must give parties like that more often,' advised Zahir-ud-din. 'It is good for people with artistic inclinations to meet together over food and drink and exchange ideas. This is how the artistic life of a city is stimulated. Only think of Paris in France: how rich it is in artistic life, all the world knows this. And why? Because it has very many restaurants where people can meet together and talk while they eat and drink.'

'Perhaps also we can come to your house,' Bahwa wistfully suggested. 'You can make party for us there, and then your father will sometimes come in and listen to our talk.'

'No,' Viddi said decisively, 'you cannot come to my house. And I cannot give party too often because then I will not be able to save sufficient money to go abroad and study literature and sociology.'

They ignored this. Zahir-ud-din said, 'We will introduce you to very many interesting people. Do you know, for instance, Meenakshi who works in the All India Radio? She is an announcer there, but really she is an actress and she is very beautiful. I think one day she will get a film-contract. You have no idea,' he told Viddi, 'how many talented and artistic people there are here in Delhi. There is really no need for you to go abroad. You can mix with very distinguished persons here. We will introduce you.'

'I am going abroad to study,' said Viddi. This line had become something of a defence mechanism with him and he intoned it quite automatically. 'Literature and sociology.'

'I will tell you,' said Tivari. 'I will let you give a party in my rooms if you cannot invite people to your house. We will ask everybody to come and the party can go on as long as we like.'

Zahir-ud-din struck his hands together and cried, 'But what a beautiful idea!' His eyes shone and he looked like a handsome and very excited little boy.

'No,' Viddi said. 'I cannot spend any more money on parties. I have to save to go – '

'We will invite Meenakshi and Leela Sinclair, and there is Mira who is learning to play the veena – '

'And do you know Agarwal, who has lately come back from America, where he has studied textile designing? And Pherozeshah Shroff the painter, and R. K. Malik who writes poetry which he sends to all the magazines – '

'No,' Viddi said. 'You see, such parties are expensive, and I have to – '

'If Ragvinder Singh is back from his exhibition in Bombay, we must ask him. He is invaluable at any party and he knows several good-looking women whom he will bring with him.'

'Please,' said Viddi, 'going to England is costly, that is why I must save and cannot – please listen to me,' he said, but nobody did.

Taking precedence in his mind over the new Deputy Minister, over the ten-lakh income tax for which the Government was suing him, over the T— case, and even – though it was intimately connected with it – over the Happy Hindustan contract, was the problem of Nimmi. Lalaji was surprised that one small frail eighteen-year-old daughter of his could so seize upon his mind and heart as even to make him absent-minded over business affairs. At the most awkward times – he might be sitting in his New Delhi office, checking bills, reading lawyers' reports, listening to supplicants – suddenly, involuntarily, he would think of Dev Raj's proposition; and then he would forget everything before him in order vehemently to tell himself that it was impossible. Why it was impossible he did not usually explain. Only sometimes, when his conscience was very urgent with him, did he try to think of a reason. She is too young, he told himself; though he knew she was not. It is necessary for her to finish her education; though he knew it was not. The match is not suitable; though it would have been hard to think of one more so. She who is worthy of a King, he would tell himself, to be married only to the son of a Director of a Trading Company ...

But that son would bring him a much wished-for contract. He really wanted that contract. It had become a matter of pride with him: it was one of the biggest works in Delhi, and it was right that it should go to him who was Delhi's biggest contractor. And quite apart from pride – which by itself would not have made him so persistent – he really needed the work. It would bring him, at a modest estimate, twenty-five lakhs, and he always needed – was there a man who did not? – twenty-five lakhs. Especially now that he had to face so many heavy expenses. He wanted to give a big name-giving ceremony for Shanta's baby, and after that there was Usha's wedding, which would cost him at least one and a half lakhs. But he could not bear the idea of sacrificing Nimmi for Usha and Shanta's baby and his own pride. She who was dearest to him! Yet there was really no question of sacrifice: he knew that if it had been either of his other daughters, Rani or Usha, he would not have thought so. On the contrary, he would have congratulated himself on being able to settle them so advantageously and at the same time, though incidentally, derive his own immediate benefit from the match. He was not a man given to self-analysis. He performed actions because they seemed good to him, and did not probe into his own motives. But here, in his uncertainty, the question of motive did arise, and then he could not help asking himself whether, when he thought of sacrifice, he thought of it not so much in connection with his daughter as in connection with himself. That he should lose her, give her away to a husband's house, not hear any more her voice ringing through his home and see her curled up on the divan eating a banana like a queen, young and graceful, dainty and fresh and fragile; his Nimmi.

He did not see much of her. He was a busy man, he had many business worries, he was always being called away, there were letters and telephone calls to be attended to, people to be interviewed, accounts to be checked, sites to be visited. Except in his thoughts, his family did not play a great part in his daily life. But what home-life he had was coloured by her more than by any of the others. When he thought of home, he thought of her. She filled his house and his thoughts like a fragrance. To come home, to think of home, and to find that fragrance missing, this was what was intolerable to him; this where the sacrifice came in. Though when the realization came to him, he scornfully negated it: it was not true, for he was the most loving of fathers and his own feelings were as nothing to him against the good of his children.

He would have liked to talk with someone about it all, and for a while he thought he would confide in Om Prakash. But he speedily rejected the idea. If he wanted advice, he wanted only the advice which would be in harmony with his own feelings. And this he knew Om would not give him. Om would say: 'But this is what we have been waiting for.' He would not be able to understand why his father was not jumping at the offer. Even if the match had not been as advantageous as in fact it was, Om would still have jumped at it, because it would get them the Happy Hindustan contract. He was like that, Lalaji knew. His sister, his brother, his own children were as nothing to him when he wanted a thing. Of course, sentiment and business must be kept apart: but not altogether. The truth about Om was, so it seemed to his father, that with him it was not a question of keeping sentiment out of business affairs, but a question of having no sentiment. Much as he loved his eldest son, Lalaji had to admit that he did not have a loving heart. Unlike himself, who had always had a loving heart and felt very tenderly not only for his own family but also for mankind in general. When he saw a poor or an unhappy man, even though he would do nothing for him, he would still feel sorry and shake his head and sigh over all the misery in the world. But Om would only shrug his shoulders, for he had no tender feelings in him. So Lalaji decided against confiding in him: only someone with a heart as loving as his own could understand his feelings for his daughter.

Even less did he wish to consult with the women of his family. What their reaction would be he knew only too well, so that he did not even .nention Dev Raj's proposition to them. But Dev Raj was too shrewd for him: he knew from which side to soften a man's opinions. A hint of the negotiations was dropped to Dev Raj's wife, who could hardly wait to get to Lalaji's house.

The moment she came in they knew she had something special to impart, for her eyes gleamed with excitement and she wore a festive blouse of blue satin. They were a little apprehensive because, whenever she came like this, she usually had something to their disadvantage to impart. However, nothing beyond the usual civilities was said at first, as she took her place among them in the courtyard where they sat enjoying the evening air. Her first concern, as usual, was with the new baby, whom she took on her lap and rocked while she looked down at it and murmured, 'Exactly her mother's face, how she takes after her mother's family,' a statement which she made so regularly that the others were weary of challenging it. And it was not until she had been sitting there for some time, drinking sherbet and eating sweetmeats and fanning herself with a fan made of peacock feathers, talking of this and that very amicably, that at last she said, 'And your Nimmi? Where is she this evening?' Lalaji's wife and Phuphiji and Rani were on the defensive immediately, and Maee sniffed suspiciously. They were well acquainted with the tactics of Shanta's mother, and took this as a reflection on Nimmi's absence.

'I have sent her,' Lalaji's wife lied defiantly, 'to the house of my sister this evening, for always my sister is asking why do you not send your children to visit in my house?'

Shanta's mother nodded very amicably and said, 'Of course, a sister's children are our own children,' and then, to everyone's surprise, dropped the point. Only to say, almost roguishly from behind her fan, 'And I hear that soon perhaps we are to be related even more closely.'

They had no idea what she could mean but took good care not to look surprised. Lalaji's wife replied non-committally, 'Ah, the ties between us are very fast,' while they waited to hear what explanation they could pick up. But Shanta, who saw no necessity to be as wary with her mother as the others, innocently cried: 'What do you mean, Mataji? How are our two families to be related even closer?' She did not realize that she had said anything wrong till she caught Phuphiji's eye.

'They have not told you?' asked her mother. 'You have not told her?' she asked the others, though by this time she had very well realized that they did not know what there was to tell.

'We thought it better – ' said Lalaji's wife, and then shouted into the kitchen, 'The rice has been cooked and the onions made ready? Tonight we will eat pilau.' To Shanta's mother she explained: 'I have to be very careful that the rice is cooked in the proper manner. If servants are left to themselves, they spoil everything.'

'That is always the way,' said Shanta's mother in polite commiseration. 'There is never any rest for the ladies of a house. I may tell her?' she asked, nodding towards Shanta.

Lalaji's wife exchanged a glance with Phuphiji and then said casually, 'Why not? There is no harm.'

Shanta's mother waited no longer: 'You know your father's cousin-brother Madan Mohan? He is married to Rampyari, and the brother of Rampyari, Ram Prasad, is married to Romeshlata, and the mother of Romeshlata has an elder brother whose name is Amar Nath. Amar Nath has three daughters and one son, all three daughters are married and for the son he has just made an offer for Nimmi.'

It was not until she had gone that they could express their feelings. And even then there was so much to express that they did not know where to start. Eventually they started on Lalaji: for this was the worst, that he should not have breathed a word to them about this admirable proposition. 'How we were shamed before that woman,' said his wife. 'I could read it in her eyes. She knew he had not told us, and she thought, "The women of this household have no power in their family at all. Even over the disposal of the daughters they are not consulted." And now she will go tell it to all her relations, how an offer was made for Nimmi and the mother and the aunt and the elder sister were not told. Such shame he brings on us with his obstinate ways.'

Phuphiji agreed with her in very strong language. It was wonderful, the way the two of them agreed on all points nowadays. It had not always been so. When Lalaji's wife had first come into the house as a young girl, thirty-seven years ago, she had suffered much from the stern rule which Phuphiji had thought fit to exercise over her. It was indeed Phuphiji's right to exert such a rule: for though she was a widow – she had been a child-widow and her husband had died when she was ten, before their marriage had even been consummated – still she was the eldest sister in the house and entitled to rule accordingly. But a few years later, when Lalaji's wife had borne two children and was firmly established in the household, she had revolted against this tyranny and there had been many fierce and terrible quarrels in the women's quarter. Phuphiji, it must be admitted, usually got the best of it, for she was a woman of strong character; which had made Lalaji's wife hate her sister-in-law with a hate which most married women reserved only for their mother-in-law. But with the passing of the years this strife had largely ceased. Whether it was that Lalaji's wife had now learned to think along the lines laid down by Phuphiji, or whether with the coming of age their tempers had mellowed, or whether they had just learned to live with one another – whatever the cause, they now regarded one another not as rivals and enemies, but as allies, and found much comfort in their accord. And nowhere was that accord greater than in their opinion of Lalaji. He was obstinate; on this they were firmly agreed. He was proud, unorthodox, irreligious and had no sense of duty towards his family – as the present instance most amply illustrated.

Even Rani, who was usually milder in judging her father, had to say: 'Why did Pitaji not tell us? Such an excellent match.' It *was* an excellent match; Shanta's mother had left them in no doubts about that. They had been fully – if obliquely – informed about the house which had cost two lakhs and was now worth four, about the other house in Prithviraj Road, about the three daughters for whom such outstanding marriages had been made and with whom fantastic dowries had been given. They had also heard about the twenty-five-lakh contract which would come to Lalaji together with the bridegroom: it was as good as receiving a dowry instead of giving one. 'Why has he not told us?' they asked one another over and over again. Lalaji's wife even forgot about the pilau for the night-meal. 'Why has he said nothing?'

'Because he has forgotten what is the duty of a brother and a father and a husband,' was Phuphiji's grim explanation. They could think of none other. It was inconceivable that he could have any doubts about accepting the proposal and making it sure as quickly as possible.

'Send for him,' Phuphiji commanded. 'At once let him come here to speak with us.'

His wife was more realistic: she knew he was not the man to be summarily sent for and made to discuss a subject which he had no desire to discuss. 'What is the use?' she said. 'You know too well how obstinate he is in his mind. His wife, his sister, his eldest daughter – he will listen to none of us. Eight children I have borne him; six of them God has prospered and allowed me to rear for him. For thirty-seven years I have served him, with my own hands I have prepared his food and laid out his clothes, and now he will not listen to me any more as if I were a servant to whom he pays a wage of forty rupees a month.'

'He *must* listen,' said Phuphiji. 'He must be made to act quickly. Such an offer we cannot afford to neglect.'

'Pitaji will not neglect,' Rani said. 'He knows very well it is a good offer. Why should he neglect?'

'Because he has no care for his children,' Phuphiji replied promptly. 'It is we who have to see to everything. He would let her get twenty-five years old and make no talk of a husband.'

Lalaji's wife let out a groan at the idea of having a daughter aged twenty-five and unprovided with a husband. Her first thought was of the triumphant commiseration of Shanta's mother, and this thought was so terrible to her that she at once began to weep. 'And such a beautiful girl,' she sobbed. 'Where else will you find such a beautiful daughter?'

'Beauty of face,' said Phuphiji, who had never had any and now found reasons for being glad of it, 'adds nothing to the good of the soul. It is only by fulfilling the work laid down for her, by doing her duty by her husband and her husband's family, that a girl will attain to goodness and beauty in the sight of God.'

'If he will find a husband for her,' Lalaji's wife wailed, 'she will do her duty by him. Only let him find.'

'Send for him,' Phuphiji commanded again.

Lalaji's wife sadly shook her head: 'It will perhaps make him more obstinate,' she said, made wise by the bitterness of her experience. Here Shanta, who had hitherto been quietly crooning to her baby, unexpectedly asked why did they not send for Om. Perhaps he could tell them something. She was not entirely disinterested in this suggestion: she wanted to see her husband, who had not come to the women's quarters for several days.

This was thought a good idea, so Phuphiji at once made it her own. 'Let the eldest son be sent for. When the father is neglectful of his duty, the burdens of the family fall on the eldest son.'

A servant was sent to the sitting-room but soon returned with the message that Om was tired and could not come. A more peremptory message was sent, and this, after some delay, brought an Om who was very cross and whose first words were, 'What do you want with me? All day I work in the office, and even in the evening I cannot sit and rest for one moment?' The truth was he had made an appointment with some friends for a very special party and was in a hurry to be off.

Shanta rocked her baby in her arms rather ostentatiously and sang to it: 'Just see who has come. Your Pappaji has come.'

'What do you want?' Om asked his mother.

'Son,' she said, 'has your father spoken with you about the proposal that has been made for your youngest sister?'

'The first-class proposal,' Phuphiji supplemented, but Om did not show any interest. It was nearly eight o'clock and they were to assemble at eight-thirty. He and seven other business men; very elaborate arrangements had been made. 'No,' he said, 'he has said nothing.' And when Shanta came and pressed the baby into his arms, he clucked his tongue at it absent-mindedly.

'Every day she looks more like you,' Shanta said, looking down, proud and shy, at father and child.

'He has said nothing?' cried Lalaji's wife.

'There,' said Phuphiji, 'did I not say so? His family are nothing to him. A first-class proposal is made and he says nothing.'

'For Nimmi?' asked Om.

'A very rich family of our community. One hundred years you can look and not find a better, and then also there is a contract . . .'

'What contract?'

'For a building,' said Phuphiji. 'It is worth twenty-five lakhs of rupees.'

'The Happy Hindustan?' Om asked. His interest was stirred, and for a moment he even forgot about the party.

The women nodded, and he looked impressed. 'It is good news,' he said.

128

'Of course it is good news!' cried Phuphiji. 'But why are we not told about such good news? Why do we hear of it only from the lips of that woman?'

'It does not matter from where you hear it,' Om said impatiently. 'The important thing is that we get the contract. It is certain?'

'Who knows what is certain? With your father, who can tell? If the Lord Krishna Himself came and asked for his daughter in marriage, one cannot be certain if he will say yes, he is so obstinate and self-willed and without proper regard for his family.'

'He has wanted this contract for a long time,' Om said. 'We have both worked hard to get it. He will not throw it away when it has dropped into his hands.' The baby began to cry, for he was holding it awkwardly. Shanta desperately tried to soothe it, saying, 'Look look, it is your own Pappaji who is holding you and loving you,' but still it cried, so that Om returned it quickly to the mother. 'She will make me wet,' he said, and anxiously looked at his trousers. He was wearing his best trousers, pale cream gaberdine, fitting tightly over his stout thighs.

Shanta also noticed the trousers; and she took in his silk-shirt, his gold cuff-links, his hair drenched in oil which gave out a sweet smell like distilled violets. She said, 'You are going out? You will not stay to eat in the house?'

'I have to go,' he replied glibly. 'I have to meet people on business; it is very important.' From this she realized that he was going to a party with friends; otherwise he would never have given her any explanation. She knew, vaguely, about these parties. They would drink a lot and there would be dancing-girls. She did not think very precisely about these dancing-girls. They were bad women, this was all she knew about them. But she accepted them, because everyone's husband went to such bad women. It was just something a wife had to pretend she did not know about. So all she said was: 'What a pity you have to go out; tonight pilau has been cooked and you like so much to eat pilau.'

But that she should even say that much irritated her husband. He shouted, 'Is it my fault that I have to work all day and also in the night to keep you and your children? I would like a life such as yours, to sit all day in the women's quarter and eat only and sleep.'

'If your father was dying of thirst,' Phuphiji said, 'and we brought him freshly made sherbet, in his obstinacy he would not take it.'

'Why do you worry,' said Om. 'I know how much he has wanted this contract.'

'With the other one also, with Usha, he waited till she was twenty,

129

though there were many good offers. It is only because we begged of him and begged that at last he has made marriage for her.'

'But with me,' Rani said, 'he made at seventeen. So also he will make for Nimmi this year, you will see.'

'He knows very well it is time for her,' Om said. 'He will not delay, especially now that such a good offer has come.'

'Why do you not speak with him!' Phuphiji cried. 'Perhaps he will listen to the son when he will not hear his elder sister or his wife.'

'What is the use of my speaking with him?' Om said crossly. 'For years I have been telling him to get an air-conditioner into the office, for years he has said, "yes, yes," and still every day I have to sit and sweat. He will not listen to one word I say – not in the office, not at home. Like a slave I work for him, but he has more confidence in his clerk than he has for his own son.'

His mother gently clicked her tongue and rocked her head from side to side. 'No, son,' she said with love and affection; 'your father thinks very highly of you. Often he has said to me, "the greatest comfort to me in my life is my eldest son".' She could not remember whether Lalaji had ever actually said anything to this effect, but it was what she liked to think of him saying. It gave her pleasure to imagine her son as the indispensable support of his father.

'Why do you not ask Mohinder to speak with him?' Om said. Mohinder was Rani's husband, himself a very successful business man of whom Lalaji was known to hold a high opinion.

But Rani said: 'What does he care? He will never stir to help any of my family. It is only when there is talk of marrying any of his own sisters that he will run here and there with his tongue hanging out of his mouth. For my sisters he does not care at all, though they are one hundred times more beautiful than his, who are all very ugly and as black as boot-polish.' She got on quite well with her husband. He minded his business and she, mostly, minded hers. But it was a continual grievance to her that he was more attached to his own family than to hers.

'He will care when he hears that with the bridegroom his father-in-law will get a contract of twenty-five lakhs,' said Om. 'A contract of twenty-five lakhs is not a little thing, he knows this very well. He also knows that it is good for his own children that their grandfather should get such a contract.' Shanta gave him a glass of sherbet, which he drank. Though as soon as he had drunk it he was sorry, because he had intended to keep his palate clean for the drinks and the sumptuous dinner which were waiting for him. This irritated him against his wife and he thought: 'why can she not leave me alone, at every step she stands in my way.'

'And he will care,' said Lalaji's wife, 'that his wife's youngest sister should be well settled in the world. I know my son-in-law Mohinder, he is very careful of the honour of the family. Not,' she added bitterly, 'like his father-in-law, whom God forgive.'

'Only for his own family he cares,' Rani repeated, 'for his mother and his ugly sisters.'

'We are all one family,' Phuphiji said. 'A disgrace for us is a disgrace also for them. And what is it,' she cried, 'but a disgrace that a girl eighteen years old should run out and show herself to all the world? At this very moment we do not know where she is and three nights ago she came home so late that no one knows how late it was, though she says she was in her bed at ten o'clock.'

'I was awake till ten o'clock,' said Lalaji's wife, 'and she never showed herself to me then. What can we do, what can we say to her, when always there is her father to say let her alone, let her do what she wishes, let her go to a College, let her go out into the world.'

'College!' exclaimed Om. 'A hundred times I have asked what is the use of sending a girl to College.' He got up, for it was really time for him to go. He did not want to miss a minute of the party; at such gatherings it was important to be there right from the beginning, so that the festive spirit could be worked to its proper pitch. 'Already it is very late,' he said, looking at his watch. 'I cannot keep these people waiting, such business we cannot afford to lose.' Shanta silently came forward with the baby, and he patted its foot.

'Thank God,' said Lalaji's wife, 'that I have a son who is a hardworking honourable boy. I will keep pilau for you. You shall eat when you come home.'

'You must speak with your father,' said Phuphiji. 'This marriage must be arranged as soon as possible.'

'Do not worry,' said Om. 'Pitaji has been in business long enough to know the value of a twenty-five lakh contract.'

It was strange, Nimmi thought, but when she was away from Pheroze she was more excited about him than she generally was when she was with him. The kiss was a case in point: for when he had actually been there, kissing her, her sole reaction had been one of amusement. But afterwards she could not keep her thoughts away from it, and then it became romantic and thrilling. Perhaps it only became real, fully experienced with all the correct accompanying emotions, in the telling of it. Before Rajen had been told, it was – if she had told herself the truth, which she did not – not quite satisfactory, not quite what she expected a kiss to be. But when, at College the next day, she had drawn Rajen aside and told her – not, of course, just like that, but with many 'please guess what happened – no, but please guess' and floods of giggles and hiding her face and pinching Rajen's arm – as she told her, it all became just as it should have been: the moonlight, the Kutb, the wishing pillar, the smell of jasmine, the silence, and a sudden passionate impulse of love which had made him draw her close and hotly seek her lips.

Rajen was properly impressed. 'He really – ?' she cried. 'You are not teasing, he really – ?' and Nimmi nodded and burst into fresh giggles. Arm in arm they walked down the corridor and Nimmi told it all over again, thinking that although Rajen had very fashionable parents, a sister in England and was herself a member of the Club, she had never been kissed by a young man. And this really did seem to be beyond even Rajen's wide experience of fashionable life. She was quite awestruck, and continued to press for further details. She did not think, she said, looking at Nimmi with admiration, that her sister had ever been kissed. And Pheroze was quite redeemed in her eyes. She no longer thought he was a bore who did not know how to make conversation; especially when Nimmi repeated to her everything he had said, how experienced he was, how well informed, how he had spoken of the Eiffel Tower in Paris which was higher than the Kutb and of cabarets in Europe; and also how he had a mechanical turn of mind and knew a lot about cars.

The evening's adventure occupied them for many days. They would retire to the Library to whisper exuberantly from behind their hands, huddle together in a corner of the Common Room, pass notes to one another during lectures with ostentatious secrecy. Other girls looked enviously on: even their great friend Indira Malik was given no more than a hint as to their great preoccupation. Nor could Indira pride herself that this hint was exclusive to herself, for in some form or other it was given to most of the other girls. It was pleasant to be shrouded in mystery, but even more pleasant to put others in a position to appreciate the greatness of the mystery by acquainting them with its outline. Soon everyone in the College knew that Nimmi Verma had a Parsi boy-friend.

Going to the Club was more exciting than ever. Hitherto, Nimmi had had a slight feeling of inferiority, because she was not really a member of the Club, because her parents were not fashionable and had no friends in fashionable circles, because she was young and inexperienced and unknown. But after she had been out with Pheroze all that was changed. She felt she had a right to be there, for she too was now experienced and fashionable. She walked through the opulent lounges with her head as high as she held it walking down the corridors of the College; and when she went to the ladies' dressing-room, she no longer moved aside apologetically when she saw some other lady wanted to use a mirror, nor did she respectfully listen to the conversation of others. Instead she monopolized a mirror for as long as she wanted, while she chattered away to Rajen about clothes and the Hot Spot and her boy-friend. And her self-confidence increased even further when she discovered that she had another admirer.

She was very quick to make this discovery – quicker than Rajen, who at first noticed nothing. But Nimmi knew at once that while they played tennis one young man watched with more than ordinary interest. Next evening he was there again – she had been looking out for him, though she did not admit it to herself – and he stayed all the time they were playing. Afterwards he came up and said, 'You know, you could play quite well if you had a little training,' but as several other young men had already said that to her – Pheroze had been the first – she was not as excited as she might otherwise have been. Anyway, she in no way encouraged him; because she was not interested, because she was in love with Pheroze and had no time for anyone else, even though this young man was also, in his way, quite nice-looking. Not, of course, as handsome as Pheroze – oh no, nowhere near; but quite nice-looking. He was not very tall and he was rather thin; but he dressed well, even though it was only in white shirt and white flannels, and he wore a pink scarf with white stripes on it tucked very rakishly into the open collar of his shirt. And he always looked so gay: this was the first thing that struck her about him. He laughed a lot, and when he walked from one place to the other he did not seem to be walking so much as skipping. Nimmi thought that he would probably be very amusing to talk to. Only at present she had no need to be amused.

On the third evening that he presented himself, even Rajen noticed him. Afterwards, while they were sitting on the lawn, drinking their customary pineapple juice, she said, 'Did you see the young man with the pink scarf? I think he likes you. He is always watching you.'

'Which young man with pink scarf?' asked Nimmi, falsely frowning as if trying hard to recollect.

'The one that came yesterday and said you only needed a little training to play well.'

'Oh, that one!' Nimmi said and gaily laughed. 'He is only a boy.' He might have been about twenty-one or twenty-two whereas Pheroze was twenty-six and therefore much more experienced and exciting.

'He looks quite nice,' said Rajen; which pleased Nimmi so much that she rejoined: 'But I think his friend, the tall one with spectacles, is interested in you. I have noticed how he cannot keep his eyes away from you.' She made a point of insinuating such things occasionally. She instinctively realized that if Rajen was to give her untarnished interest to Nimmi's affairs, she would have to be given some hopes for herself.

It always worked, and Rajen always reacted in the same way. She gave a false little laugh and said, 'What nonsense! You are imagining things.'

'All right. I am imagining things. Perhaps I have not had enough experience and do not know when a man is attracted to a girl.' To this Rajen knew no answer, for in such matters Nimmi was now the acknowledged expert.

'It would be nice,' Nimmi resumed after a while, 'if we could all go out together, Pheroze and I, and you with your friend. We will book a table at the Hot Spot, and when we dance we can exchange partners. Also we can make up a four for tennis.'

'But what about the other one? The one with the pink scarf? He will be very hurt if he has to be left alone while you go with Pheroze.'

'Oh, that one!' said Nimmi. 'I do not think he is interested in me at all. I will tell you what I think: his friend, the one who is interested in you, he is rather shy – he looks shy, doesn't he – so he has asked his friend, the one with the pink scarf, to talk with us so that he can get to know you. Bearer!' she called – she was getting as expert at ordering now as Rajen – 'bring us more pineapple juice and a plate of potato chips with chutney.' Then she slipped her feet out of her sandals and rubbed them to and fro on the lawn, under the table. 'How cool is the grass,' she said. So Rajen also shuffled her sandals off, and they both sat cooling their feet on the grass.

After a while Nimmi said: 'My family would be very angry if they knew I went out with Pheroze.' Lately she had become a little more outspoken about her family; at any rate with Rajen, if not with Pheroze. She felt that Rajen had now accepted her as an equal and that her position in the social world had become, by her own efforts, quite secure; secure enough for her to relax some of her self-imposed censorship on her family background. It was more comfortable that way too; she could talk almost freely with Rajen instead of having to be on her guard all the time.

'What nonsense,' said Rajen. 'I am sure Mummy and Daddy would not mind at all, on the contrary, they always say that young people must get together.'

'My eldest sister,' Nimmi said, 'was married when she was seventeen, and she never knew any young man before that.' She was not even sure that Rani had known or seen her husband before she was married to him, but she did not mention this.

'That is what makes Daddy so angry,' Rajen said. 'He says it is a primitive custom to marry girls young, without giving them any education, even if you can afford it, or without letting them see anything of the world. He says this is what retards our progress.'

'My other sister,' Nimmi continued, 'is also to be married in two–three months. She is twenty now. She was sent to College and had education; but she failed in Inter three times so she was taken away. I do not think she ever spoke to any young man.' Usha had been allowed to meet her future husband once or twice, but only for a very short time and with many people present. Even then Phuphiji had protested that it was unorthodox and unfitting that the bridegroom should be allowed to gaze on the face of his future bride.

'She likes the young man she is to marry?' Rajen asked.

Nimmi shrugged her shoulders. 'Like?' she said. 'How can you like someone you do not know? Could I like even Pheroze if I did not know him?'

'Your poor sister! How unhappy she must be. Thank Heaven that Mummy and Daddy do not believe in arranged marriages!'

'No,' Nimmi said slowly, thinking it over, 'I do not think she is unhappy.' She had never given the matter any thought before. Like everybody else in the family, she just accepted the fact that Usha was to be married. And Usha never talked to anyone of her feelings.

'My auntie,' said Rajen, 'also arranged a marriage for my cousin last year. But she chose the bridegroom very carefully. Of course, he was of our own class and community and he was very well educated and America-returned, so it was all right and they are very happy together. Just now they have gone to Switzerland for holiday. Nimmi,' she said, 'if your parents arrange for your sisters, will they not also arrange for you?'

'Oh,' said Nimmi and laughed. That was the way she always answered this question when it occurred to her, or when it was forcibly suggested to her by her mother and her aunt. 'Oh, I will never marry!' And just then she became aware of the young man in the pink scarf, who had settled himself with a group of friends at a nearby table. She lowered her head and studied her hands and said with a very faint smile – the last vestige of a vast amusement which she struggled hard to suppress – 'Look, Rajen. Here is your friend with the spectacles come to sit near you.'

After this it was impossible to carry on conversation as before, though they tried hard to look unconcerned. Nimmi was greatly aware of the young man with the pink scarf and Rajen of the one with the spectacles. 'It is rather hot this evening,' said Rajen, her feet groping for her sandals because it was not nice to sit with naked feet, even if they were hidden under the table.

The young man with the pink scarf sat in an easy attitude, his arm resting on the back of his tilted chair, his legs crossed and one foot swinging. He laughed a lot, Nimmi noticed, and made the others laugh a lot. He was drinking orange squash.

'Is he looking at me?' asked Rajen in a low voice. Nimmi darted a look at the other table. All she saw was her own admirer, gazing at her intently. She quickly looked away again. 'Oh yes,' she said; 'he is looking at you so hard his spectacles are nearly bursting.' Rajen giggled and said, 'How you tell lies.'

Nimmi was almost surprised when Pheroze joined them. Not that she was not expecting him; she was always expecting him. But it so happened that just at that moment she was not thinking about him.

'Please sit down, Pheroze,' she said, with dignity and as if she owned him. As really she did: he was her boy-friend. It was nice to have him come up and join them like this, as a matter of course; very different from that time, no more than a week ago, when she had to sit there and hope and tensely pretend she did not notice him.

'It is rather hot this evening,' said Pheroze. Both girls hastened to agree to this and to add their own comments. Rajen also was on her best behaviour, for she had a very great respect for Pheroze now. 'In Bombay,' said Pheroze, 'the air is more pleasant, especially by the seaside.' Nimmi could still hear the voice of the young man in the pink scarf and he was still laughing.

'Do you not feel the heat very much on your head?' Pheroze asked her, 'with so much hair?' Her hand went up to those heavy coils and Rajen's also went, a little complacently, to her short curls. 'Yes,' said Rajen, 'it must be very hot for you. Why do you not have it cut? You would look so nice and it would be more comfortable.'

Nimmi pouted at Pheroze. She had never before confronted him with so undignified an expression; but she knew it suited her and the occasion seemed to call for it. So she pouted and said, 'Oh, but you said once you liked the way I did my hair. Why do you now say you do not like it?'

He smiled indulgently; the pout had gone down well. 'My dear Nimmi,' he said, almost paternally, and she loved him that way, 'I have not said I do not like it. Only I asked if it was not uncomfortably hot for you?'

'But how nice you would look if you had it cut!' cried Rajen. 'Do you not think so, Mr Batliwala?'

He considered the question with great seriousness. Nimmi wondered whether he knew the name of the young man in the pink scarf and whether she would dare ask him. 'Yes,' Pheroze at last delivered his opinion, 'I think it would suit you very well. And it is more fashionable.'

'There,' said Rajen, 'always I tell her so. But she says her parents will not allow her to have it cut.'

Nimmi was annoyed. There was no need for Pheroze to know that her parents were not fashionable people. Why could Rajen not keep her mouth shut? Was she being spiteful or just stupid? 'No,' she said, frowning, 'I like to wear it like this. I think it suits me better.' She thought I suppose Rajen is still imagining the young man in the spectacles is looking at her; she can talk for four hours about her sister in Cambridge, England, and her Mummy and Daddy who go to parties at the Embassies, but still no one will look at her. 'We were thinking,' she told Pheroze, 'that perhaps one evening we could go out, four of us together, you and I and Rajen and her boy-friend.' Rajen looked embarrassed: perhaps she had a boy-friend in the offing, but one could hardly as yet talk so confidently of him and already make appointments for him. Nimmi noticed her embarrassment and thought defiantly: 'Well, she should not have said that about my parents.'

'Yes,' said Pheroze, not very enthusiastically, as she had known he would not be. Of course he would prefer to be alone with her. How could he kiss her if there were two other people present? Tomorrow night he was going to take her out again; and she had been wondering, ever since he had made the appointment, whether he was going to kiss her this time too.

It was a very large party. A cocktail party it was called, and Viddi was immensely proud to be host at a cocktail party. But he would have been happier if it had been made clear that he *was* the host, at any rate that he was paying the bill, though all the guests had been invited by Tivari and the party took place on the lawn of the house in which he lodged. Tivari took no pains to enlighten people that really it was Viddi who was giving the party. Even when he introduced him to some of the guests, he made no mention of his true function, so that Viddi could not help feeling just like another guest and a very unimportant one at that. He would have liked to speak to Tivari about this, but felt it would not be quite nice to do so.

Besides, Tivari was far too busy to listen to him. He did not even have time to introduce Viddi properly, but would just break off – rather impatiently – in the middle of amusing conversation to wave his hand and mutter a few names which Viddi failed to catch. Zahir-ud-din was even more preoccupied, dancing round a number of attractive young ladies, and it was only when Viddi stared at him very insistently that he would as much as wave at him across the lawn and flash a brilliant smile which was left over from someone else. As for Bahwa, he seemed to know as few people as Viddi. In fact, Bahwa, Viddi noticed at once, did not belong at all. It was a pity he had been invited, for he lowered the tone of the party. Not only was he shabbily dressed but he also made himself a nuisance by trying to sell tickets for his play to people who stared at him coldly.

Bahwa was the only misfit: otherwise the tone of the party was very high. Viddi was impressed. He had not known that there were so many fashionable and advanced people in Delhi. Most of the girls behaved as freely as he thought European girls behaved, and some of them even smoked cigarettes. Unfortunately, Viddi was not introduced to them, so that he could only hover on the outskirts of individual groups where no one took any notice of him. Once or twice he tried to assume the air of host and gave peremptory orders to the bearers who walked about with trays of drinks; but they only said, 'Very good, Sahib,' and carried on as before. He wandered from one group to the other, his hands behind his back, and from time to time cleared his throat in a preoccupied manner. It was a warm languid night, the garden full of tall stiff flowers, the lawn smoothly mown, and lights had been fixed in the foliage of the trees so that the underside of leaves glimmered a faint golden green. There was a buffet, a long table covered with a white cloth bearing glasses and bottles and plates full of potato chips and sandwiches. Viddi felt a little uncomfortable when he thought of what it was all going to cost. It would certainly eat deep into his next month's allowance, and again he would not be able to save for his education in Europe. For the moment he did not mind: this was an education in itself, all these elegant people laughing and talking together, mostly about Clubs and restaurants and parties and sometimes about Art.

'Ved Prakash Verma,' Tivari muttered, waving his hand, as Viddi insistently appeared by his side; and this time he added, 'He is the son of Lala Narayan Dass Verma.'

Viddi was much annoyed at that, but noticed that people seemed to look at him with more interest. One man said: 'Oh, we have all heard of your father,' and a girl asked: 'Why have we not seen you before?' She was a very pretty girl, rather artistic-looking, with straight shingled hair and a lot of lipstick. She was smoking a cigarette.

Viddi gulped. 'I often go to the Rendezvous and sometimes to the Swiss Miss.'

'But those places are so dull,' she said, flicking ash, 'and they are becoming really vulgar.'

'Yes,' said Viddi, 'they are very dull and also vulgar. I think so too.' But she had already turned away to talk to someone else, so that he had to address the latter half of his sentence to a young man standing beside him. This young man was looking at him with great attention. 'So you are the son of Lala Narayan Dass Verma.'

Since this was the only opening he had, Viddi had to brush away his feeling of annoyance. 'You know my father?'

'Everybody knows your father,' the young man answered, and laughed, though not offensively. He was just a young man who liked to laugh. 'I have also seen your sister,' he said, 'she comes to our Club and plays tennis.'

'Oh! do I know her?' cried the girl with the cigarette. 'Who is she, Kuku?'

The young man called Kuku did not answer but he took her hand and said: 'Let me tell your fortune.'

'Can you tell fortunes?' asked Viddi, looking enviously at Kuku who could be so familiar with this pretty girl.

'He cannot do anything except be silly,' said the girl, snatching away her hand, though not before he had held it for a little while.

'I think you mean my sister-in-law Kanta,' Viddi said. 'She goes to Club and I think she plays tennis.'

'No,' said Kuku. 'I mean your sister. Her name is Nimmi.'

'Nimmi?' said the girl. 'Who is Nimmi?'

'My youngest sister,' said Viddi. But Kuku had already turned away to join another group, and when he walked he did not seem to be so much walking as skipping. The girl followed him, and because there was no one else who seemed inclined to talk to him, Viddi trailed behind them. The group they joined included Zahir-ud-din who, though Viddi stared at him very hard, made no attempt to introduce him. Viddi noticed that Zahir-ud-din's own position among these people did not seem to be very secure: he was working hard at being agreeable and he asked all the girls: 'When will you let me paint you?' Kuku said, 'This is the only way of approach he knows,' and then he took Viddi's arm and said to the others, 'Please meet my friend, the son of Lala Narayan Dass Verma.'

'Ah yes,' cried Zahir-ud-din, 'his father is a very great man. I shall paint his portrait – you have fixed it up for me?'

'Do not listen to him,' said Kuku. 'For months he has been trying to come and paint my father's portrait too.'

Zahir-ud-din laughed heartily at that, throwing back his head. 'A poor artist has to live,' he said.

Viddi asked: 'You are sure the Nimmi you know is my sister? I do not think she goes to any Club. She is only a student.'

'But who is this Nimmi?' cried the girl with the cigarette.

'She is his sister,' said Kuku, and Zahir-ud-din asked: 'She is pretty? Shall I come and paint her?'

Viddi did not answer because he did not like Zahir-ud-din to talk so easily of his sister. Kuku also did not seem to like it. 'No, you will not paint her,' he said with such decision that Viddi wondered just how well he knew Nimmi.

'I think you people are not very interested in Art,' Zahir-ud-din replied. 'You are too materialistic.'

'I am not materialistic,' Viddi answered, for he did not wish to appear in a bad light before his new acquaintances. 'I like Art very much.'

'Of course,' said the girl with the cigarette impatiently, 'we all like Art.'

'And dancing,' said Kuku, 'and parties and drinks and tennis.' He hummed a tune and threw his arm round the girl with the cigarette, who shook him off with a great show of indignation.

'It is easy for you to like these things,' said Zahir-ud-din, sulking a little. 'You have a rich father. For us poor artists it is not so easy.'

'There is very little fashionable life in Delhi,' said Viddi. 'Unfortunately we live in a backward country. It would be interesting to write a thesis on social life in India,' but no one took him up on this. Only Kuku said, 'I like being backward,' and the girl with the cigarette laughed affectedly and said: 'Oh yes, you are backward. You only belong to three Clubs and go to five parties a week. You are very backward!' Viddi looked at him and was much impressed. He is no older than I am, he thought, but he knows how to live.

'Kuku is wiser than you are,' Zahir-ud-din told him. 'You see, he knows how fortunate he is in his birth and he has gone into his father's business and has a lot of money.'

'I am going to Europe to study. Literature and Art and Sociology,' Viddi said.

'Your father is sending you?' Kuku asked.

'I am saving out of my allowance, which is 500 rupees a month': and this reminded him that he was – at any rate financially – the host of this party and he said: 'Why do you not have one more cocktail?' He wished that he could state his importance at this gathering more directly. Zahir-ud-din also gave no hint of it, which Viddi thought mean, considering how much he was drinking at his expense.

'They are not very nice cocktails,' said the girl with the cigarette, wrinkling her nose at the glass in her hand. 'Last week I went to a cocktail party at the house of an American lady and there they were much better.'

'This is not a very nice party,' said Kuku. 'It is very dull. All the people are dull.'

140

The girl with the cigarette said: 'They are people who are never asked to really nice parties, so they come here.' Viddi ceased to devise plans by which he could explain himself as the host.

'Come on,' said Kuku, 'we will go somewhere else. We have been here long enough.' Everyone thought this a good idea, except Zahir-ud-din, who wanted to stay longer because there might be some useful people present. Viddi wondered whether he was also included in the general invitation to go somewhere else. Certainly he no longer wanted to stay, he had no interest in a party at which only people who were not invited anywhere else were present. As he stood hesitating, Kuku called over his shoulder: 'You also come with us, son of Lala Narayan Dass Verma,' and Viddi said to the girl with the cigarette who did not hear him: 'Yes, I think I will go too. This is a very dull party.'

They piled into their cars, and Viddi was fortunate enough to get into Kuku's car, though it was already very full. Nobody said anything about where they were going and Viddi was quite content to let himself be taken wherever they chose. They all complained what an awfully dull party it had been, but then what could you expect from someone like Tivari? 'He never has any money,' they said. 'Whenever you meet him he wants you to pay for his drinks.'

'Where did he get the money for this party from?' someone asked, but Viddi kept quiet.

'And that Zahir-ud-din,' said the girl with the cigarette. 'How tired I am of his talk about poor artists. All artists are poor, it is a well-known fact. In Paris, France, they all live in garrets and starve, but they do not mind because they live only for their Art.'

'Zahir-ud-din does not think of Art at all, he thinks only of making money.'

'That is what I say. He is not a true artist. True artists do not care about making money. And who was that man who said he had written a play for which he wanted us all to buy tickets? How badly dressed he was, he looked like a servant. Why does Tivari ask us to come to parties with such people.'

They stopped at a restaurant and the doorman swung the portals open for them. It was very full. Well-fed people were piled on gilt chairs and damascened sofas which looked too fragile to hold them. A few couples were dancing, but most people concentrated on eating. Bearers swayed under overladen trays and thrust vast steaming dishes between closely packed shoulders. Preoccupation with food and drink had swamped the dainty western-style elegance of the interior decoration, and even the dancers and the band, its jazzy little tunes so bravely played, could not hold out against the bulging bearded cheeks of chewing men.

The manager bowed deeply to Kuku and his party, but when he wanted to show them to a table, they said it was not a nice place, and they all returned to the cars and drove to another nightclub. Kuku pretended to be drunk; he zigzagged the car along the road, took his hands off the wheel and cried, 'Look no hands!' and all the girls shrieked.

At the other nightclub there was a cabaret in progress; an Indonesian girl in a tight skirt and a brassière walked up and down, jerking one hip and clacking castanets. They ordered drinks and kebabs and some of them danced. Viddi, unfortunately, did not know how to dance, but he liked watching, sitting there with a whisky-glass in one hand and a kebab in the other. He thought: 'Yes, this is what I want; this is Life.'

The leader of the band was a European; an oldish man with a bald head, but very gay, he made encouraging gestures to the dancers, flexed his knees and shouted things at the band which made them break into smiles at once. Kuku said, 'He has been in India twenty-five years and now he wants to go home, but he has no money.' The girl with the cigarette ate an enormous ice-cream, licked her spoon and said, 'I love ice-cream, everybody knows that.' Viddi smoked a cigarette; he sat with his legs crossed and leaning far back in his chair blew puffs of smoke which would not turn into rings. Waiters stumbled over his feet and apologized. He thought with contempt of the Rendezvous and also of Tivari and Zahir-ud-din and Bahwa. Then the Indonesian girl came back for another number; she had slim brown arms and bright-red fingernails so long that they seemed to bend over at the tips.

Kuku leaned over to him and said in a low voice: 'There is your sister over there.' Indeed there was Nimmi, sedately eating dinner at a table for two with a young Parsi in evening-dress. Viddi drew in his feet and sat up. He was surprised, and his first thought was what the family would say if they saw Nimmi sitting in a place like this, alone with a young man who was a Parsi. But it was a thought he checked immediately; of which he was even ashamed, because it was right for his sister to be here, to be emancipated. It raised his own status in the fashionable world to have such a sister.

Kuku said, 'You see, she is only a student, but she knows the right places.'

'I will introduce you if you like,' Viddi replied. He was proud of himself and proud of Nimmi, for it was not every brother who could offer to introduce his sister to a young man whom he had met at a party and whose very name and community he did not know. But Kuku laughed and said, 'That will not be necessary now,' and then the girl with the cigarette took him off to dance.

142

# Part Three

None of them felt at ease, not even Lalaji, who did not usually suffer from embarrassment. Nor would he have done so now, if it had not been for the children. But the children made him unhappy. They were his grandchildren, he wanted to love them, he *did* love them, but when he gathered them into his arms and drew them close, they squirmed away from him and then stood staring at him from a distance. Lalaji looked back at them and made sweet noises with his mouth; 'come my little ones, come,' he said, but they only giggled more. Kanta admonished them, and they stopped giggling, but they would not come closer; nor did she encourage them to. Lalaji thought of his other grandchildren, Rani's children and Om's, and how they came running to him and rubbed themselves against his chest. His eyes became melancholy and he said to Chandra in a gentle voice: 'You have not taught your children to love their father's father.'

'They are a little shy,' said Kanta. 'They do not usually kiss other people.'

'And the Grandfather is also other people?' Lalaji asked. Chandra fidgeted and looked reproachfully at Kanta. They could not afford to annoy his father. But Kanta assumed an expression of defiance; she did not care, she was not going to be more polite than necessary. She had not asked him to come, and the sooner he went away again the better. Every time he came to the house, and this was by no means frequently (it must have been at least two years since the last visit), she felt the same. Her one wish was always that he would be gone again as quickly as possible. Afterwards she would tidy the room, shake out the cushions and arrange the doilies, and feel restless because his presence still lingered in the house long after he had gone.

'All right,' she said to the children, 'you can go off now to play.' They walked to the door slowly but without protest, and looked back over their shoulder at their grandfather.

Lalaji sighed and rubbed his knees. They were very obedient children and very quiet, not like his other grandchildren. Perhaps that was a good thing, but he himself had always liked lively children. His own children

143

had been lively; all day and half the night the house had rung with their voices. Chandra Prakash himself had been very lively and Lalaji had loved him extremely.

'Why do you not bring my grandchildren to our house?' Lalaji asked his son.

'They are very busy at school,' Kanta replied; 'and then they go to dancing classes twice a week.' Mrs Ghosh's children went to dancing classes too; it was very fashionable.

Lalaji made no comment, though many occurred to him. He did not wish to speak harshly to Kanta. She was his son's wife, she had borne his son's children, and even though she came from a different community and her ways were not their ways, he had always tried to love her as a daughter.

'We want them to have a good education,' Chandra said, almost apologetically.

'Yes,' said his father, and then again, 'yes.'

'The early years are very important,' said Kanta. She spoke authoritatively.

'Yes,' said Lalaji.

'They must have a good grounding,' Kanta said. 'Unfortunately, education in India is not very good, but, of course, later they will go to University in England.'

'That is still a long way off,' said Chandra. He was nervously squeezing his bony ankle between two bony fingers.

'Yes,' said Kanta, 'but one must plan ahead.' She spoke with decision; she was not going to be compromising before her father-in-law. On the contrary, she intended to make it quite clear that her children were going to be educated along lines which would remove them far from him and his family: they were going to be educated beyond any point of contact. 'In a few years' time,' she said, 'they will be sent to boarding-school in the hills. These are still the best schools in India; they are run on English lines and the children are taught good manners and also good English. I do not care for my children to learn too much Hindi.'

'You will send them away to the hills?' Lalaji asked his son. 'They will not be at home with you?'

'They will come only for holidays,' Kanta said. 'It is best for children to be away from their parents. It is the English system.'

Lalaji was scandalized. He looked at Chandra who did not dare to meet his eye. 'Best for children to be away from parents!' Lalaji repeated in a dazed manner. What did this mean? He did not understand how such a thing could be said. How could parents live without children or children

144

without parents? He thought of his own home, all the homes he had had. What would they have been without children? For it was only the children – running from the women's quarters to the men's, into the kitchen, into the neighbouring houses – it was only they who united a family, united a neighbourhood, brought life to a society. Mothers, grandmothers, aunts, uncles, neighbours, servants – they could be run together only on that one thread: children. The kissing and the petting, the scolding and the smacking, children's laughter on festival days, their excitement at weddings, their wide-eyed amazement at funerals – he could not imagine life without them. There was no life without them; they were as the sounds and the smells of a home, its soul.

'And parents also must lead their own life,' said Kanta.

He gave it up. There was really nothing to be said to that. So he said only, 'Jio,' meaning bless you, live long, live well, live the way you like; meaning I have nothing further to say to you. It was at once tolerant and contemptuous and dismissed the topic.

'But such an education,' he said, subtly changing the theme, 'will bring great expense.'

'For children,' said Kanta, 'no expense is too great.' This was a sentiment, the first she had uttered, with which he could perfectly agree. But not on this occasion, for on this occasion she had missed his point.

Chandra, however, had not. Nervously twitching his nose and looking away from his father, he said: 'Yes, of the expense we will have to think.'

'As long as I am here,' Lalaji answered smoothly, 'there will be no worry.'

Kanta was irritated. There was no need for him to mention the fact that he sometimes had to help them out. He was Chandra's father and it was only natural that he should do so; it was his duty. And Heaven knew, he owed them something, considering all the embarrassment and inconvenience to which he put them. She was convinced that Chandra's career was hampered by his connection with his father; he would have been made Deputy Head of Department last year, she was sure, if everybody had not been suspicious of his father's name. Such things counted heavily against one in Government circles.

'I am your father,' said Lalaji. 'It is my duty to help you.' But though this was to some extent a voicing of her own thoughts, Kanta was not pleased. Certainly it is your duty, she answered him with silent indignation, and she felt that their demands on him were really far too modest. After all, his other children – except perhaps Rani, who had a rich husband of her own – lived on him completely. In face of that, what was a cocktail cabinet here, a summer holiday there, an occasional cheque – they were as nothing; he did nothing for them.

'I do not want to fail in my duty towards my son,' said Lalaji.

Chandra twisted his fingers and at the same time twisted his thoughts in accordance with his father's. He knew that what Lalaji was really saying was not, 'I am your father; I must not fail in my duty towards you,' but, 'You are my son; you must not fail in your duty towards me.' And Chandra's thoughts crept reluctantly to the one spot from which he had urgently tried to keep them: to the back of his wardrobe, to the file, to the letter. 'Pitaji,' he said miserably, 'what will you take? A sherbet, tea, fruit-juice?'

Kanta threw him an angry look. This was almost like a reproach to herself, for as the mistress of the house it was her place to offer refreshment to the guest. She had deliberately refrained from doing so because, for one thing, her father-in-law had come uninvited and – except for a few intimate friends like the Ghoshs and the SankarLingams, and members of her own family – she only received people in her house who came by special invitation. Secondly, she did not want him to settle down there and be comfortable, but to go as soon as possible. How would it be if someone came and saw him sitting there on her settee with the English upholstery? Sitting there chewing his pān, his naked feet tucked under him, in his muslin kurta-pyjama, solid and placid as a bull, imperturbable.

Lalaji had noted her omission. At his own house, anyone who came, at any time, on any business, would be offered something by way of courtesy and hospitality. Neither his wife nor himself would let a visitor leave the house unrefreshed any more than they would turn him from the door. But he did not condemn Kanta for her omission. Her ways were different. 'I will take water only,' he said to Chandra, for it would have been as discourteous to refuse to take refreshment as it was not to offer it. 'Yes,' he said slowly and as if speaking to himself, 'you are my son. I have given you everything I could. I have even sent you abroad, though it was very costly and all the family blamed me for it.'

'Whatever it cost,' said Kanta defiantly, 'has it not been worth it? Chandra has become independent. He is not a burden to you, but earns his own money and supports his own family. He has shown himself worthy of his education and everything you say you have done for him.'

Lalaji swayed his head and appeared lost in thought. Chandra asked himself uneasily what his father was thinking; he was almost angry with his wife for what he considered provoking the old man. But Lalaji was not provoked. He was only surprised and tried to adjust himself to the idea of a woman who spoke her husband's name so freely and addressed a man, who was not only older than she was but was her father-in-law, with such lack of respect. Certainly Kanta's ways were very strange. But he did not want to be angry with her because of that. He was determined not to be angry; so he tried to adjust his ideas of old and young, of husband and wife, of respect and duty, according to hers. It was difficult for him because he was an old man and the people among whom he had lived all his life had a rigid code concerning such things.

Lalaji's silence became oppressive. Even Kanta felt disturbed, but this only made her look defiantly at her husband. It was the truth that I spoke, she told him with her eyes. Chandra would not look at her; he continued to squeeze his ankle between his fingers.

'Yes,' Lalaji said at last, and again as if he were speaking only to himself. 'I have spent much money on your education. More than I have spent on your other brothers.'

Chandra's thoughts, to his disgust, involuntarily turned to Viddi. He remembered his brother sitting there, just where the father was sitting now, though not so insistently, not so possessively, and saying, 'You speak with Pitaji for me.' Yes, Chandra thought bitterly, that is what you would like me to do, to plead for you now. As if it is not difficult enough for me to deal with him over my own problems.

Lalaji also thought of Viddi. He said, 'Your younger brother wants to go abroad. But I have refused him. I did not refuse you.'

'Naturally,' said Kanta, 'the case of Chandra was quite different. Ved Prakash has not such a good mind.' But Lalaji could not take her words in: he caught only the name Chandra and, though he tried to accept it, it jarred on him when she spoke it so boldly. He knew that his wife, his daughter Rani, his daughter-in-law Shanta would have plucked out their tongues rather than pronounce their husbands' name.

'I do not say you have not shown yourself worthy of what has been done for you,' he told his son. 'No, you are a good son to me. I know you are a good son.'

Chandra paced up and down. His nerves felt taut and strained. He could not bear it. He was a man who needed peace and quiet, and peace and quiet for him depended on certainty. He had to be certain what he was dealing with, have it all clearly defined before him in the shape of a minute or a report with correctly headed sections. He did not know how to face, how to deal with things that depended not on cerebral clarity but on emotion, cunning, psychological astuteness. His work had taught him to ignore these things. He was an administrative officer, he knew only facts and figures; in dealing with any situation he was helpless until he had the facts and figures before him; he could not deal with things indirectly.

Suddenly he stopped short in his pacing and, looking towards his father with unhappy eyes, he blurted it out: 'Pitaji, I have the file with me, it is lying here at home at the back of the wardrobe.' Kanta looked at him with astonishment, for what, she asked herself, was the point of bringing this unpleasant subject up without any provocation?

Lalaji continued to sit there, placid and immovable. He only shifted his pān from one corner of his mouth to the other. Inwardly he was shocked at his son's clumsiness. No, he thought, he would have done no good in business. For this was not the way things were done, so abruptly, tactlessly, crudely. Lalaji's mind, and the minds of those with whom he was accustomed to deal, worked the other way round from that of his son. For him facts and figures were a vague goal in the distance. The ultimate desire was to reach that goal, but before this could be done there were many obstacles that had to be overcome. And these obstacles all lay in the minds and feelings of the man with whom one had to deal. A man could not be expected to state his meaning directly; one had to guess what it was. Then one had to allow him to guess one's own; because, again, it would have been indelicate, as well as injudicious, to voice it outright. And when one was sure that mutual understanding had been achieved, then, slowly, warily, one drew near to the point, by hints and circumlocutions, by apt parables and philosophical generalities.

'It is quite safe with me,' Chandra was saying; 'you need not worry. For some time I can keep it with me.'

'Son,' Lalaji said quietly, 'why do you not give me the letter?'

'But that is impossible!' Kanta cried. 'Chandra cannot remove a letter from a Government file!'

'It is so simple,' Lalaji told his son. 'You will take the letter out and return the file. That is only right. The letter belóngs to me, it came from my office.'

'Pitaji,' Chandra said, 'please try to understand my position.'

'It does not belong to you!' Kanta cried. She was really furious; not only because of what her father-in-law was saying, but also because he so completely ignored her. 'It belongs to Government, and Chandra who is a Government officer is responsible for it.'

'It is a private letter,' Lalaji said to Chandra. 'It was written to T— privately, as a friend, and it was only by mistake that it was put in a file. Such mistakes must be put right. Government files are very important things; you cannot put your own private letters into them. It looks very bad.'

'That is not for us to decide,' Kanta said. 'A Government officer cannot take letters out of files as he pleases. Even the Head of Department cannot do such a thing.'

Lalaji wanted almost to laugh. To say this to him, who had had so many documents inserted or extracted at will; not by any Heads of Department or gazetted officers, but by ordinary Grade-3 clerks for a few rupees. But to Chandra he said: 'Just think, if I wrote you a letter, "Dear son, today I am going on a pilgrimage to Kumbh and will return in three weeks; your mother sends her blessings," and instead of keeping this letter at home or throwing it away after reading it, instead of this you take it into your office and place it in an important file? Would the Government not have every right to be angry with you and to tell you to remove this letter?'

'The file came to my office,' Chandra said desperately. 'I had to give my signature to it and when it leaves my office I will also have to give my signature. How can I sign if I take the letter out? Without this letter the file will no longer be the same file, it will be a different file. I cannot pass a different file under my signature.'

'Of course not,' said Kanta. 'The signature of a gazetted Government officer is a very important thing. Everyone trusts it, it is like a mark of guarantee on something you buy in a good shop in Connaught Place.'

'Listen, son,' Lalaji said, 'if someone eats a mango in your office and then throws the stone which he has sucked on the floor, can you not tell the sweeper to pick it up, can you not say to him, "take this dirty thing out of my office at once," because if he takes it out it will no longer be the same office?'

'A letter in a Government file,' Kanta said, 'is not a dirty mango-stone on the floor. It is a very important thing. The Head of Department himself has no right to take it out.'

'Please Pitaji, try to understand my position. I am a gazetted officer, every gazetted officer has a record and if anything bad goes into this record it is detrimental to his career. So far I have a good record and, if things go right, in three–four years perhaps I will be made Deputy Head of Department. I say perhaps, because in Government departments such things can never be stated for certain. Pitaji, to become Deputy Head of Department will mean a lot to me; it will mean more money and higher position, and also it will mean that perhaps in another eight–nine years I have chance to become Head of Department. A Head of Department draws 1,300 rupees a month and he is next in rank to the Deputy Secretary. Pitaji, it is a very high and a very honourable position; a man's whole family is honoured when he is made Head of Department.'

'Son,' Lalaji said, and he spoke very calmly, 'I have told you this letter is a private letter, a letter like you might write to a friend any day or perhaps to your wife when she has gone for the summer to the hills. It is just such a letter, a private letter which concerns only two people.'

'Then what harm is there,' Kanta asked, 'if it stays in the file? Let it stay there. Why do you concern yourself?'

'I do not say,' Lalaji told Chandra, 'that the people who make public inquiries are bad people. On the contrary, they care very much about their duty, which is a good thing in any profession or business. They care so much that they will spare no pains and sometimes they will even do something that is not moral in order simply to make out a case. For instance, if they find a letter written by one friend to another they will read it from here to there and backwards and forwards and upside down till they have succeeded in thinking something into it which will help their case. It is only their case they think of. The innocent man whom they will call for witness and whose name will be printed in the newspaper and whose business perhaps will suffer, of him they do not think.'

'No public prosecutor,' said Kanta, 'will do harm to an innocent man. If he is called it will be because he is guilty.'

'They do not think of him,' Lalaji said, shaking his head, and as if no interruption had taken place. 'Neither of him nor of his family. Just think, such a man may have relatives who are in responsible positions, perhaps they may even be working for Government – how will it be for them when the name of their relative is printed in all the newspapers and spoken in all the bazaars? Will they not suffer too?' And driving home his point before the others could even begin to consider the matter: 'And also, such a man when he is called for witness, people will perhaps not trust him so much, his business will suffer, consequently his family will suffer. For whereas before he could give them money and help them out of difficulty whenever needed, now this will not be so easy for him and perhaps it will be necessary for him to refuse them when they come to him to ask for help.' With which he slowly gathered himself together, drew out his feet on which he had been sitting and, with great dignity, assumed his shoes. 'Your house is so cool,' he said. 'It is pleasant to sit here.'

Nimmi, looking defiantly casual, came sauntering into the sitting-room. Only her father was sitting there. He was laughing absent-mindedly into the telephone and at the same time checking some bills. She got into her favourite position curled up on the sofa and waited for him to finish his telephone conversation. She felt nervous and did her best not to show it, so that her ease of manner was somewhat exaggerated. But even when he had put down the receiver he still did not notice her.

'Hallo, Pitaji,' she said, studying her nails. He looked up for a moment, grunted and returned at once to his bills. She stopped studying her nails. He does not even notice, she thought. She was not so much disappointed as disgusted. Viddi was right: he could only think of money. They were all nothing to him; if he could, he would sell them all for money. She swung herself down from the sofa and made for the door. 'Where are you going?' he asked without looking up, and did not notice that she failed to answer.

She had hoped to go to the women's quarter with his approval; or, if not approval, at least with his resigned consent. And he would have given her that, she knew, if only he had noticed. He was not the man to make a fuss over something that was finished and done. Her hair was gone – very well; after the initial shock that was what he would have said – very well. If it is gone, it is gone, and however much he might rage, he could not bring it back again; so he would not have raged. Not so her mother and her aunt: no consideration of the inevitable would restrain them. She hoped at least that Rani was there, for Rani knew that short hair was fashionable and she might be able to point this out with some effect to the others.

Rani was not there. Only her mother and Phuphiji and Shanta. And they noticed at once. Their reaction could have been predicted. Even Shanta let out a gasp and looked at Nimmi with horror; her first thought was how angry Om would be to see his younger sister thus; afterwards he would be angry with his wife too. Maee, hearing the uproar, came running into the courtyard, and when she saw the cause, at once joined in: 'Her beauty is gone! How will we find a husband now?' Lalaji's wife clasped her face between her hands and rocked it to and fro: what would Shanta's mother say?

'Have I not told you a hundred times,' cried Phuphiji, 'that such things and worse will happen if a girl is allowed to go to a College and no husband found for her!'

All the servants came running out of the kitchen and stood gaping at Nimmi. Even the sweeper timidly thrust his head out of the W.C. which he was cleaning.

'Go tell him!' Phuphiji screamed. 'Go tell him what his daughter has done!'

'Pitaji has seen me,' Nimmi said sulkily.

'He has seen?' cried her mother.

'And he says nothing?' cried Phuphiji. The two women looked at one another, Phuphiji with bitter triumph, Lalaji's wife in great distress. 'Now we know what sort of father he is,' Phuphiji said.

'No, he said nothing,' said Nimmi. 'Why should he?'

'Insolence,' cried Phuphiji, 'how do you dare speak to your father's elder sister and to your mother thus! You owe us all honour – more honour than you owe to your father, because it is we who have done everything for you and who will do everything. He is careless and neglectful, but we will see to it that a husband is found for you, now, at once, quickly! Together with your sister you will be married and the first who will take you will have you!'

Nimmi put her hands over her ears and ran straight up to her bedroom. Usha was sitting on the floor, looking at some sheets which were part of her dowry. When she saw Nimmi, she clapped her hand before her mouth and gasped: 'O, you have cut your hair.'

'So I have cut my hair!' Nimmi shouted. 'Perhaps you also will have something to say?'

Usha smoothed out a sheet. Then she turned it round and smoothed it from the other side.

'It is impossible for me to live with such people,' Nimmi muttered; and she longed to be Rajen, or at least to be the child of Rajen's parents, who thought it good that a girl should be smart and fashionable, and never spoke of marriage. She had thrown herself on to the bed, but she got up again and sat in front of the mirror. She looked so unfamiliar, she had quite a shock. She might have been a boy, her hair was so short – but her full mouth, her eyes, the rounded contours of her face were not those of a boy. She shook her head, then put her hand up to pass it over her hair. Tears came into her eyes. She wished she had not done it. Her thick heavy braided coils that had shone brown-black and could be twined about with fresh jasmine . . . if at least she had curly hair, like Rajen, short curls might have looked attractive.

'I think it looks nice,' Usha said quietly from behind her.

Nimmi frowned and took up a comb. 'You do not have to try and please me,' she said without turning round. She looked at herself in profile – the short straight hair fell rather prettily around her ear.

'No,' said Usha, 'but I think it looks nice.'

They had given her a short fringe. She liked the fringe. She ran the comb through it and pushed it over to one side, studying the effect. The most important question was: would Pheroze like it? If he liked it, nothing else mattered. Oh he would like it, surely he would like it. He had said he liked short hair. If he had not said so, she would never have done it.

'Really?' she said and turned around. 'You really think it looks nice? You think it suits me?'

'Yes,' Usha said; but then added very anxiously, 'What will Matiji and Phuphiji say?'

Nimmi sighed and replied, 'They have said already,' and threw herself on the bed again. She lay there thinking, looking up at the fan spinning on the ceiling, her arms under her head. 'Usha,' she said, after she had thought for a while, 'do you not think it is very bad that our family is so old-fashioned?'

'Old-fashioned?' asked Usha and laughed.

'Yes, what else? They understand nothing. For instance, they do not understand that it is fashionable for a girl to go to Club and have her hair cut and meet young men. They think all these things are bad because they do not understand them.'

Usha, sitting on the floor, turned over another sheet and lovingly ran her hand along its surface. 'Perhaps it is not very good,' she suggested, 'for girls like us to meet young men ...'

'What nonsense!' cried Nimmi as Rajen might have cried. 'Are you not ashamed to say such things, Usha, you who have had education?'

'I failed in Inter three times,' Usha pointed out and laughed again.

'It is easy to see why.'

'Yes, I am not very clever and Om says I am stupid.'

'No,' Nimmi said, 'it is not that. You failed because you have no ideas of your own. You do and say only what Matiji and Phuphiji tell you to do and say. You never think for yourself.' This latter was a favourite expression of one of her lecturers which had much impressed her.

'But what shall I think?' Usha enquired.

'What shall I think? Really, Usha, sometimes I feel Om is right: you *are* stupid. How can you say such a thing when there is so much to think? And all you do is sit with hands joined together and your eyes downcast and say yes to everything Matiji and Phuphiji tell you.'

After a while Usha replied in a diffident manner: 'They know how things should be done, that is why I say yes when they tell me to do something: because I know it is right.'

Nimmi rolled over on to her side and, supporting her head on her hand, looked at her sister with interest. 'Is that why you said yes when they came to you and said in four months you are to be married and this man is to be your husband?'

Usha did not answer. She pretended to be very busy with her sheets.

'Oh,' Nimmi cried and rolled on to her back again, 'you are terrible!'

'Why am I terrible?' her sister asked in a gentle voice. 'Every girl has to be married, what else is there? How could I not say yes? There was nothing else for me to say.'

'There was much else for you to say,' Nimmi replied decisively. 'You could have said I do not know this man, therefore how can I marry him? This is what you could have said. This is what you ought to have said. Now *I*,' she said, and by the way her tone changed one could tell with what intensity, with what scrupulosity she regarded this I, '*I* will never say yes if they come to me with a husband they have kindly found for me. On the contrary, I will tell them: Thank you, I am grateful to you for your trouble, but if you do not mind I will find my own husband; this is a work I will do for myself.'

'Perhaps it is different for you.'

'How should it be different for me than for you?'

'Oh,' said Usha, smiling, 'you are not like me. Everybody knows this. Everybody knows you are beautiful and clever ...'

Nimmi jumped up from the bed and squatted beside her sister, throwing her arms around her neck. 'You also are beautiful and clever. Who says you are not?'

Usha returned her caresses very affectionately. 'I am so proud of you,' she murmured. 'When you first came to the College and I was still there, how proud I was when I saw you walk down the corridors and I could tell everybody: this is my sister.'

'How sweet you are! Usha, I love you more than I love any of the others.' And she rubbed her face against her sister's shoulder. Usha stroked her short straight hair and said, 'Where did you leave the rest?'

'I brought it with me. It is downstairs in a paper bag. There was so much of it, I did not want to leave it at the hairdresser's. I tell you what I will do – I will stuff a cushion with it and give you for a wedding-present. Oh Usha,' she cried, 'will you really be married?' And when she got no answer, 'Do you really want to be married?'

Usha faintly smiled. 'Why not?' she asked. 'Some day it will have to be, so why not now?'

'But you do not even know him!'

'I have been allowed to see him.'

'Only to see is not to know.' For instance, she had only *seen* the young man in the pink scarf, she could not say she *knew* him.

'Afterwards there will be plenty of time to know him.'

'Yes,' Nimmi said, not very hopefully. She also had seen Usha's future husband, and she had not been impressed. He had sat there silently, his hands dangling between his knees, and had stared with bovine eyes – not at Usha but at herself. He had hardly glanced at Usha. Perhaps he too had thought there would be plenty of time afterwards.

'Do you like my sheets?' Usha asked proudly.

'But Usha, you do not want to become like Shanta?'

'Like Shanta?'

'Yes, like Shanta, only to sit all day in the women's quarter with your mother-in-law and your aunt and have babies all the time and feed them so that your breasts are ruined and you become fat and old and ugly and stupid.'

'I do not think Shanta is fat and old and ugly and stupid. And I want to be like her.'

'What! You want to be like Shanta?'

'Yes,' said Usha almost obstinately. 'I think she is very happy. She has three children and they are all her own and she can wash them and feed them and dress them and play with them the whole day long.' Her hand rested on her sheets and her eyes became dreamy as she thought of herself washing and feeding and dressing babies all day long. 'And also she can sew clothes for them,' she added, remembering another pleasure.

'And when your husband comes,' Nimmi said in disgust, 'you will not dare raise your eyes to his face and you will never speak his name and you will do everything that he tells you to do and if he likes, you will let him beat you?'

'Om does not beat Shanta.'

'He does,' Nimmi said, 'I have heard him. And she did not even dare cry out. And what is worse. I think he goes to other women – '

'Nimmi!'

'Where else do you think he goes,' Nimmi said scornfully, 'when he wears silk bush-shirts and rings on his fingers and pours a bottle of oil on his hair to make it shine? You think he goes out to meet people on business with such a smirk on his face?' She tried to imitate this smirk, and then gave a sound of disgust.

'Do not say these things,' Usha pleaded. 'Please, Nimmi, I do not like to hear such things spoken.'

'But it is life,' Nimmi told her. 'If you are to be married, you must hear such things spoken. You must learn that men are sensual.'

'Are what?'

'Sensual.' Or was it sensuous?

Usha pushed aside the sheets and got up. 'Nimmi,' she said, 'what would Matiji and Phuphiji say if they heard you speak in this manner?'

'Matiji and Phuphiji!' Nimmi said contemptuously. 'They know nothing of these things. They are so ignorant. They have never come out of the women's quarter, so how can they know what life is?' What it is, for instance, to be kissed by Pheroze Batliwala at Kutb in moonlight.

'But how do you know what life is?'

Nimmi did not reply to that. She only looked mysterious. For besides Pheroze, there had been guarded discussions with Rajen, and with Neena before her father was sent as Ambassador to Indonesia, and she never failed to look up a word which interested her in the dictionary.

'You are wrong,' Usha said quite fiercely. 'You do not understand at all.' Nimmi was surprised. Usha, who was always happy and smiling and eating sweets, to speak so fiercely. 'You understand nothing!' Usha shouted even more loudly. She did not want to believe these things that Nimmi was telling her; and because she did not want to believe, she did not want to hear. When she had been at College and girls had whispered such things or passed books and pictures round, Usha had always looked the other way, soft, smiling, tolerant, but adamant. There was nothing in life except bearing babies and looking after them and sitting in the women's quarter amid servants and the smell of cooking; nothing, except perhaps for a gentle lovely love for one's husband, which made the babies come. 'Why do you speak, when you understand nothing!' she shouted.

Nimmi did not get angry. On the contrary, she felt sorry for Usha because she was so ignorant, and thought it was her duty to enlighten her. 'My dear sweet sister,' she said in a patient tone, 'what do you think marriage is? Do you not know that men – '

'Please,' Usha cried, 'I am not listening!' Stumbling over her sheets, she ran from the room, down the stairs, into the women's quarter. She sobbed once or twice as she ran. Nimmi could hear her.

Nimmi was very much surprised. She could not understand what had happened to Usha. Something must have upset her, and she wondered what it could have been for it took much to upset Usha. But she did not wonder for long. She had too many important problems of her own to think about to spare much time for her sister's. The most pressing at present was: would Pheroze like her hair? She looked at herself in the mirror again, front and side and back, and began to like it better. She hummed a little tune, then remembered that the bag of shorn hair was still lying somewhere downstairs. It would be better, she thought, to retrieve it before someone found it and got into a fury over it. On the stairs she met Viddi who said: 'Oh, you have had your hair cut.'

'Yes,' she said defiantly, 'I have had my hair cut.'

He looked at her critically and then decided, 'It looks nice. It is very fashionable for girls to have short hair.' He thought of the girl with the cigarette and added: 'All modern girls have their hair cut.'

Nimmi laughed out loud and measured him up and down with amused eyes. 'What do you know about fashionable and modern?' she asked. And then it struck her – how he had changed. He was no longer the fat slovenly young student she knew. Instead he had become sleek and stout and smart, wore expensive clothes and what was almost a worldly air.

Viddi drew up his eyebrows and smiled. But he only said, 'Yesterday I met a friend of yours.'

'Yes?' she said casually. This was to give him the impression that she had so many friends that she could not be expected to keep a track of them all; they could be met by anyone at any time in any place.

'Yes,' said Viddi. His smile deepened and his eyebrows rose higher. 'And it was not only your friend I met. I met you too.'

'Where did you meet me?' she asked and almost succeeded in sounding indifferent.

'In a place where I did not think to meet you. And also with a person with whom I did not think to meet you.'

'Viddi,' she said, 'you did not . . .'

'Yes I did. I saw you in the Pipal Tree having dinner with a Parsi. Oh you need not be afraid: I will say nothing to the family.'

Nimmi curled her lip in a fine attempt at defiance. 'I do not care if you do tell. What is it to me? Viddi,' she asked quickly, both to take his mind off the subject and because she really wanted to know, 'who was the friend of mine you said you met?'

'Please guess.'

'No I cannot guess – it was Rajen Mathur?'

'It was Kuku.'

'Kuku?'

'Kuku.'

'But I know no one called Kuku,' she said. 'Who is she?'

'Do not try to pretend with me. You know very well Kuku is no she.'

'A boy? I know no boy called Kuku.'

'He is not a boy,' Viddi said with dignity. 'He is about my age. You know very well.'

'I swear to you, Viddi . . . he says he is a friend of mine?'

'He says he knows you. Of course he knows you – it was he who first saw you in the Pipal Tree, he said, "there is your sister Nimmi". Why do you pretend with me? You know I am not like the others – it does not matter to me whom you know and whom you do not know. I have other things to think about.'

'But I am not pretending. Viddi, did this Kuku who is my friend wear a pink scarf around his neck?'

'Certainly not. He wore very nice clothes, evening clothes. He looked like a gentleman.'

Lalaji appeared at the bottom of the stairs. He held a paper bag into which he peered with a very puzzled expression on his face. He looked up at them and asked, 'What is this?'

Nimmi could not help laughing. She leant over the banisters and called down, 'Pitaji, it is my hair!' He looked even more puzzled, and this made her throw back her head and laugh very gaily.

Phuphiji had had her bath and now sat saying her prayers in the prayer-room. She sat on the mosaic floor, very stiff and still with her legs tucked under her, surrounded by gaudy gods and goddesses of clay and garlanded pictures of gilded ascetics. It was a peaceful morning. Shanta, having sent the two older children to school, was feeding the baby while Maee washed its nappies. Lalaji's wife squatted in the kitchen and kneaded dough for the midday meal. Usha sat and ate sweetmeats, smilingly content. Warm, sleepy, restful, the women's quarter droned with household noises – pots clattering, servants coughing, the voice of Phuphiji in prayer, naked feet padding on the stone floor, grains of rice sharply tossed from a sieve. The baby sucked audibly and Shanta, with her eyes shut, rocked herself to and fro and hummed a lullaby. The smell of spices melting in clarified butter came floating out of the kitchen. 'Oh God, God,' moaned Lalaji's wife, while her practised right hand pulled and pushed the dough as if it were a wet shirt. Usha yawned and helped herself to another sweetmeat.

Into this peace came Shanta's mother, accompanied by her niece Lakshmi. Shanta's mother wore her triumphant smile and satin blouse, while Lakshmi, trailing behind her, had her eyes downcast and an air of modesty and self-effacement. Lalaji's wife came out of the kitchen to make them welcome, bits of dry dough dropping from her hand. Though she smiled in a very happy manner, she was inwardly distressed because she was sure that Shanta's mother had come to talk about Nimmi's hair. Phuphiji, hearing who had come – only a curtain separated the prayer-room from the main women's room – slurred over a few verses and came shuffling in, very clean and withered and as if she had scrubbed herself away in her bath.

'Ah,' said Shanta's mother, luxuriantly lowering herself on to a mat. She looked so sleek and clean and oiled, so complacent. Lalaji's wife felt very much at a disadvantage, for she had not yet had a bath nor combed her hair, which drooped in a weak pigtail down her back. Surreptitiously she tried to wipe the dough from her hand by passing it down her old cotton sari.

But then Rani came and Shanta's mother was eclipsed. For Rani looked even sleeker. Tall – she was taller than any other woman in the family – with her ample bosom in a tight shining blouse, a heavy silk sari, jewellery, gleaming hair, brilliant eyes sparkling self-confidently in her rather too plump and faintly moustached face: Rani, at thirty-six, smelt not only directly of scent and hair-oil, but also indirectly of good living and a rich husband. Beside her Shanta's mother shrank and withered; and at once it could be noticed that her satin blouse did not fit very well.

'Come daughter,' said Lalaji's wife, 'come and entertain our guests.' She was glad that Rani had come, for she would be able to deal with the fact of Nimmi's hair better than any of them. And she was quite sure that this was what Shanta's mother had primarily come to discuss. Why else the look of triumph? She had probably brought Lakshmi only to show that the girls in *her* family, even if they went to College, kept the long hair suitable to women. Lalaji's wife wished that she could manage to introduce the topic of Nimmi's hair before her visitor did; introduce it lightly, almost laughingly, pointing out how fashionable it was nowadays for a young girl to wear short hair, as Rani had pointed out to her the day before.

'Oh my pretty one, oh my lovely one, oh my pride, my beauty,' said Shanta's mother to the baby which sucked rapturously at its mother's breasts.

'Every day she grows fatter and more beautiful,' said Lalaji's wife; and added with cunning humour: 'Just see what a fashionable one is our child, see she wears her hair short just like a modern lady, oh the little queen.' Shanta laughed heartily at that. She looked down at her baby and said, 'So you are a fashionable lady, do you hear? What will your Pappa say? Will he like you to be a fashionable lady?'

Shanta's mother also smiled. 'Like her father's youngest sister she is,' she said and looked at Lalaji's wife, who came in very hurriedly with, 'Yes, our Nimmi also wears her hair short now – what can you do when these young girls take it into their minds to be fashionable? We can only say: Bless you, child, do as you wish, my beauty.'

'What else,' Shanta's mother surprisingly agreed.

Rani said: 'Of course it is right to move with the times. If I were a young girl still, I also would have my hair cut short. It is very modern and also more convenient.' Phuphiji too would have liked to add something to confound Shanta's mother, but she could not betray her principles. So she only intoned to herself part of the prayer which she had rather skimped.

'She has done like her friend Rajen Mathur,' said Lakshmi. 'Her friend Rajen Mathur also wears her hair short.' She took a sweetmeat and as she chewed her little gold earrings shook.

'Lakshmi,' said Shanta's mother severely, 'please do not eat so many sweetmeats. You know it does harm to your skin. You will get more pimples.'

'It is not nice to see pimples on a young girl's face,' said Lalaji's wife.

'Very ugly,' Rani said, drawing a hand over her own smooth soft opulent skin.

Phuphiji said, 'If a girl purifies herself with saying the correct prayers, her skin will also become pure.'

'All the girls in our family have pimples,' said Shanta. 'When I was younger, I also had. With childbirth they go.'

Her mother frowned and said: 'Please do not speak such things. When we gave you in marriage your face was like a flower, and also your sisters' faces. Lakshmi,' she said, 'you are acquainted with the friends of Nimmi?'

'I know her friend Rajen Mathur and also her friend Indira Malik,' Lakshmi replied.

'She has no other friends?'

'Oh yes,' said Lakshmi placidly, 'she has many friends. She also has a boyfriend. He is a Parsi and England-returned.'

Shanta's mother pulled down her satin blouse which had wriggled up to her midriff, and tucked it firmly into the top of her petticoat.

To everyone's surprise it was Shanta who spoke first. She spoke indignantly: 'Lakshmi,' she said, 'how can you say such lies about my husband's sister?'

'But it is true,' said Lakshmi. 'Everyone in the College knows. She goes out with him and has dinner in restaurants with him, and they dance.' Her voice was full of admiration; she was not censuring, only stating enviable facts.

'Your cousin does not tell lies, Shanta,' said Shanta's mother in a gentle voice. 'She is your mother's sister's daughter.'

'And Nimmi is my husband's sister,' said Shanta with unwonted spirit. 'My husband will be very angry if he hears my cousin speak such lies about his youngest sister. It brings dishonour on his family, and my children also will suffer.'

'Shanta,' said Lalaji's wife, 'have you no shame, no respect, to speak in this manner to your mother?'

'Let be,' said that mother sweetly. 'My child has just recovered from childbirth. A woman in such condition is weak and her nerves are bad. We must make allowances for her.'

'Please do not bring Lakshmi to our house any more!' Shanta cried, sounding not at all weak. 'I do not want ever to see her again in my husband's father's house!'

'It *is* true,' said Lakshmi. 'Every girl in the College knows. We have many talks about how she goes with him and dances.'

'Be quiet!' Shanta cried.

Lakshmi assumed a sulky expression. She defiantly helped herself to another sweetmeat, for which no one reproached her. On the contrary, Lalaji's wife murmured, 'Take, child, take; eat your fill.'

'Come, Lakshmi,' said Shanta's mother. She heaved herself to her feet, clutching her left knee which suffered from stiffness. 'We still have other visits to make. We have to go to the house of my relative Amar Nath, who is Director of the Happy Hindustan Trading Company. I have things to say to his wife. Please no ceremony,' she said to Lalaji's wife who made to accompany her to the door. 'This is my own home. I will send for you this afternoon a jar of mango pickle. It is made with mangoes from our own garden; you will enjoy.'

Usha sat there and frankly cried. Fat tears rolled mournfully down her cheeks and dropped on her knee unchecked. Because it was all her fault. Yesterday Nimmi had told her that there was no harm in a young girl going out to meet men and, beyond a mild protest, she had said nothing. She had not even thought of it; perhaps deliberately not thought of it, because she could not bear the idea of her sister exposed to such dangers. She had persuaded herself that Nimmi had been talking generally, not particularly about herself. She had persuaded herself that there was nothing to worry about, when perhaps she had known all the time that there was something to worry about – and had been too lazy, too cowardly, too comfortable to face it. 'I am selfish,' she thought; 'I think only of my own happiness; my sister's is nothing to me.' She had not wanted to think about Nimmi, because she had wanted to think only of her sheets which meant dowry, which meant marriage, which meant babies. 'I do not deserve happiness,' she thought; 'I do not deserve babies'; and wept.

The others did not notice her distress. They were too engrossed in their own, though theirs expressed itself more pungently. Phuphiji kept beating her temples with tight fists and shouted, 'Send for him! Tell him this!' Lalaji's wife held her hands before her face and rocked herself to and fro.

'Pitaji must be told at once,' said Rani, her face flushed, her bosom heaving up and down. 'How can I go home to my husband's house when soon all the world will know of this disgrace?'

Shanta bit her lip and thought about how angry Om would be. Her eyes were round with distress.

'Send for him! Tell him this!' cried Phuphiji.

'How can I go back to that house?' Rani said. 'Always my husband's sisters have been jealous of my sisters, and now how happy they will be! How can I go back and see the triumph in their ugly black faces?'

'A Parsi!' cried Lalaji's wife from behind her hands. 'Not even a boy from our own community!'

'That is what they will talk about most,' said Rani. 'Always, whenever they can, they say things to me about my brother Chandra Prakash because he has married a girl from a different community. And now also Nimmi – my life in that house will become intolerable.'

'Send for him!'

'How can we send for him?' wailed Lalaji's wife. 'He is in his office, he will not come. If the house is burnt over our heads he will not come.'

'All day they will say to me, "Your sister Nimmi" – I will go out and telephone to Pitaji,' Rani said resolutely, 'and also I will call Om Prakash.'

'Go!' cried Phuphiji. 'Let the eldest son come to teach his father his duty.'

'You will call him?' said Shanta anxiously. 'You will make my husband come?'

Rani was already out by the telephone. A servant handed her the receiver, and she dialled with a very determined look on her face. 'At once,' she told her father. 'You must come at once. It is very important. My brother also must come.' Lalaji could hear the determination in her voice and knew this was serious. If it had been his wife or his sister, he would have laughed and said: 'I am coming home in the evening, please have a good dinner ready for me.' But with Rani it was different.

'He is coming?' cried Phuphiji as soon as she got back. 'And the son also is coming? Now we will see.'

Om Prakash was very hot and very cross. His first words on entering were, 'Is it not enough that I must sit all day in an office that has no air-conditioner, but now also you must call me away from my work to listen to your women's chatter?' He angrily wiped his face with a handkerchief which was already soaked in perspiration. Shanta hurried to get iced drinking-water, and in her agitation she made the mistake of serving her husband before her father-in-law. But no one noticed and Lalaji good-humouredly took the second glass.

He too was hot, but unlike his son he was quite calm and even wore a tolerant little smile which said: 'These women, we must humour them sometimes.' He sat himself cross-legged on a mat and comfortably scratched his thigh. His calm radiated out into the room, though it did not communicate itself to the women – they could not allow it to do that. Their case depended on the vigour and heat with which they put it forward.

Yet his presence had a reassuring effect on them: they were no longer helpless and alone.

But the frenzy had to be kept up, the seriousness of the situation driven amply home to him. Phuphiji opened the chorus: 'To all the world will that woman tell the disgrace that has befallen our family!'

'My husband's sisters will hear of it and my life will be a plague!'

'Even now she has gone to the house of Amar Nath and we will lose his son!'

Usha began to cry again, because it was all her fault, and Shanta looked anxiously at her husband.

'A Parsi!' cried Lalaji's wife. 'This is the worst, that she should disgrace us with a Parsi!'

'They go into public places,' cried Phuphiji, 'and they dance! She dances – a daughter of our family!' Dancing to her was something that was done by girls of low repute, with ankle bells and coy smiles and suggestive hand-gestures. She had no idea of modern ballroom dancing and would have been even more shocked if she could have visualized Nimmi dancing in the arms of a young man who was a Parsi.

'This is what has happened because she has been allowed to become eighteen years old and no husband found for her!'

'And has been sent to a College!'

Om Prakash, though he understood that all this referred to Nimmi, could not piece things together. He was puzzled and therefore more cross. 'At least tell us what happened,' he said. 'You call us out from our office and now all you can do is shout about Parsis.'

But Lalaji needed no further explanation. The whole thing was as clear to him as if it had been stated in a few precise sentences: Nimmi had been seen with a Parsi, Shanta's mother had heard of it and had taken the news to the house of the Director of the Happy Hindustan Trading Company. It *was* serious then. The smile had vanished from his face and he sat sunk in thought, picking his teeth.

Shanta told the whole story to her husband; the others punctuated the recital with their own vehement comments. When it was done, Om's face seemed to swell with rage. He jumped up and paced about the room for a while and then confronted his father: 'Why did you not arrange it?' he shouted. 'Why did you sit and do nothing when this offer came to you? Now perhaps we have lost that contract for ever. Chunni Lal will get it, and not only that but also our whole family is dishonoured through my sister who has been allowed to go to a College!'

Lalaji did not appear to be listening to him. He nodded absent-mindedly and continued to pick his teeth.

'For months, for years we have been telling you,' Phuphiji cried, 'arrange for her, as is right and fitting!'

Om shouted: 'A better offer we can never hope for! Is a contract of twenty-five lakhs a joke perhaps?' Lalaji glanced up at him and said gently, 'Sit down, son. Let us speak quietly.'

'Speak quietly!' Om cried. The flesh of his jowl quivered and a pulse throbbed visibly in his neck. 'This is no time to speak quietly! Before this there was time to speak quietly, there was time to sit down and discuss terms with the Director of the Happy Hindustan, time to arrange the dowry and the contract, the date of the betrothal and the wedding – but now all of that has been lost because you would do nothing, would not even speak when the one offer we wanted came to us!'

'Sit down!' Lalaji suddenly roared. There was a silence and Om sat down.

'All of you eating my life up,' Lalaji said, more calmly. 'Let me think at least.'

His wife said, 'Shall I get you some buttermilk?' Phuphiji would have liked to point out that the thinking should have been done earlier; but she refrained.

'Please think, Pitaji,' Rani said. 'Please, now, you must do something. I will not go back to my husband's house till you have promised me that you will do something.'

He said patiently: 'What do you want me to do?' She lost no time in patly replying: 'The best thing will be you send to this Amar Nath and arrange with him. Perhaps he has not heard yet – '

'Not heard!' cried Lalaji's wife. 'This very moment that woman is sitting in his house and telling him who knows what lies about our family.'

'Perhaps he will not believe her,' said Rani. 'All the world knows that she does not know the meaning of truth. Please, Pitaji, send to him, quickly, today, arrange with him.'

'It may not be too late,' said Om. 'I saw one of Chunni Lal's men today, and though he talked with a big mouth I could tell that he was not certain of the contract.'

'Chunni Lal has only one daughter,' said Lalaji's wife. 'He has six sons, and his wife thinks she is better than other women because she has given birth to six sons and only one daughter. She is a stupid woman and she keeps her house very dirty.'

'Arrange with Amar Nath,' Rani urged. 'My husband's sisters will look with a different face when they hear what sort of a marriage has been arranged for my sister.'

'And take the girl away from this College,' said Phuphiji through tight

164

lips. 'She must stay at home here with us and not move out of the women's quarter. Then we will hear no more talk of Parsis.'

Lalaji shrugged his shoulders and said quietly, 'Do as you like.' The women looked at one another and were triumphant.

But Lalaji was very unhappy. Because now, after all, it had come to this: that he had to give her in marriage, and quickly. There was no other alternative, for to leave her unbetrothed now would be dangerous for her, dangerous for them all. His heart was heavy, but he did not know whether he grieved more for her or for himself. Not for one moment did he blame her. He thought: she is young, she does not know the world, she does not know what she is doing. He had no doubt that she had, at any rate, not done much. The possibility that she might have done anything beyond going out to restaurants and dancing did not occur to him, as indeed it did not occur to the others. Such a possibility lay too far outside the orbit of their society. Such things did not happen to girls of good family.

There was, however, another danger. If a girl was seen out in public places with a young man – and worse, much worse, with a young man from a different community – her reputation in her own community would suffer; which would make it very difficult to find a suitable husband for her. So the only thing to do when there was a threat to the reputation was to find the husband, quickly, at once, before the canker spread.

Seeing him in such a resigned and pliable mood, Phuphiji thought it expedient to bring up another topic close to her heart. 'And that other one,' she said, 'your youngest son. Is it not time you settled him also, before he brings disgrace on our family?'

'I will take care of him,' Lalaji said, with indifference.

'You are taking him into the business?' his wife cried eagerly. 'You are arranging marriage for him?'

'First let Pitaji settle my sister,' Rani said, 'then afterwards there will be time for the brother.' Her husband's sisters did not extend their interest to her brothers.

'Do not worry,' said Om. 'We will take care of him. And of her also.'

Lalaji got up with a sigh. His sadness was a contrast to the satisfaction that shone on the faces of the others.

'Sit, sit,' his wife said complacently. 'Take rest. We will cook for you, horseradish pancake we will cook for you, why should you run to your office now?'

But he would stay no longer, even though horseradish pancake was his favourite dish.

Viddi sauntered into the Rendezvous. True, it was dull and vulgar, but then he had nothing else to do and was bored. As soon as he came in, Zahir-ud-din stood up and waved to him. Viddi made his way towards that table, but nonchalantly and looking round to see whether there were no other friends. 'Please sit,' said Zahir-ud-din. 'We have kept a place for you.'

Bahwa sat with his heavy head supported on both hands. He said, 'You did not come yesterday,' in a manner that was at once despondent and accusing.

'Only fourteen people came to this play,' Zahir-ud-din explained. 'And the critic from the newspaper said very bad things about it.'

'I will sue him,' Bahwa groaned.

'And apart from the critic, all the other people were friends of Mrs Iqbal Singh, who was the leading lady.'

Bahwa lifted his head and said, 'Nobody cares about Art in this town. And the critic knows nothing. What does he mean when he says my play lacked emotional form? It is full of emotion and also full of form.'

Viddi made a mental note of the expression 'emotional form'. He looked forward to using it on some suitable occasion. 'Who is the critic?' he asked.

'He is a lecturer in a College,' Bahwa said. 'The paper pays him ten rupees for every play he writes about. But what does a lecturer in a College know about plays? About living drama?'

'This time he will be sorry for what he has written,' said Zahir-ud-din. 'Captain Iqbal Singh will be very angry for what has been said about his wife, and the friends of Captain Iqbal Singh, who are all military, will also be angry.'

'But it was not a good play,' Viddi said suddenly. Bahwa raised his head and stared at him.

'That is not a kind thing to tell your friend,' said Tivari.

'I do not care who is my friend and who is not my friend,' Viddi said. 'In art I must have my own opinions.'

There was a short silence. Bahwa continued to stare with round and unbelieving eyes. After a while Tivari said, 'Yes, with 500 rupees a month you can have your own opinions about art.'

'Art has nothing to do with money,' Viddi said vigorously. He looked at Zahir-ud-din and added, 'A man who thinks about money is not a true artist.'

'Two hundred rupees the set cost,' said Bahwa in despair, 'and fifty rupees I paid for the hall.'

'There are too many characters in your drama,' Viddi informed him. 'And they all say too much and what they say is not real, it is not what

166

people would say in real life. In a good play characters speak like people in real life. You should read classical plays like by Sir James Barrie and Shaw. You would learn from them.' He called the waiter and said, 'Bring me one strawberry milkshake with ice-cream.'

Bahwa said, 'For years I have studied the dramatic works of Kalidasa, of Bhavabuti, of Shudraka. I have steeped myself in our great National Heritage, in our Culture which is 5,000 years old – perhaps that is nothing?'

'Those people,' Viddi said with a shrug. 'They are all very well for Colleges and students and examination papers, but for artists it is necessary to read and study the work of modern English and American writers. It is only from these works that you can learn.'

Tivari looked at him and said: 'Lately you have learnt a lot about literature.' Viddi could smell his whisky breath across the table. Tivari was slightly drunk; his eyes looked sodden and his mouth hung loose. Viddi allowed himself to be disgusted. Drunkenness was something that could be tolerated only in non-Hindus and the lower classes. Not, he told himself, that he was narrowminded: it was quite all right for a Hindu gentleman to drink so long as he never showed the effects of drink.

'Why did you not bring your father to my play?' Bahwa said. 'He would have appreciated.'

'My father is a very busy man,' Viddi said and sucked his milkshake through a straw. He was aware that the others were watching him enjoying it, but he persuaded himself not to mind. If they wanted milkshakes they could buy their own; they were not all that poor. Or if they were, they had no right to come and sit in expensive restaurants.

'And also your father does not like drama,' Tivari said. 'You told us he had no taste for literature.'

'Why should he like bad drama?' Viddi said. 'Let Bahwa write a good drama, then I will bring my father.'

Bahwa looked at him with sad eyes and said, 'I thought you were my friend.'

'I am giving you the frank criticism that only a friend can give,' Viddi said. But he sounded indifferent: he was not very anxious to proclaim himself Bahwa's friend. He still remembered how odd the dramatist had looked at the party and how people had asked who is that dirty man hawking tickets.

'Remember,' said Zahir-ud-din, 'you promised to be our patron. A patron must always give encouragement and constructive criticism. It is his duty.'

'How can I be a patron when I have only 500 rupees a month? My expenses are heavy, you must realize that. For instance, this month already

I have no money left. I will have to ask my father for advance and the Manager of this restaurant will have to give me credit.'

'That reminds me,' said Tivari, patting the breast-pocket of his shirt. 'I have this for you.' And he laid before Viddi a piece of paper which could be recognized at once as a bill.

Viddi looked at it. It was a caterer's bill for supplying drinks, snacks, bearers, lights and glasses to a cocktail party on 24 October. Viddi looked only at the total: 762 rupees 4 annas. It was of course impossible. He could not pay so much money; he had no intention of paying it. Next month's allowance was already allotted to an evening-suit such as Kuku wore and the membership fee of the Club which he intended to join, besides books and gramophone records and the saving for his education in Europe. He pushed the bill back towards Tivari and said, 'Why do you give this to me?'

Tivari laughed. 'Is not your name written on it?'

'It was not my party. You gave the party. It was at your house and you invited all the guests and you did not even once tell them that I was the host. You did not even introduce me.'

'Everybody knew you were the host,' said Tivari. 'In good society one does not stand on a platform and announce who is paying the bill.'

'The people at your party were not good society. They were only people who are never asked to other parties.'

'Why do you complain then that I did not introduce you to them?'

'And we did introduce you,' Zahir-ud-din said. 'We introduced you to very many people. For instance, we introduced you to Kuku; he is a very useful man to know. His father is Director of the Happy Hindustan Trading Company and he himself is also on the pay-roll of the Company. He draws very big salary.'

'I do not care how much salary he draws,' said Viddi, 'or who his father is. You think too much about money. An artist should never think about money; he should think only about his art.'

Zahir-ud-din smiled pleasantly. He had heard this often before, and had learnt long since that it was no use replying. No one was interested in his wife and three children, nor in the fact that however much he cut his household expenses, they refused to go below 150 rupees a month. On the contrary, if he mentioned these things, people looked impatient and turned away to talk to someone else; so he never mentioned them.

'I am writing a new drama,' said Bahwa. 'This one is also very interesting – it deals with birth control. But putting on a drama is very expensive. No one is interested in good drama, therefore it is difficult to cover expenses. It will be better for me to have someone who will sponsor me.'

168

'I do not think I shall be in Delhi much longer,' Viddi said. 'Soon I will be going abroad to study.'

'My drama will take only three weeks to write.'

'Well we will see,' Viddi said. He had often heard his father say this when people came to him with requests which he had no intention of gratifying. 'But now I am in a hurry to go, because of appointment for lunch.'

'Please do not forget to take your bill,' said Tivari.

Viddi, already on his feet, looked down at it lying on the table. Then he looked at Tivari. 'There is a mistake,' he said. 'It is your bill.'

'I do not think so. Look, it has your name. This is your name?'

'It is a mistake,' Viddi said obstinately. He saw the manager deferentially greeting him from behind the bar, but he did not bother to acknowledge it. The Rendezvous was a dull and vulgar place; what could you expect of a place which had murals done by Zahir-ud-din? He did not think he would come here again.

'Well,' said Tivari good-humouredly, 'leave it then, if you think it is a mistake. The caterer will send you another bill. He is used to this, for there are many people like you who think bills are sent to them by mistake.'

Though he left with a shrug, Viddi was worried. He had never had any bills made out to him before and knew of no technique to avoid payment. But he was quite determined to avoid it: Tivari could do what he liked, and the caterer could do what he liked, but he was not going to pay. He had better uses for his money than to spend it on someone else's unsuccessful parties.

He strolled around the shopping arcade, his lips silently moving, his hands gesticulating as he remonstrated with his adversaries. Fortunately there was no one to see him, for it was midday and the arcade deserted. Even the hawkers who usually squatted between the pillars had packed up and departed. Shops were locked and shuttered and tattered figures lay curled up in their doorways. Beyond the arcade the street was abandoned to the flood of white sunlight. A tonga sheltered beneath a tree, the driver fast asleep, the horse shifting its legs and placidly chewing.

Viddi thought: 'If only I could consult with someone; someone who has had more experience in these matters.' And he thought of Kuku, but did not know where to find him. He strolled on, thinking hard, and only noticed that he had come full circle when he saw the Rendezvous again. Coming towards him was a cluster of business men, on their way to lunch. They were fat and merry and looked very successful. The doors of the Rendezvous swung open and swallowed them up, and Viddi heard a last burst of their rich laughter. Then he knew where to go.

He walked as casually as before, for he did not allow himself to become quite conscious of his destination. Stopping outside an optician's shop, he looked in the window; the optician sold blue sunglasses and also fountain pens and Japanese earrings on cards. Two storeys above the shop was Lalaji's office. When he had examined every item in the window, Viddi went through the side-door and climbed slowly up the narrow wooden stairs. A peon lay there asleep, with his mouth open and one arm outstretched, and as he walked round him Viddi thought to whom else should a son go for advice if not to his father?

The door of the office stood ajar; he peeped inside and saw that it was empty. Chairs stood aslant, as if they had just been abandoned; in the little washroom the typist's typewriter stood alone with a piece of paper inserted. Viddi pushed the door further and saw Om Prakash sitting there behind his desk, his lunch on one chair, his feet put up to rest on another. Viddi sat down and said, 'Where is Pitaji?'

'Out,' Om said. He bent low over his lunch-container and picked up vegetables between his thumb and forefinger. 'Of course he is out,' he said with his mouth full. 'After one o'clock why should he stay here when it is so hot and no air-conditioner? Only I have to stay to melt in the heat.'

'It is not very hot,' Viddi said and peered across the desk to see what Om Prakash had for his lunch.

'For you – no. For people who sit all day in air-conditioned restaurants and drink iced drinks, for them it is not hot. For years I have been telling him,' he said on a new wave of exasperation, 'get an air-conditioner. At least let us sit in the office like human beings.'

'But where is he?'

Om scooped up another pile of vegetables and said, 'Why do you want him? You know he does not like to be disturbed in business hours.'

Viddi said, 'When is it not his business hours?'

'If it were not his business hours twenty-four hours a day, you would be standing in the sun and working with your hands instead of sitting all day in air-conditioned restaurants.'

'You also,' Viddi said.

'Do I sit in air-conditioned restaurants? I sit here in the heat and do the work of six clerks, so my younger brother can go to College and be comfortable.'

Viddi dropped the argument, for he had at present no wish to quarrel. 'Where can I find Pitaji? I must speak with him.'

'What do you want with him? If you want to ask him to send you to Europe, you need not speak with him. He will never send you. I will see to it myself. One England-returned brother is enough for me.'

Viddi assumed a superior smile. He thought of his 500 rupees a month and how he could save out of that for his study-trip to Europe. One day, when he had saved enough, he would simply tell them: 'Tomorrow I am going to Europe.' Then Om would look with a different face. But thinking of his 500 rupees brought a sharp reminder of the bill for 762 rupees, and his smile disappeared. 'I have urgent business with Pitaji,' he said.

'You can speak with me,' said Om, licking the tips of all his fingers.

Viddi considered. Certainly it might not be a bad idea to talk to Om; he would be just the person to know about a thing like this. Not as well as his father of course; but still, he had been working with his father for many years now and must have learnt a lot. 'This is the thing – ' he said.

Om brought his lunch-container on to the table and said, 'You have eaten?'

'No, and I am hungry.' He plunged his hand in, while Om from the other side plunged in his. 'Enough to feed ten people she sends me every day,' Om said. Shanta always prepared his lunch with her own hands and saw to it that it reached him punctually and hot. 'I do not like to see food wasted. She thinks perhaps I am a millionaire.'

'Pitaji is,' Viddi said.

'He did not become one by *wasting* money. It is best to marry a wife from a poor home. At least she knows the value of money. What do you want to say to me?'

'The thing is this,' said Viddi, taking another mouthful of food. 'A bill has come to me. A bill for a party.'

'You gave a party?'

'No, I did not. This is what I want to tell you. Someone else gave the party and he invited people whom I do not like and now he wants me to pay the bill.'

'What sort of party?' Om asked with interest. He thought of the party he himself had attended a few days before and the thought put him in a good humour. It had been very successful.

'A cocktail party,' Viddi said proudly. He knew Om had never attended a cocktail party and perhaps might not even know what it was. 'Cocktail party,' Om repeated and laughed. 'Listen, brother, one day when you are a little older and more experienced, I will take you to a real party.'

Viddi knew what his brother meant by a real party; so he said: 'At this party also there were many girls present.' He had found out long ago what sort of parties his brother went to with his business friends. At one time – this was before he had any idea of fashionable life – he had longed to accompany him to such gatherings in order to report on them to his College friends.

'You had girls there?' Om said. He did not like this. He had very strong moral principles and did not approve of his younger brother attending such parties. These things were for older men, married men who knew about life.

'Of course, what is a party without girls?' Viddi asked casually, digging to the bottom of the lunch-container.

'Have you no shame to say such things to your elder brother?' cried Om, genuinely shocked.

Viddi felt an urge to boast: he wanted to show his brother that he too was now grown-up and led a life far more exciting than anything Om had ever known. But because he wanted his advice on the bill, he did not wish to provoke him any further; so he merely said: 'They were all girls from good family. It was a fashionable party. In a fashionable life respectable girls go to parties just like men.'

'Fashionable-pashionable – do not bring such talk to me. I know these respectable girls. If any of them were my sisters, I would lock them up in the house and straightaway marry them to the first that will offer.' Which was, he thought, just what they had done or were going to do to Nimmi. In his family, thank God, such fashionable girls had no chance of survival.

Viddi sighed but did not press the point: his brother would never understand, he had no idea of elegant living. 'But this bill which has come to me – '

'Why should you pay for giving parties to such respectable girls? Did you invite them?'

'I told you – no. But the man who gave the party has no money, so he told the caterer to send the bill to me.'

'He is a very wonderful man. A man of ideas. Tomorrow I will order three new suits to be made and I will tell the tailor to send the bill to my brother-in-law.'

'What shall I do?'

'What would my brother-in-law do if such a bill came to him from my tailor? He would send it back and say – are they my suits that I should pay for them?'

'But this man will tell the caterer that it was I who gave the party. Then he will send me another bill.'

'And then you will sit quiet.'

'He will send me another.'

'Again you will sit quiet.'

'He will file a suit against me.'

Om Prakash threw his head back and laughed. 'With great pleasure, let him file ten suits against us, we will be very happy.'

'But, brother – I will have to go into court and pay much money for lawyers and afterwards I will have to pay a heavy fine as well as the bill ...'

Om laughed again, even more heartily. Then he leant across the desk and said with a rather superior smile on his face, 'Listen, brother, we know more about these things than any caterer. He will be very careful before he starts with us. Do you know how many lawsuits we have against us now? About fourteen, fifteen – I do not quite know how many. Some of them have been going on for five years, some for four, some for six. If you have a clever lawyer you can make them go on for ever – till the other party will wish he had never started and will come and beg with joined hands for a settlement out of court. And by that time it is we who say what are the terms of the settlement. Oh, brother, people will be very careful before they come and speak about lawsuits to us.' He dabbled his fingers in his drinking-glass in order to wash them and said with an unamused laugh, 'They know we are not so easy to play with.'

Viddi felt very comfortable. He had eaten well and his mind was at rest. He liked the way Om kept saying 'we', it gave him a sense of solidarity. The problem of the bill was no longer his alone but also that of his father and his brother. They stood behind him, they guarded him, and in their wisdom and experience they would see that no trouble came to him. He thought contemptuously of Tivari: what was he but a poorly paid journalist, dependent on his monthly salary, with no power, no influence behind him? He would learn that the son of Lala Narayan Dass Verma was not so easy to play with. Let him bring ten caterers' bills, let him prove that Viddi had undertaken to pay for the party, let him learn how far he would get, with the power of wealth, of experience, of influence ranged against him.

'You want pān?' Om asked and bellowed for the peon who appeared with sleepy eyes in the doorway. 'Never worry about these things,' he said. 'We have learnt long ago how to deal with people who bring bills.'

Viddi yawned and comfortably scratched his shoulder. He thought: 'Om has had much experience, it is good to have a brother like him.' He said, 'You know Pitaji gives me 500 rupees a month?'

Om nodded. He knew that, and also that soon the 500 rupees would be increased to 800, and that the business of the sweepers' hutments was practically settled. Only that morning Lalaji had spoken over the telephone with a clerk of the Works office who was eager to serve him.

'It is not very much,' Viddi ventured. And it really was not very much. He needed money for clothes, he needed money for membership of a

Club, he needed money for entertaining – as the son of his father he had to keep up a certain standard of life.

'Soon Pitaji will make it more,' Om said and also yawned.

'He has said so?'

Om, deeply immersed in his yawn, only nodded. But it was enough to make Viddi happy. He would get more money, he would be able to buy more things. One day soon, when he had made many fashionable friends, he would give a really first-class party of his own. Everybody would talk about the party he had given. And since his allowance was to be increased soon, there was no need for him to start saving for his trip to Europe now; he could start later. It was difficult – no, impossible, as he had already found – to save out of only 500 rupees.

'Only stay here with us,' Om said, 'and we will take care of you. All things will come to you.'

'Yes,' Viddi said absently. For there was no need to speak of the money he intended to save to go to England; when he had saved enough, he would simply go and no one would be able to stop him. And he was determined to start saving soon; as soon as his allowance was increased. He felt pleased and satisfied.

Om also felt pleased and satisfied. He was flattered that Viddi had asked for his advice and reassured because Viddi was coming into the business. He began to think quite kindly of his youngest brother. In time perhaps he could come to be his friend, his companion. And Om felt much in need of a friend and companion. It was true he had many business friends with whom he arranged clandestine parties after business hours, but he knew that within business hours their friendship would not stretch very far. With a brother it was different: he and his brother could be friends and companions without suspicion, for their interests were as one. Later, when Viddi was older and had been married for a few years, he could take him along on all his pleasures, introduce him into the world; it would be good to have a brother to share these things with him. He richly burped and said, 'Always she cooks my food in too much ghee, she will ruin my digestion.'

The match was too good for them to raise any difficulties. Lalaji had known it. If they had heard that she had been seen with ten Parsis, still they would have been glad enough to have her: for such a prize was not to be had every day. He had only to give a slight hint over the telephone and Dev Raj had come hurrying over. 'Do not worry,' Dev Raj said; 'I will arrange everything.'

Lalaji had no doubts about it: this is what he feared, that everything would be arranged, quickly, smoothly and without any chance of drawing back; as if the girl to be given were just an ordinary girl. They would talk about her, settle the terms, there would be some haggling, but everybody would be very good humoured and soon complete agreement would be reached. Dev Raj was already in high good humour, and he told one or two stories which Lalaji's clerk, bent over his ledgers, pretended not to hear. Lalaji's laugh came only from his throat.

'Listen,' said Dev Raj at last. 'I know how it is with you. Parting with a daughter is never easy.' Lalaji heaved a sigh and thought: 'What does he know? He talks as if she were just any daughter.'

'But such a good family,' Dev Raj urged, 'such a beautiful boy! For the rest of your life you will rejoice and your daughter also.'

Lalaji smiled, ruefully and unconvinced, but he said nothing. Dev Raj became uneasy. 'These are modern times,' he said. 'If you like, the boy and the girl can be made to meet, and then if she does not like, we can . . .' He trailed off, looking at Lalaji who only nodded absently. 'Listen,' said Dev Raj, rather desperately, 'we will do like this, we will have picnic – they can meet at picnic – soon it will be cool enough, we will go to Kutb or the river at Okhla or anywhere you choose.'

'Yes,' said Lalaji without enthusiasm, 'we will have picnic.'

Dev Raj looked at him and nervously drummed his hand on his thigh. He did not know what else to suggest, and he was in a hurry to be off, to speak with his relative before Lalaji could say that he had changed his mind.

Left alone with his clerk, Lalaji sat cross-legged on the carpet and thought and sighed. The clerk crouched humbly and intently over his ledger. It was very still in the room, only the fan turning and from behind the shuttered windows the muffled monotonous sounds of a crowded city lane. At last Lalaji said, with a sigh deeper than all the rest, 'It is very hard for a father to part with his daughter.' This was the clerk's cue and he spoke up – he had it all ready – in his weak clear old voice. 'It is written that a daughter is but a loan to her parents; when it is time for her to go to her husband's house, they must return this loan. This is written in the work of our great Sanskrit poet Kalidasa.'

'True,' sighed Lalaji, 'it is true.' Everything that was written was true, he knew it. But it was difficult to accept it into one's own life. He looked towards his clerk with envy, for here was a man who had steeped not only his mind in the wisdom of the Vedas and the Gita and all the old writings, but also his whole life. He was pure, withdrawn, detached. As he often quoted to Lalaji, 'The Supreme Self of the self-subjugated and serene-minded is ever undisturbed in heat and cold, pleasure and pain, as well as in honour and dishonour', which Lalaji translated to himself as 'a wise man is indifferent whether he earns a salary of 75 rupees or 750 or 7,500 a month'. And it should be so: one should be content with, indifferent to, what one had and concentrate one's life only on spiritual things. Perhaps, Lalaji ruefully reflected, that was why he was now so unhappy; because he had not concentrated his life on spiritual things.

And he thought of his life. It was true he had wanted only the things of the world. And yet he had been happier when he had had only a few of them. Now he lived in a big house, with many servants, he had motor cars and bank accounts and shares and jewellery and properties; but what difference did these things make to him? He had been equally a man when he had possessed only two shirts and a few silver pieces and had lived with his whole family in two rooms in a city tenement. He had always had enough to eat and to keep his family – what more could he have wanted? But he had, nevertheless, always wanted more. When he had been poor, he had wanted to be rich, when he had been rich, he had wanted to be richer. Something had always been driving him on, he did not know what.

Usually he told himself that it was his love for his children; that he had wanted to become rich in order to give position and security to his sons, large dowries and fabulous marriage celebrations to his daughters. When they had been small and he had been poor, he had often thought about this; he had sat at night in the courtyard which he shared with the other tenants, and thought about the things he would do for his children. Well, he had done them, but they had brought him no satisfaction: for still he worked, and thought of ways of making himself greater. Was it the greatness he valued? That men should respect and admire and envy him? It was good to have power, he knew; good to have influence. But power and influence were only a means, they were not an ultimate satisfaction. He did not want them for themselves; he did not want to set himself up above other men. On the contrary, he liked nothing so much as when other men came to him and treated him as a brother, jokingly insulted him, jovially slapped him on the back. He had no sense of superiority and was ready to treat the humblest sub-contractor as an equal. He did not think himself different from or better than others only because he had money and power. He knew that money and power were ultimately worthless and had no meaning.

Once his clerk had explained to him that every man is born with a certain nature, and that it is his task in life to act according to that nature. 'Man attains perfection,' he had quoted, 'being engaged in his own duty. He who does the duty born of his own nature incurs no sin.' This information had been very interesting to Lalaji, for he had construed from it that it was not the desire for money or for power that had driven him on, but the nature with which he had been born. He had been endowed with the nature of a rich man, this he clearly understood: hence it had been his duty to *make* himself a rich man. In his pursuit of wealth he had only been following the path of his duty; he had done as God meant him to do, he had done well. And yet, nevertheless, he had not attained perfection, neither was he free from sin. On the contrary, in his unhappiness he felt that the older and the richer he had become the more imperfect and the more sinful he had become. He had not obtained the serenity of mind which was the reward promised a man who did his duty. He had had more serenity of mind in his beginnings, when he had been a poor man and had hardly started on his path of duty. There had been no Deputy Minister to worry him, no T— case, the Government had not been pursuing him for ten lakhs of income tax arrears; and his children had been a happiness to him.

As always when he was much troubled, his thoughts turned to retirement, to withdrawal. He imagined himself back in his native village, an old man come home to sit quietly under a tree. For this was the ideal which every man looked forward to during all his working life: the return to the native village, the ultimate peace. Yet even this was denied him: his native village in the Punjab had been incorporated into Pakistan and the ancestral strip of land was lost to him and his. The only home he had now was in the city, if a home in the city could be called a home. He had to die there because, like any outcast, he had nowhere to go back to. Retreat was impossible for him, reflection and meditation were impossible. How could he reflect and meditate caught up here in the midst of life, of activity?

He glanced at his clerk who managed to be serene and withdrawn even while he worked and lived in the city. But then, Lalaji argued, it was easy to be serene and withdrawn on only seventy-five rupees a month. Easy, he bitterly told himself, to be without attachment if one had nothing to which to attach oneself. If a man had no prospect of ever earning 7,500 rupees a month, he could say without pain that a wise man is indifferent whether he earns a salary of 75 rupees or 750 or 7,500 a month. Had he been born without the nature of a rich man, Lalaji himself could have said so without pain. As perhaps he could also have said that a daughter is but a loan, if he had not had a daughter like Nimmi. All men wish in their hearts for wealth and for beautiful daughters; and yet, thought Lalaji, there is great sorrow both in wealth and in beautiful daughters. Since the one has to be kept up, and the other given away.

Nimmi looked at Rajen with eyes stretched wide: 'And that is all he said?'

177

She was not clear what she had hoped he would say, but it was certainly not this.

'Yes,' Rajen said, 'I went to him as you told me to – '

'You told him that I had sent you?'

'Of course not. I went to him – he had just played tennis and was drinking lime-water. I was surprised to see him drinking lime-water because, when we are there, he always calls for whisky. Do you think he calls for whisky only to make himself look big?'

Nimmi urged: 'But what did you tell him?'

'I sat down beside him and he asked: "Where is Nimmi?"'

'Yes?'

'And when I said she has not come because her parents will not let her, he asked me what I would like to drink. Oh Nimmi, you know the boy with the spectacles – the one who goes with the one in the pink scarf – he was sitting very near and I think he was looking all the time and wondering what I was saying to Pheroze.'

'When you said Nimmi's parents will not allow her to come, he asked only what you would like to drink?'

'Yes. But I said I did not want anything, because I had just drunk pineapple juice with Indira. Nimmi, do you think he is jealous?'

'Pheroze?'

'No, no! The one with the spectacles. Because I think he was watching all the time. Oh no,' she said and laughed, 'I think you are wrong, he is not interested in me at all,' and laughed some more.

'And then what did he say?'

'He said the nights are cooler now and I said yes, soon it will be winter. And he asked me do I come every day to the Club in the winter also.'

'He asked you that?'

'Yes, and I told him no, in the winter I do not come so often. But I think this winter I will go at least twice a week, I can play squash and badminton there. Those are very good sports. And Indira will be so disappointed if I do not take her, now that she has started going she enjoys it very much.'

'But what did you say to him about me?'

'I told you,' Rajen said impatiently. 'I said Nimmi is soon to be married, her family have arranged for her.'

'And he, what did he say?' For she wanted to hear it again; Rajen must have left something out in her first recital.

'He said you must please congratulate her for me, I told you, and then he called for another lime-water and asked me was I sure I did not want to drink anything. And I said no thank you, I must go now, because I did not want to stay any longer. Indira was waiting for me and also I did not like the one with the spectacles looking so much.'

That really was all then. She did not know what she had hoped for. She only knew that all her hopes had been centred on him. It was galling to hear that all he had sent her to satisfy them were his congratulations.

'And he is not at all interesting to talk with,' Rajen said. 'Really, Nimmi, I do not know why you like him. He is quite handsome but not very handsome. He has no style. And he can speak only about the weather and that is not very interesting.'

Nimmi was in no mood to defend him. She was hardly listening to what Rajen was saying. Now she admitted to herself that she had hoped that he would say, 'I will not allow it; she must not marry anybody else.' He had taken her out to dinner, he had danced with her, he had kissed her; and now that he heard she was to be married, it was his duty to want to marry her himself. There was nothing else for him to do, she felt, now that things had come to this head. It was his only hope of keeping her – more, it was the only hope she had of escaping the marriage that had been arranged for her. She found it hard to believe that he – he who had kissed her! – should be willing to lose her altogether; and harder still to believe that the escape she had been expecting almost confidently should after all be denied to her.

'I will tell you the truth,' Rajen said coyly, scratching her fingernail along the table and looking down at it, smiling a little. 'I left him so quickly because I thought the one with the spectacles would think Pheroze is my boy-friend.' She looked up and laughter trembled on her lips, spilt out of her eyes; but there was no response in Nimmi's face. 'Though I am not really interested in him,' Rajen added, 'and I do not think he is interested in me. Why did you think he is interested in me? Did you see him looking at me often?'

'Yes,' Nimmi said absently. She was asking herself: 'Why did he kiss me if he did not love me?' Men kissed only if they were in love; and if he was in love, why should he give her up so readily?

'What nonsense,' Rajen said with a giggle. 'Oh yes, and the one with the pink scarf was with him yesterday. Only he wore a blue scarf. And he also looked while I talked with Pheroze. I think perhaps he was asking himself where is Nimmi?'

'He does not know my name,' Nimmi said. She thought of the young man in the pink scarf and wondered how it would have been if it had been he and not Pheroze who had taken her out dancing and had kissed her at Kutb. She asked herself whether he too, on hearing the news of her impending marriage, would have sent her his congratulations.

'I think he is nicer than Pheroze, the one with the pink scarf,' Rajen said. 'Why did you not let him be your friend? Of course, he is not so handsome as Pheroze but he has more style and I am sure he knows better how to make conversation.'

But Nimmi had no time for such idle speculations now. She did not even have time to think more about Pheroze. That hope of escape having proved hopeless, she searched about for another; and because nothing occurred to her, she appealed to Rajen, 'What shall I do now?'

'Now it is too late. If you are to be married soon, how can you make him your friend now?'

'I do not know what to do,' Nimmi said and tears came into her eyes.

'I wonder if he would be interested in Indira? Nimmi, do you think he would be interested in Indira, the one with the pink scarf?'

'There is no one to help me, and my family will not allow me to go out of the house. Even here to College they would not let me come, until I said I would hunger-strike.'

'That is a good idea,' Rajen said, her interest stirred. 'Why do you not hunger-strike? When someone wants something they always hunger-strike, like Gandhiji, and then it is written in the papers and they have to be given whatever they want because otherwise they will die. Why do you not tell your family: if you arrange this marriage I will kill myself by not eating. Then they cannot arrange. It is so easy.'

'What do they care if I die,' Nimmi replied bitterly. 'Even when I am lying there dying, still they will make marriage for me, once it is their wish.'

'I think it is better to be dead than to marry someone you do not want to marry,' Rajen said.

Nimmi remembered how she had imagined herself jumping down from Kutb or throwing herself into the Jumna for love. Perhaps, after all, if everything else failed, she would have to do that. 'Yes,' she said, 'I think so too,' and more tears came into her eyes as she thought of herself floating dead in the Jumna.

'Or why do you not run away from home?'

'Where can I run to?' Nimmi said hopelessly. The personal urgency of the problem gave her a more practical turn.

'There are so many places. People are always running away from home – do you not read the advertisements their families put in the newspapers? Only yesterday I read about an old Sikh gentleman of eighty-five who had run away from home and his family wrote in the paper: "Please Uncle come back to us, we will do everything you wish." Your family will also put in an advertisement like that and then you can write to them and say:

"I will come home if you promise not to arrange marriage for me." And you can also say that you will stay away till they promise to send you to Cambridge. Nimmi, do that, it will be such fun if we can all be together in Cambridge.'

'But where can I stay if I run away from home?'

'You can stay with some relations – surely you have relations out of Delhi?'

'Oh yes, I have many aunts and uncles in Cawnpore and Agra and even in Bombay. But if I go to them, they will at once write to Pitaji and he will come and fetch me home, and then they will make marriage for me.'

'You can go to stay in a hotel. Only you must not give your real name. Then if people read your family's advertisement in the newspaper, nobody will know it is you.'

'I have no money to go to a hotel, it is very costly. You know I have only my allowance and I spend it all.'

'Always money,' Rajen said with a sigh, and Nimmi sighed in unison. Hitherto money had been for her merely something of which her father had plenty.

'But you can get work and earn money,' Rajen said on a new inspiration.

'What work can I do for which people will pay me money?' On any other occasion Nimmi would have entered into these schemes with enthusiasm. But the thing was too close now, and the practical considerations too pressing.

'Oh there is so much! For instance, you could go to Bombay and be a filmstar – though you have not a good singing voice. That will perhaps be a difficulty. Or you can become a teacher if you like. You have passed your matriculation and you have studied almost two years in degree course.'

'What!' Nimmi cried, quite indignantly, for this suggestion horrified her even more than the idea of her forthcoming marriage. 'You want me to go and be a teacher in an ordinary school with poor people's children!'

'No, of course not that sort of teacher – only girls from low-class families become teachers like that. But you can start a school of your own, a sort of nursery school, and you will only take children from the best families. If you charge high fees, only people from the best families will come to you. There are several ladies in Delhi who have started nursery schools, and they all make a lot of money and also they are very highly thought of.'

'Where will I teach the children? If I leave home, I will have no house in which I can make a school.'

'Really, Nimmi,' Rajen said, quite annoyed, as who would not be to have all these brilliant suggestions countered in such humdrum fashion, 'I did not think you had so little spirit of adventure. Daddy always says that young people must be adventurous and make their own way in the world.'

'It is easy enough to talk,' Nimmi said with trembling lips, and then she burst outright into tears. Rajen looked at her uncomfortably and asked, 'You want a handkerchief?' Whereupon Nimmi shook her head and drew out her own and dabbed it against her eyes. 'What can I do,' she said, dabbing, 'when I have to marry and nowhere to go and no one to help me. You can talk, but how does that help me? Still they will make marriage for me, and I do not want – oh I do not want.' And with that came a fresh gush of tears as she thought of herself becoming like Shanta and sitting all day in the women's quarter, feeding babies.

'It is terrible,' Rajen said with indignation. 'How can your family do such a thing? It is like selling you as a slave. Daddy always says arranged marriage is a primitive custom and should not be allowed. Would you like him to go and speak with your father? I will ask him if you want.'

Nimmi only shook her head. Rajen did not understand, and it was no use explaining. Perhaps until now she had not fully understood herself how much, how completely, she belonged to her family. She had wondered how Usha could submit so meekly to the marriage they had arranged for her; now she understood that there was nothing for it but to submit. The independence on which she had so prided herself, her differentness from the other women in her family, were only an illusion. In reality her position was no different from Usha's and, ultimately, from Shanta's. They expected her, they expected them all, to become like Shanta. 'Oh Rajen,' she said – for what was the use now of pretending that she came from an advanced family? – 'you do not know what it is like for a girl in my family, how everybody expects us to sit all day in the women's quarter and learn how to cook and afterwards to be married and have children and never go out anywhere.'

'It makes me so angry,' Rajen said sympathetically. 'How can you have democracy if women are not emancipated?' This was another favourite phrase of her father's.

'I will never be allowed to go to Club or restaurants or lead a fashionable life,' Nimmi said tearfully. The best she could expect – if she was lucky and married to a tolerant husband – was to lead a very second-rate social life, like her sister Rani, who was always over-dressed and belonged to a Club patronized by newly rich business men who did not know how to use knives and forks properly and burped after meals. Nimmi thought that rather than associate with such people she would stay at home and be like

Shanta. But this urged her to new tears and she sobbed to Rajen: 'I will become like my sister-in-law, who does not speak English and never goes out of the house. I do not think she even knows what a restaurant is.'

Rajen clicked her tongue and said in an adult manner: 'This is why our progress is so retarded, because our women are kept in such ignorance.'

'And always I will be thinking of you and Indira studying in Cambridge and leading a gay life.' Nimmi wept into her handkerchief as she thought of her friends leading a gay social life while she herself had to sit with a mother-in-law, wear cotton saris and cook her husband's food.

'Poor Nimmi,' Rajen said and patted her hand, and after a while she said, 'Will you come to the Library? I have to speak with Indira to fix this evening's tennis programme.'

Kanta arranged her sari gracefully over her shoulder and said, 'It is finished now. Do not think about it any more.'

'I cannot help thinking about it.' Chandra said gloomily. 'Even in the night I lie awake and think about it.'

'It will do you good to go out this evening, it will distract your thoughts. And Mrs Ghosh's brother from Jamshedpur will be there. She told me over the telephone he is in Delhi for a few days. Such a pleasant surprise!'

'But what else could I do!' he cried.

'Nothing else, of course. Anybody in your position would have had to do the same thing.'

'If they find out that will be no excuse.'

She sat down rather quickly and said: 'There is no chance of anyone finding out. You told me so yourself.'

'I did not say there is no chance. I said it is not probable. But it is possible – everything is possible, especially in a Government office, where so many records are kept and no one can tell when someone will not make a check of the records. Suddenly they will ask, "where is this letter?"'

'But they do not keep record of every letter that is put in a file?'

'Sometimes they do. Who can tell? Or an officer may have seen this letter and he will remember, and when he goes to look it up and finds it missing, he will check up who took out the file and when. And my signature is there and also the date.'

'You told me yourself there is no chance ...'

'I did not tell you! I never told you so!'

'Please do not shout at me,' she said, quiet and severe, which made him hold his head in his hands and reply in a weak voice, 'I did not mean to shout at you, of course not, but my nerves – Kanta, the strain is terrible.' She moved nearer to him and laid her hand soothingly on his knee. 'Now, darling, let us sit quite quiet and you tell me everything. Mrs Ghosh is expecting us at eight, but even if we go to her house at nine, we can always say we were held up by the children.'

'What can I tell you, you know everything. It is only the worry that is eating me up.'

'Why should you worry? No one will ever know about it. How can they know about one single letter in a file when there are so many letters and so many files?'

'I told you – everywhere there are records and also someone might remember . . . and what will they think when they see the file has been with me, knowing who my father is? At once they will guess what has been done and then what will happen to me?'

'Oh!' Kanta cried and took her hand from his knee. 'I knew that only trouble we will get through being related to your father! Such a man can bring ruin even to innocent people!'

'Can I help it that he is my father? I did not ask him to become my father.'

'Once you were married to me, it was your duty to see that you had no more to do with him.'

'How could I do that? Where would we have lived if he had not given us this house – '

She quickly said, 'But you need not have got involved in his business. What have we to do with such things? For us T— is only someone we read about in the newspaper.'

'What could I do when he came and told me all these things. You heard him yourself.'

'You did not have to give him the letter!'

'Oh!' said Chandra Prakash and he looked at her quite shocked. 'But you yourself told me to give it to him. You remember, after he came here, you said, "You had better give it to him so he will leave us alone." Those were your words.'

'Well,' she cried, 'and did you have to listen to me – you are a man, it is your duty to decide on these matters, what do I know of them?' And when he kept quiet, only continued to look at her in shocked amazement, she burst out, 'Everything you say is my fault!' and ran out of the room to the bedroom, where she would have flung herself on the bed to cry, if she had not remembered that she had already applied her make-up, ready for Mrs Ghosh's little dinner-party. So she sat herself in front of the dressing-table and furiously dabbed more scent behind her ears, muttering, 'For everything he blames me.' But when she noticed in the mirror that anger made her look older and also rather ugly, she altered her expression, settling it into one suitable to a lady guest at a dinner-party; this calmed her. After a while she returned to the lounge where Chandra still sat in the same position as before, squeezing his ankle. She sat down beside him and said gently, 'Darling, why do you quarrel with me? I wish only to help you. We must share all our worries.'

Limply he held out his hand for her to fondle and, as she did so, told her, 'My nerves are so bad, this affair has made me quite ill.'

'I know, darling,' she said, cracking his finger-joints, which always gave him pleasure. 'You are so sensitive and also so honourable, you cannot bear to be involved in anything that is dishonest.'

'I have done nothing that is dishonest,' he said, not so much stating a fact as making an appeal to her.

'Of course not,' she hastened to say, 'nobody will ever say such a thing about you. It is only your father who has acted dishonestly.'

'But if they find out, they will think that I also – oh Kanta, they will suspend me perhaps and make an inquiry, and even if the inquiry is favourable to me, still my reputation will be ruined and I will never be able to rise to Deputy Head of Department, let alone Head of Department.'

At that Kanta was about to give vent to strong emotion again, but she checked herself in time and managed to say in a soothing voice, 'Nonsense, darling, nobody will ever think anything bad about you or make any inquiries. Everybody knows what you are and what your father is, and they will know at once that if anything dishonest has been done, it is he alone that is to blame.'

'Yes,' he said, somewhat comforted, 'he is to blame. I have done nothing wrong. But people might think – you see, because I signed for the file and someone might have noticed the letter before it was taken away, that is why I worry, even though I have done nothing wrong.'

'Do you think someone will notice that it has been taken away?'

'Who can tell? If they do not notice today, then they will tomorrow or next year perhaps, or after five years. One can never know.'

'Or perhaps they will never notice!'

'That also is possible.'

'It is perhaps most possible of all?'

'Yes,' he conceded, 'but as I said, you can never tell. Of course nobody knows every letter in every file but there may be a record somewhere, and what peace of mind can there be for me when all the time I must be thinking that someone may notice?'

'But if they do notice, what blame can they give to you?'

'I told you, I signed for the file and, of course, everybody knows who is my father and that he had connection with T—.'

'You are not your father!'

'No, but if they find out that the letter has gone, they will think that I too had connection with T—, and it is a criminal offence to take any letter out of a Government file, especially for a gazetted officer in a position of responsibility.'

'You did not take it out! It was your father.'

'It is true,' Chandra said. 'It was he who made me take it out.'

'Naturally it is the person who makes the other person take it out who is responsible. The other person is only his instrument, he does not even know what he is doing, so how can he be made responsible.'

'Yes,' Chandra said, struggling hard to suppress the working of his own more logical mind.

'That is common sense,' added Kanta. 'Nobody can say that you took the letter out when it was he who made you. And how could you help yourself, what could you do when your own father came to you and blackmailed you?'

'That is what he did,' Chandra said and he sounded more cheerful, 'he blackmailed me, that is the word for it.'

'What else? How shameful that a father should come and blackmail his son! And it was not you alone he threatened but, worse, your wife and your children ... Just think, if you had refused, the whole future of your children would have suffered. What would have happened to their education? Also my health would have been affected because you know, and your father knows too, that I cannot bear the heat in the plains. I have to go to the hills for the summer ...'

'They are his grandchildren and you are his daughter-in-law,' Chandra said, 'and yet he would sacrifice you all for a letter.'

'There are such people in the world,' Kanta said with a resigned sigh. 'If one has to have dealings with them, the only thing to do is to say yes to everything they want, otherwise God alone knows what they will do to you.'

Chandra nodded wisely. He had straightened up by this time and looked altogether more like a responsible Government officer. He tapped his front-teeth with his fingernail. But he kept quiet, for he wanted to hear more; he hoped she would be able to convince him.

'They know you are a family man and that you had to do as your father said, because otherwise he would have ruined us all. They will understand that – everybody knows what kind of a man your father is.'

'Yes,' he said, and had to reluctantly add: 'But you see what people think in private is not always what they think officially. In private they will know that I was not to blame, but officially, as public servants, they may think it is their duty to investigate the whole matter and then perhaps,' and his face fell into deeply worried folds again, 'there will be an official inquiry and my career – '

'There will never be an official inquiry!' she cried.

'How can you know?'

'Darling,' she said, 'of course it is very bad that things are so and that a man like your father should have so much power through bribing people ...' She sighed and smoothed her sari over her lap, looking down at her hand as it smoothed.

Her idea very swiftly communicated itself to him. It made him almost a happy man, but he owed it to his conscience to look displeased. 'It is true,' he said in a voice which conveyed gloom he did not feel. 'He has much power, even in Government circles, so if it should come to an inquiry ... Unfortunately, Kanta,' he continued in a severe lecturing tone, 'there are always officials, people in high places, who care more about money than about their duty and responsibility, and it is just these people who put so much power into Pitaji's hands.'

'It is a terrible thing,' she said. 'Bribery and corruption.' She laid her hand lightly on his shoulder. 'Of course you and I and all the people we know, like the Ghoshs and the SankarLingams, are very much against it, but what can a few honest people do when it is so deeply rooted in political life.'

'It will take generations,' he said gravely, 'to eradicate this evil from our midst.' Kanta nodded with a very serious expression on her face, and then she glanced at the clock and said, 'Mrs Ghosh will think we have forgotten.'

'I shall enjoy this little dinner-party,' he said. 'It will be good to talk with people who think like ourselves. Honest responsible people of advanced ideas.'

'I do not know that they are so very advanced,' Kanta said. 'Now for instance, Mrs SankarLingam wears very unfashionable blouses, I would not call her advanced at all, and Mrs Ghosh, even though she has been to England, has no idea how to arrange a room in the more modern manner. Though, of course, they are more advanced than your family, there is no question.' Chandra sighed and straightened his spectacles on his nose. 'Darling,' she said, 'we owe it to the children to have as little connection with your family as possible. I have told you a hundred times.'

'I know,' he said and sighed again, though he no longer looked unhappy.

'They will only learn bad morals and bad manners from them – not only from your father but from the whole family. Oh I forgot to tell you, this afternoon your sister Nimmi was here. She sat with me for a long time and she cried because they are arranging marriage for her.'

'Oh,' said Chandra Prakash with polite fraternal interest. 'Who with?'

'She does not even know, poor girl. I feel sorry for her, because she is a good-looking girl – she has good complexion and figure and also she has quite good manners and speaks English. She is better than the others in your family. But now that she is to be married, of course all this will go and she will become just like them. It is a pity.'

'What can you do? She is a victim of the society into which she was born.'

'This is exactly what I told her. I said I am sorry for you, but what can I do? She begged me to speak with her family, to use my influence, but I was quite firm. I told her I had no influence there, nothing I could say would do any good. Certainly I have no wish to speak with them or take any part in their affairs. The less I have to do with them the better it will be for me and my children.'

Chandra nodded and said, 'Quite right. This is what I also told Viddi when he asked me to speak with Pitaji about him. I told him: "I cannot interfere, I have my own life to lead and my own family to care for."'

'It is very selfish of them to ask us. They know quite well that we have enough worries of our own. Darling – we must go, it is so late already. I am looking forward to seeing Mrs Ghosh's brother from Jamshedpur. He is an engineer with Tata Iron and Steel Company, he draws very good salary Mrs Ghosh tells me. 1,100 a month she says.'

Kuku said, 'You will see, we will have jolly times together.' Nimmi's lips twitched irresistibly into the shadow of a smile; this was the only indication – and she tried hard to suppress it – that she was very happy. For it was almost as good as having a proposal of marriage; almost as good as choosing one's own husband. Of course Kuku did not ask her: 'Will you marry me?' He only told her all the things they would do when they were married. But he looked so nice, so young, so charming – he was wearing a gaily-flowered bush-shirt and suede shoes – that it was quite easy to imagine they were young lovers and their marriage of their own choosing. And he told her, 'Once I saw you at a wedding, and then I said to my father: "If you must arrange marriage for me, then please arrange it with this girl only."' Again Nimmi tried hard to control the twitching of her lips, and she gave a little tug at her sari to make it fall more gracefully round her feet.

He was leaning against a pillar of the pavilion, which was not really a pavilion but a mausoleum with three dateless grey stone tombs down the middle. He leant there quite at his ease and smoked a cigarette through a holder. It was cool and dark inside, but through the pillars they could see the patches of sunlight. Their families sat in the distance, within the shadow of an old wall – they could see them framed between two pillars – surrounded by picnic tins and baskets. They could not hear them talking, but from time to time a burst of man's laughter or a woman's shrill command to a servant came across the sunlight. Kuku smoked his cigarette and looked at her and smiled. He said, 'You do not regret?'

She assumed a pout and replied, 'I wanted to finish my College education.'

'College!' he said. 'What use is that to you? You will learn nothing there.'

She could not help feeling that he was right. What, in the end, had she to do with English literature and John Keats? They did very well to pass away the time till one could begin to live in earnest, but beyond that there was nothing in them. Pretty girls from rich families did not have to bother themselves with such things; they were of value only to plain girls from poorer families who had to think of making a living by teaching. She felt sorry for such girls.

'And your Parsi friend?' Kuku asked and smiled again.

'Oh that one,' she said scornfully. 'He is so boring, he does not know how to make conversation at all. Are you a member of the Club?'

'Of course.'

'And will I also be a member of the Club?'

'Oh yes, as soon as we are married you will be a member automatically, as my wife. We will pay subscription in our joint names. Mr and Mrs Prem Nath,' he said and listened to it.

She tried to look indifferent; but she was jubilant. She would be, at last, a member of the Club in her own right. She and her husband would drive up in their car, he sober in evening-clothes, she gorgeous in sari and jewellery. They would dance in the ballroom and eat dinner on the lawn. Afterwards they would go on to a nightclub and dance some more. 'And my father promised me,' he said, 'that after I am married he will let me go to Europe. We will go next year, we will go to England and also to the Continent and live in hotels.'

'Will we also visit Cambridge in England?'

'If you like.'

She would go and call on Rajen and Indira. They would be very happy to see her and she would invite them to dinner at her hotel and introduce them to her husband. They would be very much astonished at the elegance of her clothes and manners.

Green parrots flew in and out of the sun and a gush of bright orange blossoms flowed down the length of the crumbling old wall. The sunlight was bright but gentle, winter sunshine full of the sound of the birds. In the distance, out on the barren plains, the broken flight of steps of a vanished palace led to nowhere and a man with a stick and a loincloth walked behind two yoked and shabby bullocks.

For the women of the three families – of Lalaji's, of Dev Raj's, of Amar Nath's – it was no different from sitting at home in their own courtyards. They thought of the food which they had prepared and which was now being unpacked by the servants; they spoke of pregnancies and relatives. Shanta's mother looked a few times towards Viddi and enquired meaningfully about his age; but Amar Nath's wife, who proved to be very amenable, said that he was young yet and there was plenty of time. Lalaji's wife liked her immediately, and already began to look forward to the many pleasant hours they would spend together in later life discussing the possibilities and resemblances of their mutual grandchildren. Probably Amar Nath's wife would come to share their opinion of Shanta's mother. Phuphiji was also prepared to like Nimmi's prospective mother-in-law, once she had ascertained that she held to the old orthodoxies. They were placid and comfortable, especially since – apart from her few glances at Viddi – Shanta's mother had nothing to hold against them. Lalaji's wife could not remember when she had felt so light of heart. It was true, there was still Viddi, but Lalaji had promised that he would provide for him; and besides, with a boy it was never of such great urgency. She had not felt so free from worry since her children had come to maturity. Her eldest grandchild, Rani's daughter, was only fourteen, so there were still two or three years before one had to start thinking about her. Her only anxieties now were over the marriage celebrations which had to be arranged, first for Usha, then for Nimmi. But those were pleasant anxieties.

At a little distance from the women, the men joked and laughed together. It was always the same jokes they made, but they enjoyed them always with the same relish. Om slapped Viddi on the back and shouted, 'Look at my little brother here! He has become a great Sahib. Soon he will be such a big contractor, he will eat us all up!' and everybody laughed. Viddi also laughed; he felt himself to be a man and liked it that the others should feel it too. He wore his new gold wristwatch and a beautiful pair of nylon trousers, made to measure. Kuku had felt the material and asked him where he had had them made. Viddi had been most pleasantly surprised to find that Kuku was to be his brother-in-law. He thought: 'What times we will have together!' and felt that now indeed he belonged to the world of Clubs and parties. He poked Om in the ribs and said, 'Soon I will teach

190

my eldest brother what it is to be a great Sahib!' and he held out his hand so that Om, bellowing with laughter, could slap his down on it in appreciation of the joke.

Lalaji was very pleased by this new accord between his eldest son and his youngest. This was how things should be between brothers. It filled him with a proud and pleasant glow. Altogether life seemed very good to him just now. He loved all gatherings – whether it was a picnic or a wedding or even a funeral – men coming together to meet in friendship, in brotherhood, with their womenfolk clustered nearby, not thought of nor looked at, but nearby. He loved to see men of his own community around him, men whose ways were his own, whose nostalgic memories were his own, whose jokes were his own. It was not the place where they met that mattered but the men and the sense of kinship they engendered. They brought their own atmosphere with them wherever they went. They brought their jokes, their familiar ragging, their good-humoured insults. They brought their success and their relaxation; and they brought their food. He inhaled deeply and yes! there it was, the smell, sweeter than the scent of jasmine, of rich spiced meat swimming in red curry. He could see the servants running up and down unpacking the boxes and hear the women shouting instructions. This was happiness.

He laughed uproariously, he slapped his thighs, he said, 'Every day of our lives we should meet together like this. Then we would all live to a hundred.' He thought with pleasure of Usha's coming marriage cele-brations, the gathering together of thousands of relatives and friends, the honeyed days of feasting and merrymaking. Ah, but people should talk for years to come of the marriage in the house of Lala Narayan Dass Verma.

And after Usha, Nimmi. Here he could hardly contain himself, when he thought of the marriage he would make for his Nimmi. If people were to talk of Usha's wedding for years to come, the memory of Nimmi's they should carry with them into their next birth. A hundred cooks and confectioners would be sitting in his house day and night to prepare for the feasting; six bands in red and gold uniforms to serenade the guests; whole streets lit up by the illuminations from his house; Delhi drained of chickens and rice and spices and sugar and ghee; all traffic blocked by the cars bringing the guests; the women of the family in saris stiff with gold, bent under the weight of their jewellery; all the richest men in Delhi, the contractors, the millowners, the Directors of companies, thronging in the wedding-marquee; Ministers, Deputy Ministers, Secretaries – the whole Government – should come to honour his daughter. And after the wedding – for he could not stop there – after she was married, he would make her life a paradise. She should have a motor car of her own, every day a new sari, lakhs worth of jewellery, dozens of servants. At every step someone to attend her, every wish to be fulfilled before she had wished it. And when she went out, all the world should turn its head and ask, 'Who is this Queen?' to be answered, 'She is the daughter of Lala Narayan Dass Verma.' His eyes filled with tears as he thought of all the happiness he would make for her.

Then he saw her. She came stepping out of the pavilion with the boy behind her. They sauntered across the plain, through the sunlight, he in his gaily-flowered bush-shirt, young and jaunty and curly-haired, skipping as he walked, she slender and slight and very proud, in a pastel sari of pale green. Lalaji watched them and was very moved.

Viddi came running after them. He cried, 'Where are you going? Wait for me!' Shanta looked up and for a moment she thought Viddi was her husband, he looked so much like him; even his voice, it seemed to her, sounded like Om's.